William Lee Rees, Lily Rees

The Life and Times of Sir George Grey, K.C.B.

Vol. 2

William Lee Rees, Lily Rees

The Life and Times of Sir George Grey, K.C.B.
Vol. 2

ISBN/EAN: 9783337094584

Printed in Europe, USA, Canada, Australia, Japan

Cover: Foto ©Raphael Reischuk / pixelio.de

More available books at **www.hansebooks.com**

THE

LIFE AND TIMES

OF

SIR GEORGE GREY, K.C.B.

BY

WILLIAM LEE REES

(Member of the House of Representatives, New Zealand)
AUTHOR OF
"SIR GILBERT LEIGH," "FROM POVERTY TO PLENTY," ETC., ETC.

AND

L. REES

IN TWO VOLUMES

VOL. II.

.

SECOND EDITION

LONDON:
HUTCHINSON & CO.,
25, PATERNOSTER SQUARE.
1892

CONTENTS OF VOL. II.

BOOK THE FIFTH.

SECOND GOVERNORSHIP OF CAPE COLONY, 1859—1861.

BOOK THE SIXTH.

SECOND GOVERNORSHIP OF NEW ZEALAND, 1861—1867.

BOOK THE SEVENTH.

SIR GEORGE GREY ENGAGES IN ENGLISH POLITICS, 1868—1870.

BOOK THE EIGHTH.

SIR GEORGE GREY'S LIFE IN NEW ZEALAND, 1870—1892.

Book the Fifth.

SECOND GOVERNORSHIP OF CAPE COLONY, 1859-1861.

CHAPTER XXXI.

PUBLIC OPINION IN ENGLAND ON THE COLONIAL QUESTION.

" Have been at a great feast of languages and stolen the scraps."
Love's Labour's Lost.

As the ship neared England, the mind of the returning Governor was somewhat perplexed as to his future course and destiny. He had long since decided to follow out what seemed to be the path of duty irrespective of consequences; and had already in New Zealand entered upon a course of independent conduct which had threatened the sudden termination of his official career.

The blow had at last fallen, and although sustained by a consciousness that he had done his duty, the sudden separation from his chosen work, which he loved so well, weighed heavily upon him. There was so much yet to be accomplished in South Africa. So many golden opportunities for usefulness presented themselves to his mind which perhaps a stranger might not perceive, or, perceiving, appreciate, that a sadness, foreign and strange to him, asserted a temporary sway.

VOL. II.   B

All the races in South Africa had endeared themselves to their late Governor. The colonists, whether of British, or Dutch, or French extraction, had welcomed him warmly, and loyally supported him. The natives, both chiefs and people, had proved themselves true-hearted and faithful.

To realise that all his plans were stopped, and that the shears of the fatal sisters had, as it were, cut asunder the threads of his political life, could not but weigh with extreme gravity upon his mind. What the future would bring forth troubled him. Who would be sent to govern those scattered and diverse races ? What counsels were to guide him ? What policy would be given him to follow ? All these questions, as he paced the deck while Northern stars rose in the heavens, harassed and saddened a heart not given to forebodings, and generally untroubled by events.

At any rate, if his connection with the colonies had ceased, he had attempted to the best of his ability to serve his Maker, his Queen, and his country.

Twenty-two years had passed since he had first traversed those seas on his outward voyage to Western Australia. They had been years of adventure, of experience, of usefulness and honour. The arbitrary will of a Secretary of State might sever his connection with the chosen work of his life, and dismiss him from the public service. But no power on earth could erase the record of that twenty-two years of public service —and in his heart he esteemed the names Western Australia, South Australia, New Zealand, the South Pacific and South Africa, more worthy and more glorious than the proudest names which were inscribed in ancient or modern times upon the standards of victorious hosts.

Nor was he altogether devoid of faith, that even this blow would turn out rather a blessing than an injury. He remembered how on his first return to England not a month had passed before his highest hopes had been exceeded. He felt that in South Africa his work was not completed. The same faith which had nerved him in the terrible difficulties of his explorations, and which had sustained him since in many scenes of trial and of responsibility, enabled him under this heavy stroke of seeming disaster, calmly to resign himself to the will of that great Master whom he desired to serve and obey.

At length the ship reached her destination. The ex-Governor had requested that any reporters from the papers who boarded the ship, might be brought to him on their arrival. In compliance with his request, the captain brought to him a reporter from the *Times*. No names were mentioned—Sir George at once asked this gentleman the question which was uppermost in his own mind.

"Can you tell me who has been appointed as the new Governor at the Cape ?"

The reporter without hesitation gave an answer which settled all doubts and fears in the mind of his questioner.

"No new Governor, sir," he said, "has been appointed. Immediately after Sir George Grey's recall, Lord Derby's Ministry resigned. When the new Ministry came into office, Sir George Grey was re-appointed, and a ship was sent out to the Cape to stop him from coming home."

The sudden and unlooked for announcement of his re-appointment filled Sir George Grey with gratitude and delight. His thoughts flew over the sea to the distant land which he had recently left, and he could hear in fancy the cheers and congratulations of the people in South Africa whose petitions were thus answered before they had been received.

His faith was not misplaced; his work was not yet done, and he felt still more assured than ever, that until that work was accomplished for which he seemed to be chosen and to be fitted, the prejudices of his superiors, and the envy and dislike of his opponents, could not and would not prevail against him.

When it became known that he had not received his re-appointment in time to prevent his return to England, messages of friendship and congratulations poured in upon him from many quarters. Leaders in science, in religion, in politics, in naval and military circles, joined in the chorus of welcome.

The Duke of Newcastle was again in charge of the Colonial Office. He did not on this occasion, as he had done on Sir George's return from New Zealand five years previously, treat the Colonial Governor with coldness, arising from a sense of disapprobation. His first act on taking the seals of the department had been, at the Queen's request, to re-appoint Grey to the Governorship at the Cape. The despatch in which he had conveyed this information had been sent to Cape Town with instructions to Sir George not to leave the colony. It had, however, crossed the returning Governor upon the way, and a copy was given to him in London on his arrival.

A private letter from the Duke of Newcastle accompanied the despatch of August 4th, 1859, sent when he first assumed the position of Secretary for the Colonies, and learnt that Sir George had been re-called from the Government of the Cape by his predecessor, Sir Edward Lytton. The letter, dated August 5th, 1859, ends thus :—

I hope you will adopt the offer I make you in my despatch. I give you full credit for a conscientious sense of duty in the course you have taken, and therefore believe that, if you feel your position allows it without sacrifice of public usefulness, the same sense will induce you to subordinate all other considerations to the hope of associating your name with the consolidation of a great branch of the British Empire, in a land which has hitherto been a fertile source of political anxiety and heavy expenditure.

Grey was grieved to find that although a new Ministry had assumed power in England, the policy of non-confederation was still definitely endorsed. The Duke, in his despatch, while giving every credit to Sir George's patriotism, his wisdom and foresight, yet conveyed the unalterable decision of the Cabinet that the confederation of the States in South Africa was not desired and must not be pursued. With great regret, while accepting the re-appointment to South Africa, Sir George acceded to the terms demanded, and wrote the following letter :—

London, October 29, 1859.

My Lord Duke,—Having carefully considered your Grace's despatch, No. 13 of the 4th of August last, and reflected upon what passed at the interview with which you recently honoured me, I beg to state that I conceive it to be my duty to carry out the course I understand your Grace to wish me to pursue, and I therefore hold myself in readiness to return to the Cape of Good Hope so soon as you may have been able to prepare such instructions as you consider necessary for my future guidance.

Much that has recently taken place will render my future position at the Cape of Good Hope a very difficult one. Had I consulted my personal feelings, I should have shrunk from entering upon it ; but from a sense of my duty to the Queen, to your Grace —who originally sent me to South Africa, and who has since treated me with so much consideration—and to the people of that country, I am prepared to encounter all the difficulties I shall have to meet, trusting that Her Majesty's Government will, in considering my future proceedings, make due allowance for these embarrassing circumstances.—I have, etc.   G. GREY.

Before this letter was written Sir George had many opportunities of testing the feeling held towards him by the Duke of Newcastle and other members of the Ministry. He was gratified to find that his conduct was held in high estimation, and that he had personally gained the approval and esteem of those with whom he had so long and earnestly worked. The veto placed upon his great project for confederating South Africa was bitter in the extreme, but he felt that he might yet be able to accomplish much for the good of the people at the Cape, even though the time had not come when his great policy could be carried out. He was convinced that sooner or later his opinions in this matter would prevail; as in many other instances he was forced to give up his own plans, and to suit his actions to narrower views and less extended counsels.

The Duke felt and sympathised with Sir George Grey in his disappointment. All that could be said to encourage and to console was uttered by the Secretary for the Colonies. Speaking of Sir George's future and the self-denial which he must practise in thus relinquishing a cardinal point in his policy in South Africa, and of the difficulties which he would inevitably meet in his future government of those dependencies, the Duke promised that when his term in South Africa was completed he should receive the highest appointment in the power of the Colonial Office, the Governor-Generalship of Canada.

Men of all political parties and of all shades of political opinions have now reason to regret that the wise policy of Sir George Grey was not pursued at that time. The blood, the treasure, the passion and the suffering which Southern Africa has cost us since, would all have been spared had Sir George's plans prevailed. Of the many sins committed by Downing Street against the welfare and the happiness of the Queen's subjects in distant lands, not the least was the blind and dogged opposition to Grey's far-seeing project of confederation in 1859.

During the course of a conversation with his friend, Mr. Greville, Sir George Grey's private secretary learned some of the particulars attending the recall of Sir George Grey. The Prime Minister, accompanied by Mr. Greville, had visited Windsor, and there Lord Derby had informed the Queen that the Cabinet had decided to advise the recall of Sir George Grey from the Cape. Her Majesty was very unwilling to assent to the advice given by her Ministers. The great services which Sir George Grey had rendered in all his governments, and especially during the late trying crisis in Imperial affairs, had disposed her strongly in his favour; and it was with feelings of repugnance that she contemplated his removal.

Lord Derby, however, pressed his advice. Ultimately the Queen yielded. Sir George Grey's recall received the royal signature, and the Premier and Mr. Greville left Windsor for London. On the journey homewards Lord Derby did not speak, nor did Mr. Greville break the silence. When parting at the railway station the Premier simply said, " I'm afraid we have done a bad thing to-day in recalling Grey from the Cape."

It afterwards gave Sir George Grey great satisfaction to know that his services had been so highly valued by the Queen, that not only did her Majesty strenuously object to his removal, but upon a change of Ministry, herself suggested to the Premier his re-appointment.

The excitement which Sir George Grey's recall had created in South Africa had no counterpart in England, but the event was of sufficient importance, and the circumstances which surrounded it so interesting, as to raise a feeling of inquiry among leading statesmen.

The Duke of Argyll invited Sir George Grey to a dinner party, at which he met a number of leading politicians and men connected with the concerns of Great Britain.

The Colonial Question, with its many ramifications, was after dinner entered into at length. Sir George Grey opened the species of discussion which ensued. He briefly touched upon the recent history of South Africa, and insisted upon the importance to Great Britain of the expansion of her colonies and the maintenance of friendly relations of the most intimate character between England and her many dependencies. In relation to the development of the colonies he proceeded to point out that in all new communities, where countries hitherto waste became the active scene of industrial and commercial life, two several species of wealth were, in fact, always created. The first consisted of the actual and tangible possessions of the new community. Its lands made valuable by the presence and the labours of men; its cities; its fleets; its flocks and herds; its stores of merchandise; its manufactures and other industries; and all possessions which could be classed as real and existing wealth. The second was found in that public credit which, though intangible, was as real and to a certain extent of as great value as the other.

In the many parts of a great but scattered nationality, especially in those where for the public benefit it became necessary to construct great public works or other improvements, this communal credit could be and ought to be, within certain limits and under wise regulations, made available for the general comfort and prosperity.

Nor should the burden of redeeming the debt so created be borne altogether by the generation then existing. Where great values and benefits were con-

ferred upon future generations, a corresponding liability might fairly be imposed.   The hoarded wealth
of different parts of the same people might well be
employed in aiding the scattered members of their
own race, who in return would give a portion of the
wealth so created to those who had thus aided in its
production.

He alluded especially to the railway which was then
in course of construction at the Cape as an illustration
of this principle, and expressed his belief that extension of assistance in this way to the outlying parts of
the Empire would tend to produce a confederation,
not limited to one part of the world, but extending to
the most distant portions of the great British Empire.
And this confederation being based, not upon government, or race, or language only, but upon a community of interest, would be likely to stand the severest
strain which future contingencies could place upon it.

The majority of those present sided with Sir George
Grey.   Lord Lawrence, a man of few words, endorsed
the opinions held by the Governor of South Africa.
Lord John Russell, before leaving the room, in alluding to the estimation in which he held Sir George,
when he had appointed him to the Governorship of
South Australia, warmly expressed to Sir George
Grey his approval of the sentiments uttered by him,
which he held to be both patriotic and wise.

Macaulay, with great eloquence, also defended
every position which Grey had advanced. Regarding
the right which the present possessed of placing burdens commensurate with benefits upon the future, the
great historian pointed out the fact that all men were
more naturally interested in that which immediately
concerned and touched them than in the cares or
triumphs of people at a distance, either in time or
space. Sir Charles Wood had urged that men would

not, and ought not, to regard the present with a
greater distinctness of purpose than that which they
bestowed upon the future : that, indeed, public men
should be guided equally by consideration for the welfare of the coming generation as of the present; and
that they should not, for the sake of a present benefit,
encumber the race which was to come after them with
burdens which might possibly prove heavy to bear.

Macaulay differed from Sir Charles Wood. However great the sympathy of the most sensitive man
might be for others in distant places or in distant
times, the present must inevitably claim the greatest
consideration. He said that when he read the reports
from China, by which it appeared that the Chinese
Commissioner Yea had put to death a hundred thousand of the Chinese rebels, he was greatly concerned
and filled with indignation. While considering this
subject he hurt his thumb, and the pain was so great
that it banished from his mind nearly all the sympathy for the hundred thousand Chinese unfortunates.
He loved those among whom he lived; it was impossible to predict with certainty what race would occupy
England in one or two hundred years, and he maintained that the present inhabitants ought not to be
called upon to bear the whole burden of provision for
the future.

Mr. Gladstone objected to some of the arguments
and principles urged by Sir George Grey. The whole
leaning of his mind appeared to be an apprehension
of the too great extension of the Empire.

The Imperial views of the majority found but little
favour with Mr. Gladstone. And the policy which
the Duke of Newcastle had enunciated as the unanimous decision of Ministers when he fettered the re-appointment of Sir George Grey to the Cape, with the
condition that the Governor must forego his plans of

confederation, was strongly and entirely endorsed by
Mr. Gladstone.

The Duke of Argyll did not himself take a prominent part in the discussion. He listened with interest
to the views expressed by the speakers, and to the
opinions of those who, coming from the distant parts
of the earth in which they had held supreme power or
prosecuted wide enquiries, were well worthy of consideration and respect.

To Sir George Grey this unstudied conference
afforded great pleasure. As his interviews with the
Queen and Prince Albert had convinced him that Her
Majesty's mind and that of her illustrious Consort
endorsed and supported his own reasonings, so this
chance discussion proved to his satisfaction that the
learning, the culture, and the intellect of his native
country were in the main favourable to those great
ideas of national extension to which, during all his
life, he had adhered.

During his stay in England, Sir George was on one
occasion the guest of the Duke of Newcastle at Clum-
ber. The party was somewhat large, and composed
of prominent politicians and statesmen. The conditions under which he was to return to the Cape were
freely canvassed. His own repugnance to the policy
of dismemberment was well known, while the determination of the Government to oppose his policy of
confederation in South Africa was equally public.
The question was one of considerable importance,
and as a consequence it was often discussed. Among
the visitors was Mr. Cooke, then editor and part pro-
prietor of the *Saturday Review*. This gentleman, who
had risen by his own exertions and talent from a
position of obscurity, was often consulted by Ministers, and his opinions were greatly respected. He
was at length definitely appealed to by the Duke of

Newcastle. Without any hesitation he decided in favour of Sir George Grey's views. "I cannot conceive," he said, "how different opinions upon this point can exist. I am astonished that successive Ministries representing both sides in politics should have so decided this important question. Sir George Grey in this matter towers above you all. I am certain that in a few years public opinion will believe you to be all in the wrong and declare Sir George Grey to be right." Public opinion did indeed change some years afterwards, but in 1859 it was inflexibly disposed against the policy of federation, and favoured the reduction of the Empire.

CHAPTER XXXII.

VISIT TO THE QUEEN AND HONOURS AT CAMBRIDGE.

> " I long
> To hear the story of your life, which must
> Take the ear strangely."
>
> *The Tempest.*

SIR GEORGE GREY was received with great cordiality and kindness both by the Queen and Prince Albert. The Prince informed him of Her Majesty's approval of the measures taken by him, and the policy of confederation which he had pursued, expressing without hesitation her opinion that the plans proposed were beneficent, worthy of a great ruler, honourable to herself, and advantageous to her people.

It was at this time that Sir George proposed the visit of Prince Alfred to South Africa. The tour of the Prince of Wales through America suggested the possibility as well as the propriety of a Royal visit to the other colonies. There were at the Cape public functions which the young Prince could perform. The breakwater was to be commenced, the public library to be opened. The colonists would be pleased beyond measure. All persons would share in the welcome— Boers of the Transvaal, Free Staters of the Orange River, Kafirs, Basutos, Colonists, Dutch, English, and colonial-born, whatever their feelings toward each other might be, would join in the heartiest welcome to Victoria's son, and so reveal their common appreciation of the great qualities of the Queen and their personal regard for her.

Prince Alfred listened with delight to stories of South African life and adventure. He was eager to embrace Sir George's offer. Without much demur, after consideration the Queen and Prince Albert consented, the matter being finally settled at Buckingham Palace. When Sir George had returned and made all necessary arrangements, the young Prince was to sail for Cape Town.

Before his departure to resume the duties of his Governorship, Sir George had opportunities of seeing and conversing with the Prince Consort. In Albert the Good he found an earnest sympathy both with the colonies and colonists, and he was beyond measure pleased to be told by the Prince that, in his opinion, if a nation ceased to take a real interest in every part of its dominions, and to do all the good it could on the outskirts of its power, it would be like a tree which had ceased to grow—the time of decay would have commenced. He perfectly agreed with Sir George's views as to opening up new country. He said that he and the Queen had read all that Sir George had written on the subject, and that it was greatly to the Queen's regret that she had been led to consent to his recall, and that she had done much to get that decision reversed.

It was during this visit to England that the University of Cambridge, following the example set by Oxford five years before, conferred its highest honours upon Sir George Grey.

The customs at Cambridge differed, as Sir George found, from those at Oxford. In place of going up alone and unattended to receive the honours of the University, as he remembered doing when the students, after cheering Prince Buonaparte, sang in his honour "The King of the Cannibal Islands," he found that it was the rule that the candidate or recipient attended at the Senate House at Cambridge accompanied by many friends.   Naturally, Sir George had but few friends or even acquaintances at the University.   This circumstance opened the way for a kind and considerate act on the part of Mr. Gladstone. Three gentlemen besides Sir George Grey were this day to receive the honorary degree—Bishop Wilberforce; Mr. Walpole, who had left the Ministry on a question of political principle, for which he had sacrificed place and power ; and Mr. Gladstone.   The latter, judging that Grey must know but few people, called for him at the Vice-Chancellor's, and the two walked up side by side, accompanied by a great number of Mr. Gladstone's friends and admirers.

Immediately before the ceremonies began, Sir George learned that an address, by way of thanks for the dignity conferred, was expected of every individual whom the University delighted to honour. He became uneasy.   Accustomed as he was to issue commands and to hold conferences upon political matters with Ministers and others, he yet felt decidedly ill at ease at the prospect before him.   When writing, his thoughts flowed readily enough, and the logic and sequence of his numerous despatches show him to have always been a master of English and a clear logician.   But he was unaccustomed to what is designated "public speaking."   To be called upon at a moment's notice to address the *alumni* of a great school of learning, to submit himself to a comparison with three well-known orators, one of whom was already looked upon by many as the greatest master of the English tongue then living, before one of the most critical audiences which England could furnish, was well calculated to render a sensitive mind anxious

and uneasy. He was at a complete loss what to say
or on what subject to dilate, and so it happened
that Sir George Grey, who had faced so many
dangers and controlled so many difficult circumstances, found himself for once absolutely
unnerved.

Mr. Gladstone was the first called upon to return
thanks. The rising statesman had not spoken for five
minutes before a sense of complete ease and comfort
spread itself over Sir George Grey's mind. Unconsciously Mr. Gladstone was giving a theme to Sir
George, and thus adding to the obligation already
bestowed by his kindness. The future Prime Minister
spoke upon the inadvisability of expending so much
strength and money in foreign missions, and urged
that their efforts should be concentrated on the great
centres of population in Great Britain, where millions
of English people were growing up in practical
heathenism.

When his turn came to speak, Sir George proceeded
to criticise and comment upon the position which he
thought had been too strongly taken up by Mr. Gladstone. To centralise and restrict missionary efforts
would be to stunt the Christian growth of the Church.
In commerce, in science, in philanthropy, expansion
ensured health and strength. He cited the personal
history and position of Mr. Gladstone himself in illustration. His wide acquaintance with foreign matters,
his converse with politics and people in many lands,
his contemplation of distant affairs in no sense impaired his energy or usefulness in England. On the
contrary, the knowledge thus gained, the sympathy
thus expanded, and the experience thus enlarged,
had, as it were, educated and fitted him more completely to fill the important positions to which the

voice of public opinion evidently called him.   He concluded a long and vigorous address amid general applause.

Next morning some of the leading newspapers, in reporting the proceedings, expressed astonishment that at such a time and place a speech of over an hour in length was listened to, not only with patience, but with pleasure.

CHAPTER XXXIII.

PRINCE ALFRED'S VISIT TO SOUTH AFRICA.

> "I thank you for your voices ; thank you ;
> Your most sweet voices."
>
> *Coriolanus.*

EARLY in the year 1860 Sir George Grey returned to
Cape Town. The news of his reappointment had
reached the colony in September of the previous year.
It had been received with a joy as unanimous and
sincere as the sorrow caused by his recall. From the
Government offices in Cape Town to the distant mission stations on the lakes and rivers, the tidings of
the reappointment of their venerated ruler gave rise
to unqualified delight. All classes and all races vied
with each other in their expressions of gratitude to the
Queen and of attachment to the Governor.

So great had been the change worked during his
administration, so prosperous had the South African
communities become during the five years of his
governorship, that the feeling of gratification at his
return was both spontaneous and irrepressible.

A great crowd assembled to welcome the Governor
upon his arrival. Music, flags, and cheers marked
his return to the Cape. The fears and sense of
insecurity which had overshadowed the whole land,
passed away, while hope and confidence were re-
established.

The event itself will never be forgotten ; and for

many years yet to come parents will tell their children the story of Sir George Grey's wise administration, of his sudden recall, and of the enthusiasm evoked by his reappearance.

It would be impossible to give even an abstract of the numerous letters which Sir George Grey received from all parts of South Africa rejoicing in his return. A translation of one, however, may be given as expressing the feeling shown in all. The writer of that we have chosen for this purpose was a chief of great importance, who ruled over the country to the south-east of the Orange Free State.

My Lord,—Our sorrow and regret is now turned into sincere joy and gratitude by the cheering news of Your Excellency's return to the shores of South Africa as the Representative of Her Majesty the Queen of Great Britain. And we beg to congratulate Your Excellency and Lady Grey upon your safe arrival into this country, amidst a people that love you, and pray that your exalted wisdom and Christian firmness may long be spared to them.

We also desire to tender our warmest thanks to Her Majesty Queen Victoria for being an eye to the blind in sending a God-fearing man as Governor and High Commissioner to this benighted land, whose philanthropic heart has done so much already for the temporal and spiritual improvement of the aborigines both here and in other countries, and whose name guarantees further blessings for the future.—I remain Your Excellency's most obedient servant, in the name of my people, CHIEF MOROKA.

The demonstrations of joy at Sir George Grey's return as Governor were hardly at an end when the people of Cape Town began to look forward eagerly to another occasion of rejoicing. This was the promised visit of Prince Alfred. Never had the Queen's subjects in South Africa seen any of the Royal Family in that portion of her dominions. Sir George knew that the presence of the Sailor Prince in their midst would not only give great pleasure to the colonists, but would also greatly strengthen their loyalty by adding warm personal attachment to their lawful obedience.

When tidings were received that H.M.S. Euryalus, with the royal midshipman on board, had sailed for Cape Colony, the greatest excitement prevailed. It was not known what port she was bound for, but the residents of Cape Town expected to see the English man-of-war with the Royal standard floating proudly from her masthead, gliding through the blue waters of Table Bay. The delight of first sighting her was, however, not for them, but for the inhabitants of Simon's Town at the other side of the Cape of Good Hope. Directly the news of her arrival at Simon's Town was made known, a pleasant excitement spread abroad—shops and places of business were deserted— triumphal arches spanned the road by which the young Prince must come to Government House at Cape Town ; flags waved from every spire and staff, streamed from windows and balconies, or floated out in the breeze in long lines of brilliant colour overhead. Thousands of expectant faces in Cape Town turned towards the road from Simon's Bay. Thousands of throats grew hoarse with cheering as the open carriage with its grey horses drew near, and the round, boyish face of their royal visitor beamed with gratification at their enthusiastic welcome.

At the entrance to Cape Town Sir George Grey was waiting on horseback to receive his distinguished guest. There Prince Alfred mounted also, and rode the rest of the way by the Governor's side. Such a mingling of races, colours, creeds, languages and dress is not often seen as the streets of Cape Town contained that day. Still less frequently does such a cosmopolitan gathering display such unanimous feeling. Boers, English, Germans, Fingoes, Zulus, and Kafirs all united in welcoming their Queen's son, and

in expressing their love for their Governor.   Suddenly
a Kafir stepped out of the crowd and caught hold of
the reins of the Prince's horse.   The movement was
momentary, and Sir George at once spoke to him and
he retired, merely saying, "I wished to do honour to
the Queen that sent us out our good Sir George Grey."

That night the capital was magnificently illuminated.
Several days were pleasantly spent at Government
House.   Balls, dinner parties, receptions, drives and
excursions to different points of interest, occupied the
time, and made Prince Alfred acquainted with the
neighbourhood and its residents.   One of the most
interesting of these excursions was a visit to the Kafir
school at Zonnebloem, founded by the Governor.   But
Sir George was desirous that the Royal lad should
see more of South African life than was shown in the
festivities at Cape Town.   He therefore planned an
excursion through Cape Colony, Kaffraria, the Orange
River Free State, and Natal.

In accordance with this programme, the party embarked in the Euryalus at Simon's Town and sailed
for Port Elizabeth, from which town they were to proceed overland to the frontier.   When Prince Alfred
stepped into the boat which was to convey them to
the man-of-war, Sir George Grey was amused and
touched by the rapid transition from a royal prince to
a simple midshipman.   Respectfully saluting, Prince
Alfred stood by and offered assistance while Sir Grey
stepped in, plainly indicating that their relative positions were changed, and that at sea His Excellency
the Governor must take precedence of the "middy."

Arriving at Port Elizabeth on the 6th of August,
the Prince was able to celebrate his birthday there
amidst rejoicings which rivalled those of Cape Town.
The citizens were hardly restrained, by the Governor's
urgent desire, from taking the six greys out of the

carriage in which Prince Alfred and he rode and drawing it themselves. Very reluctantly they relinquished their purpose. Visits were paid to the Grey Institute (where the scholars received a holiday on the recommendation of the founder and patron of their establishment), and several other public buildings. In the evening a large ball was given in honour of the visitors.

A hunt across the Amsterdam flats commenced the ride from Port Elizabeth to Grahamstown. For three hours the vice-regal party and royal guest coursed over the plains at a glorious rate. The royal middy was foremost in the chase and thoroughly enjoyed the rousing gallop.

Crossing the rivers on pontoon bridges, stopping for meals and sleeping at comfortable inns, spending the hours of daylight in the saddle amidst the romantic scenery of the mountain passes or the park-like beauty of the undulating plains—the journey to Grahamstown would have been enjoyable enough to the ordinary tourist. But a special delight was afforded Prince Alfred by the manifestations of welcome and joy at his coming. The enthusiasm of the people was shown not only by the decorations on the road, but by their assembling from far distant parts of the country to greet the party.

The entrance to Grahamstown was made under triumphal arches and waving flags, amid the thunders of artillery, the stirring strains of military music, and the deafening cheers of the populace. Above the kaleidoscopic changing of the brilliant but harmonious colour in the street, the motto on one triumphal arch was a paradox :

"With all the bright colours this world can display,
    The frontier avers there is nothing like *Grey*."

King Williamstown was reached six day later. Then

the young Prince saw the magnificent memorial which English troops had erected in the shape of the Grey Hospital.

From this point the expedition turned away from the coast and proceeded nearly due north. For ten days they rode on towards Bloemfontein in the Orange Free State. Such a journey was an entirely new experience to Prince Alfred. As the cavalcade passed along the grassy and woodless plateaux of Kaffraria, or forded the rapid mountain torrents which rushed down from the western heights and cut their way through deep, wooded ravines to the sea, everything was novel and pleasing to him.

As he and Sir George Grey dismounted from their horses, stiff and tired, and watched the gorgeous colours of the South African sunset lighting up the busy scene of camping, the clumsy Cape waggons drawn up and out-spanned for the night, and the usual evening preparations being made; or later, after a hearty meal of plain fare had been eaten with more relish than any banquet ever spread in palaces, with the camp fire brightly burning, and the more steadfast and brilliant shining of the southern constellations overhead, the English boy felt all the fascination of the scene. Even the discomforts of the excursion had a charm of their own. Fatigue, hunger, rough lodging, and the absence of many small every-day luxuries and indulgences are (one or all) attendant upon most of the favourite sports and pastimes of his race, and a certain pleasure in occasionally " roughing it " is felt by the Anglo-Saxon.

To Sir George Grey, who had known real deprivation, and looked starvation steadily in the face, whose immense powers of endurance had been taxed to their utmost limit, and whose determination alone had conquered physical weakness and saved the lives of

his party in the Australian exploration twenty years
before, the present was merely a picnic. Indeed, it
made very little difference in his usual habits, which
were simple in the extreme. He was always abste-
mious, and seldom indulged in anything beyond the
barest necessaries of life. The scenes through which
they passed had not the novelty for him that they
possessed for Prince Alfred, but he heartily enjoyed
his visitor's youthful enthusiasm and delight.

While hunting one day on the borders of the
Transvaal, the young Prince and the Governor became separated from the rest of the party. They had
breakfasted about four o'clock, and as the hours went
by the idea of lunch became more and more pleasant,
though less hopeful. The sight of a Boer's hut about
two o'clock in the afternoon was gladly welcomed,
especially by the younger of the two riders, whose
healthy appetite had been sharpened by the fresh air
and long abstinence.

They were hospitably entertained by the occupant
of the little dwelling, an old woman, who cooked
some exceedingly greasy pancakes for them. The
Prince's appetite was not at all spoiled by the fact
that the appointments of the table were rather more
primitive than at Buckingham Palace. In the absence of spoons and forks, he rolled up his pancake
and ate it from his fingers with intense relish, telling
Sir George it was " the most delicious pancake " he
had ever tasted. His companion, less hungry, and
accustomed to much longer fasting, was quietly
amused at such high appreciation of the greasy compound.

When, on leaving, the Governor told the kind
hostess who her guest was, the old woman was
almost overcome with the thought that she had been
entertaining " the son of the Queen." It is easy to

believe that there are certain objects regarded as sacred relics in that remote hut in the Transvaal, and jealously guarded to this day.

The Governor and his party crossed the Drakensberg Mountains through wide, shrubby kloofs. High above them towered lofty inaccessible peaks, their rugged outlines rendered wilder looking by the stiff, pointed foliage of countless euphorbias and aloes, whose bristles bid defiance alike to fire and drought. They passed through numerous settlements, native villages, mission stations, and everywhere the same enthusiastic welcome met them.

As they penetrated more deeply into the country, Prince Alfred was regarded with much curiosity by the natives. "The Queen" had hardly hitherto been a real personage to them, but rather a powerful deity, and they were much surprised to see her son real flesh and blood. But with Sir George Grey it was different. He was their "father," their friend. They had heard that he was taken away from them and was never coming back—and then, to their joy, he had returned. Now, for the first time since that return, he had come amongst them ; and the greatest cause they had to thank the Gracious Queen was, that she had sent them back their good Governor.

At every town or settlement they entered, addresses were presented to the Prince and the Governor, all testifying to the loyalty and hearty affection of the people for their distant Queen, and their satisfaction with the Government. One from the Kafirs of St. Mark's Mission Station contained the following passage :—

"We beg leave to express our great pleasure on seeing the son of Queen Victoria. We wish to express to him our feelings of love towards our Queen for having sent so wise a man as Sir George Grey to rule over this country. We have seen the good things which he has done, and we ourselves were saved from death by him after we had blindly followed the words of the false prophet, Umhlakaza, in killing our cattle and destroying our corn. We ourselves are living under the Christian law, and many of us have joined heartily in the Christian faith. Our children are taught in the Mission schools the law of Christ, and through the kindness of Sir George Grey our sons are learning useful trades, whereby they will shortly be able to earn a good living."

At the conclusion of the address Sir George Grey shook hands with many of the natives, and asked for some writing that had been done in the schools to be given to the Prince, and when this was complied with, Prince Alfred declared, to the great gratification of the scholars, that he would take the writing to England and show it to the Queen. The Tambookie tribes, anxious to see Prince Alfred, assembled at a certain point on the road. Not knowing the exact date at which he might be expected, they were there two days before he came. Then they heard that he had taken a shorter way. Fortunately, Prince Alfred had not gone very far when he heard what disappointment his non-appearance would cause, and turned back. The natives showed great delight and enthusiasm, singing their best war-songs and chants of welcome, the latter consisting chiefly of the words: "We have seen the child of heaven. We have seen the son of our Queen." Some of the chiefs were introduced to the young Prince, and one presented him with an assegai as a token of respect.

" His Excellency Sir George Grey conversed freely with the chiefs, exhorted them to continue firm in their loyalty to Her Majesty, and took particular pains to impress upon them the great interest which our beloved Queen took in their welfare, as well as in that of all her other South African subjects, a greater proof of which she could not have given than that of thus sending her son, whom she so dearly loved, to this distant country as her representative. The chiefs were loud in their expressions of gratitude and promises of loyalty, and they also expressed in glowing language the satisfaction they felt at the return of Sir George Grey again to be their Governor, calling him their father and their best friend, and promising implicit obedience to all his commands."*

The inhabitants of Queenstown had drawn up addresses of welcome and congratulation to Sir George Grey on again resuming the government of the colony, which they wished to present publicly. The Governor, however, declined to take any prominent position in receiving them, preferring that the young Prince should always occupy the most important place.

At Lesseytown the natives assembled and sang songs of welcome. "Never did black faces beam with greater delight than did those of these people as they looked for the first time on a Prince of the Royal House, and as they greeted once more their venerated and much-loved Governor. On Sir George Grey they seem to look as upon a father."†

They presented an address, from which the following quotation is made :

"We pray thee to convey our thanks to our Queen for the great good-luck of seeing thee, and also for all the great and good things she has done for us by the hands of our beloved Governor, Sir George Grey."

The institution to which these people belonged owed its origin to Sir George Grey and the interest which

* Extract from newspaper account of proceedings.—*Free Press*, Queenstown.
† Queenstown paper.

he took in the advancement of the natives. A Queenstown paper thus speaks of the impressions generally
made by the visitors:

"We had read and heard much of the affability,
courtesy, condescension, sense, and friendly bearing
of Prince Alfred, and of the more than paternal care
with which Sir George Grey watches over him, and
the manner in which the excellent qualities of the
two combined at once strike home to the heart and
take hold upon a people's affections. But the half
had not been told us. Their visit was brief, but it has
left many pleasant reminiscences; and often and fer-
vently shall we wish and pray for long life and happiness to our Royal Prince Alfred, and long life and
happiness to our noble Governor, Sir George Grey."

On August 19th they met the great chief Moshesh
at Aliwal. He had left his own place and, at a great
age, undertaken a long and trying journey in order to
shake hands with them.

Next day they arrived at Smithfield, which presented the same festive appearance as all the other
towns they had passed through. Crossing into the
Free States they reached Bloemfontein, the capital,
on August 23rd. The keynote to the feeling of the
inhabitants was supplied by the motto of a triumphal
arch, "Loyal, tho' discarded." Adam Kok here
awaited the Prince and the Governor.

Some of the most enthusiastic sportsmen in the
Orange Free State were determined that Prince Alfred
should take part in a more magnificent hunt than any
Royal Prince had ever seen. Accordingly for some
days before his arrival about a thousand Barolongs,
under their chief, Moroka, were busily occupied in
beating up the game from the adjacent country close
to Bloemfontein. On the morning of the 24th the
hunt commenced. The Barolongs divided into two

parties and rode off right and left, dropping a man every hundred yards or so. After forming a continuous straight line for some miles, both parties turned inwards till they met, thus completing the circle. The quantity of game shut in by the hunters could not have been less than twenty-five thousand head.

A member of the Royal party, who took an active part in the hunt, gives the following account:

"The several kinds of game—ostriches, Burchell's zebras, wildebeestes, bonteboks, springboks—kept generally each kind in separate herds or droves, crossing and re-crossing one another in the greatest confusion and terror, as they careered along the line seeking for a point through which they might break. A drove of wildebeestes, fierce with terror, would make a wild rush at some apparently weak point in the living fence, and—amidst clouds of dust, the falling of the dying ones, the tumbling of those living over those who were slain, the roar caused by the trampling of so many galloping feet over the ground, the bellowing of the wounded wildebeestes, the shouts and cries of the Barolongs, the continual popping of the guns and rifles—would resolutely break through the line, and madly career off into the apparently boundless plain. At some points would be seen riders falling, horse and all; at others, horses whose riders were thrown, galloping here and there with the game."

Beside the larger game mentioned a great number of Cape jerboas, of meerkats, cobras, and oribis (a small and graceful species of antelope), were driven in with the surging mass, while a vast crowd of vultures hovered in the air or swooped upon the dead bodies.

The Royal party proceeded as far north as Winburg, and then turned eastward, crossing the Drakensberg Mountains, entering Natal upon the 31st. The inhabitants of Pietermaritzburg were nowise behind those of the other towns visited in their demonstrations of loyalty and pleasure at seeing Prince Alfred. A local paper, alluding to the most important members of the young Prince's party, first speaks of Sir George Grey as " the most intelligent of statesmen, the best and most popular of Governors, the political benefactor of Natal, the friend and defender of the people. God bless him! say we and many another grateful heart."

They left Pietermaritzburg for D'Urban on the 5th of September, and found the Euryalus waiting for them at the latter place. Embarking, they returned to Cape Town, landing once more in Simon's Town on the 14th of September.

The overland tour that had been taken amounted to fully twelve hundred miles. The distance was covered in a month. The average rate of forty miles a day on horseback or in the waggons, over such rough roads and broken country, was very fair.

" It was certainly a progress such as no Royal Prince had ever 'done' before—among wild beasts and wild men, over mountain ranges and desert tracts, and fertile pastures; from the homes of European civilization to the huts of barbarism, from the centre of the hostile hordes who for so many long years waged war upon our advancing colonisation, to the rapidly progressing prosperity of Natal, then (though not now) Britain's youngest colonial settlement in Africa. And wherever he appeared, the welcome that greeted him was alike cordial and enthusiastic. The English settler and the Dutch boer were equally sincere in their fervent loyalty; and the natives, whether aboriginal, Hottentot, Fingo, Kafir, Basuto, or Zulu, were more loudly demonstrative still. But of all the characteristic features that marked this jour-

ney, perhaps the most striking and suggestive, and
certainly not the least gratifying, was the extent to
which the self-reliant spirit of the European inhabitants of South Africa displayed itself, in the organisation of volunteer corps and burgher forces for mutual
defence, against all encroachments of an enemy.*

Sandilli, the paramount chief of the Tambookies,
with his councillors, accepted an invitation to accompany the Prince's party from Natal to Cape Town in
the Euryalus.   The voyage was a rough one, and the
Kafirs, whose dread of the ocean is unconquerable,
suffered horribly.   A great impression was made on
their minds by the sight of Prince Alfred, the loved,
admired, and venerated royal visitor, fresh from the
triumphs and adulation of his tour through South
Africa, resuming his ordinary middy's duties.   They
saw the boy whose coming had caused tens of thousands of hearts to beat more quickly, and had aroused
unbounded enthusiasm and delight in four great
States and many different races, now rising with the
dawn to assist in washing down the decks.   As he
splashed about barefooted, all distinctions of rank
merged, not in equality, but in the discipline and
priority of the naval service, they wondered.

The following translation of an address, which they
presented to Captain Tarleton before leaving the
Euryalus, amply expresses their feelings :—

Sandilli and his councillors give thanks.   By the invitation of
the great Chief, the son of the Queen of the English people, are
we this day on board this mighty vessel.

The invitation was accepted with fear.   With dread we came
on board, and in trouble have we witnessed the dangers of the
great waters, but through your skill have we passed through this
tribulation.

* "The Progress of Prince Alfred through South Africa."—
S. S. Solomon and Co., Cape Town, 1861.

We have seen what our ancestors heard not of.   Now have we grown old and learned wisdom.   The might of England has been fully illustrated to us, and now we behold our madness in taking up arms to resist the authority of our mighty and gracious Sovereign.   Up to this time have we not ceased to be amazed at the wonderful things we have witnessed, and which are beyond our comprehension.   But one thing we understand, the reason of England's greatness, when the son of her great Queen becomes subject to a subject that he may learn wisdom ; when the sons of England's chiefs and nobles leave the homes and wealth of their fathers, and with their young Prince endure hardships and sufferings in order that they may be wise, and become a defence to their country.   When we behold these things, we see why the English are a great and mighty nation.

What we have now learnt shall be transmitted to our wondering countrymen, and handed down to our children, who will be wiser than their fathers, and your mighty Queen shall be their Sovereign and ours in all time coming.

CHAPTER XXXIV.

"One touch of nature makes the whole world kin."
Shakespeare.

"Peace hath her victories,
No less renowned than war."
Milton.

PRINCE ALFRED could only spend a few days at the Cape on his return from the tour through the colony. A great many ceremonies had to be compressed into that time. Landing on Friday, arrangements were immediately made for a fête and fancy fair in the Botanic Gardens to be held next day, succeeded by a dinner and ball at Government House.

Monday, September 17th, was the most memorable day of the Prince's whole visit, for it was signalised by the commencement of the breakwater in Table Bay—the principal object with which he had come to Cape Colony.

The great drawback to the progress of Cape Town was its dangerous harbour. Without shelter from the westerly or southerly gales, all shipping was liable to destruction which might be caught in Table Bay by the fierce winds occasionally sweeping the surges of the Atlantic to the foot of Table Mountain. For two hundred years the Dutch and English colonists had suffered from this cause. Many a gallant bark, unable to put to sea, had, in the violent storms which burst upon that coast, strewn the beach with its timbers and its crew.

From the moment of his first landing as Governor, Sir George had contemplated the possibility of constructing a breakwater, which would be at once a harbour of refuge, a convenience to commerce, and an inestimable public blessing. Busy as the Governor was with the many duties and engagements of his official life, he yet from time to time thought of the project with pleasure, but was unable to enter actively into its prosecution. Strolling one morning with some visitors along the beach to the eastward of Cape Town, his foot slipped from the crest of a little ridge of sand. Surprised at the circumstance, the Governor looked for the cause. A skull was partially uncovered where his foot had slipped, and from the bleached bone there floated a lock of golden hair.

The story was soon told. A ship bearing as its passengers a large number of female convicts sent abroad to New South Wales—many of them for incredibly trivial offences, had cast anchor in the Bay. During the night a gale sprang up—the ship dragged her anchors, and by the morning had gone to pieces—not a soul, it is believed, being saved. The bodies had been buried beneath the ridge on which they were then standing.

As Sir George looked at the silent skull and golden hair, he thought of the agony which must have wrung the heart of the poor girl and her comrades, and on the instant determined to lose no time, and spare no effort to raise a haven of safety in Table Bay for all future time.

He began to gather information. He sounded the public leaders so as to gain the opinions and wishes of the people. Estimates of expense, of labour, and of time were made, a correspondence with the great engineer, Sir John Coode, ensued, and all steps were taken which could lead to the commencement and final completion of this necessary public work.

When recalled by the despatch of Sir E. Bulwer Lytton, he left behind him a Bill which he had proposed to lay before the Parliament at its next sitting, providing for the construction of the harbour. It was one among the many causes of regret at his sudden departure from South Africa, that this project remained unfulfilled. He commended it to all public men, and left it as a sacred trust to his successor.

Upon his return from England he found the Parliament in session, but to his surprise and mortification, a great disaster had befallen his favourite plan. General Wynyard, the Acting-Governor, knowing the strong desire of Sir George Grey for the successful passage of the Act, and not being sure of the disposition of any Governor who might succeed him, and influenced, it may be, by a laudable ambition to have his name connected with the gift of a harbour to Cape Town, had pushed the Bill somewhat hurriedly in the Legislature.

A debate had arisen, during which it became evident that the conservative instinct of the Boers was very strong. Their fathers had been able to do without a harbour. Why should not they? Table Bay had afforded sufficient accommodation for the generations past. Why should it not still be sufficient? The expense would be very great. Who was to bear it? Years would elapse before any benefit at all would be derived. Possibly the structure itself would be a failure, in which case the dangers of the harbour would be increased instead of lessened. Their fathers, who were as clever as people in these days, had failed to build. Were men nowadays likely to succeed?

Finally the question went to a division, and the Bill was thrown out.

A few days after this, Sir George Grey arrived to resume his duties. With somewhat hesitating tones, General Wynyard told him of the ill-fate which had attended the Harbour Bill. But the Governor was equal to the occasion. He was determined that the breakwater should be built.

At the first Council meeting he made known his determination to his advisers. They were in despair. Having once resolved to refuse the Bill, they believed that the members would stubbornly adhere to their determination, and the probability of a struggle between the Governor and the Parliament immediately after his triumphant return from England filled them with dismay. But Sir George was not to be denied. The estimates for the year had not yet been submitted to the Assembly. He inserted the amount necessary for the beginning of the work, and declared his resolution to pass no vote for the expenditure unless this item was included in it.

The much-feared struggle was soon ended. Many of the members, delighted at the return of their beloved Governor, were willing to yield to his personal influence what they would not sanction in the prior debate. A single night's discussion ended the matter. The vote was carried by a small majority, and the estimates were passed.

On the 17th of September the most numerous assemblage of Europeans ever gathered together in South Africa stood upon the rising ground fronting the sea, to witness the laying of the first stone of the harbour by Prince Alfred. Sudden storms marred the beauty of the day, but they did not last long, and between them the sun shone out brilliantly. Beneath the shadow of that mountain, whose flat crest had given the name to itself and the bay beneath it, twenty thousand people took part in a ceremony which was in the highest sense historical.

Before the proceedings commenced, amid a deep and reverential silence, a special prayer, composed for the occasion, was offered up to God. Then the Prince, pulling a trigger, dropped into the sea the first stones of that splendid breakwater which now gives safety and comfort to the commerce of South Africa.

On Tuesday morning the Prince laid the foundation stone of the "Alfred Sailors' Home," which was erected as a special memorial of his visit. In the afternoon he inaugurated the new Library and Museum. This building had been commenced three years before under the influence and encouragement of Sir George Grey. The collection of books numbered between thirty and forty thousand volumes. Sir John Herschell called it "the bright eye of the Cape."

Sir George Grey's address on this occasion was received with unbounded enthusiasm. He commenced by pointing out the full significance of Prince Alfred's visit, and particularly his action that day. "A youthful Prince has come to visit us here, upon the extremity of this ancient continent, which was the cradle of civilisation and art, when Egypt was in its glory and its prime, with its teeming populations, its skilful artisans, its gorgeous and massive buildings, while the greater part of Europe still slumbered in savage barbarism. He comes from a land which, when the north of this continent on which we stand was old in science and art, was regarded as almost beyond the confines of the habitable earth, and was only peopled by hordes of painted and lawless savages ; and yet he comes to us, a poor, a scattered, and still struggling people, from what is now the centre of Christianity and of civilisation—from that great heart, the ceaseless pulsations of which scatter truth, swarms of industrious immigrants, crowds of traders, and streams of commerce throughout the world. Europe, which in its comparative youth of civilisation adopted Christianity, has sent to us, as well as to so many other parts of the earth, all that can render this life valuable to man or prepare him for a future state. This ancient continent has sent us little to brighten or embellish life, but has strewn thickly, with perils and difficulties, the path which lies before the now rising and future nations of South Africa." He then went on to show how time after time the slight beginnings of civilisation and learning had been swept away by ignorance, sloth, and barbarism in Africa; while in Europe gross superstition and degrading customs had been steadily replaced by Christianity and freedom.

"Yet, with apparently such slight encouragement before us, we here in the South of Africa have again boldly entered on the attempt to establish civilisation and Christianity in this continent, and to spread their blessings through the boundless territories which lie beyond our borders. . . . We are a small and scattered people, with many dangers and enemies around us and in our front, and with a task before us requiring all our energies and well and ripely-matured plans if we hope to accomplish it. And we do not doubt that we shall succeed, for the cause we labour for is the promotion of truth and knowledge, and the carrying out of God's service upon earth."

The first book placed upon the bookshelves by His Royal Highness was a rare and priceless MS. in Greek of the Gospels, the gift of Sir George Grey. After Prince Alfred had also presented Knight's

Shakespeare and *Pictorial History of England* as his own gift to the institution, he returned to the daïs, and gave through Sir George Grey to the people and Legislature of the Cape Colony a splendid portrait of the Queen. The national anthem was sung, and the Prince declared the institution opened.

Mr. Porter, the Attorney-General, fittingly acknowledged, on behalf of the Library Committee and the public, the honour which the Prince had done them, and their gratitude to Sir George Grey. In the course of his remarks he said, "Of Sir George Grey I need not speak. His character as a lover of learning is well and widely known ; and a lover of learning he ought to be, because he is not merely one of the large class who write books, but one of the rarer class about whom books are written ; and because independently of belonging to both these classes, he knows and feels that good books are great blessings, and that knowledge is not merely power but enjoyment. . . . Let His Royal Highness be assured that he carries away with him the heartiest good wishes of all ranks, races, creeds, and colours in South Africa ; that the people here, confident that in after life he will tread no path but that of honour, will watch with interest his future career, and that they will ever reckon it as one of the many services rendered to them by their Governor, Sir George Grey (cheers), that through his instrumentality the auspicious visit of Prince Alfred was arranged—a visit which has, as it were, annihilated ocean spaces, and brought us in feeling so close to the old Mother Country that we seem to see her cliffs again." In concluding his address, he called upon all present to give way to their enthusiasm, and thus testify their gratitude to Prince Alfred and Sir George Grey. The response was given in such cheers as are seldom heard, while the large assembly, throwing off conventional restraints, gave way to unbounded joy.

Next morning (September 19th) the Prince embarked. Before leaving the shores of South Africa he took part in one final ceremony. That was to declare the recently finished Prince Alfred's Jetty open for public traffic. This he did after having driven in the last silver bolt. Then shaking hands with many of his new friends, he entered his barge and proceeded to the Euryalus, realising with regret that his visit to South Africa was at an end.

Among those who accompanied Prince Alfred to the end of the jetty was the old chief Sandilli. As the Royal party passed between the two lines of soldiery, these lines closed in behind them. Sandilli told Sir George afterwards that it was with terrible misgivings he saw that impenetrable military force blocking up the pathway by which he had come. Suspicious of treachery, and accustomed to the cunning strategy of his barbaric foes, he realised with a sinking heart how completely he was in the power of the Governor. If, when the boat was reached, Sir George Grey should order him to take his seat in it, he felt that resistance would be vain. With every step he took, two more armed men closed in and added to the force which made retreat impossible. His fear was very real, though no trace of it appeared in the proud bearing of the old warrior.

The friendship cemented in South Africa between the Prince and the Governor has never been broken nor even disturbed. During the few months in which the guardianship of Prince Alfred was, as it were, confided to Sir George Grey, the latter made every effort to direct the mind of the Sailor Prince to the proper consideration of public affairs. In the Prince's presence, the Representative of the Queen received the native chiefs and discussed matters of state with them. When the Executive Council sat, Prince Alfred had a seat at the Council Board, and watched with interest the proceedings. To his hand was entrusted the commencement of those great public undertakings which made the history of that time memorable in Southern Africa. Nor did Sir George fail to impress upon the mind of his young and illustrious guest those lessons of wisdom and of faithfulness in government of which he himself had learned the value both in theory and practice.

Yet, amid this stately procession of wise counsels and great undertakings, the visit of the Duke of Edinburgh was one continued series of festivities and rejoicing. The universal welcome never ceased; the natural beauties of that part of the earth were seen and admired; and the pleasures of the chase were not forgotten or neglected.

It is not surprising that the Queen and Prince Albert felt grateful to Sir George Grey for the care and kindness lavished upon their son. In the letter which Her Majesty addressed to Sir George the heart of the mother speaks more strongly than the voice of the Queen:

"Though Sir George Grey will receive the official expression of the Queen's high sense of the manner in which Prince Alfred has been received at the Cape, she is anxious to express personally both the Prince Consort's and her own thanks for the very great kindness Sir George Grey showed our child during his most interesting tour in that fine colony; and she trusts that the effect produced on the nation and people in general will be as lasting and beneficial as it must have been on Prince Alfred to have witnessed the manner in which Sir George Grey devotes his whole time and energy to promote the happiness and welfare of his fellow-creatures."

The Queen sent to Sir George not merely a letter of thanks, which, though it would be remembered must be laid aside for preservation, but another memento which, being perpetually in the personal care and manual possession of the recipient, would always remind him of those days in South Africa when Prince Alfred and he were together—a pocket chronometer with an inscription such as a grateful Queen might indite to her faithful servant, was sent by Her Majesty to Sir George. For more than thirty years that timepiece has been his constant companion, and thus has continually reminded him of the pleasant past.

Nor will the Duke of Edinburgh, when he reads these pages, be displeased to hear that Sir George Grey has followed his career of public duty with increasing interest and pleasure.

It is strangely remarkable that the greatest chief of the native tribes in our South African dominions should instantly have recognised that the performance of the ordinary duties of the State by its princes, in common with and by the side of subjects of the Crown, is the surest evidence of public virtue, and the surest guarantee of public safety. Bearing this in mind, he observed that with the highest civilisation the necessity of the most noble setting such an example was recognised as a duty of paramount importance, although among uncivilised people such a thing was regarded as a terrible degradaton.

CHAPTER XXXV.

THE GREY COLLEGE.

" Not in vain the distance beacons. Forward, forward let us range,
  Let the great world spin for ever down the ringing grooves of change ;
  Thro' the shadow of the globe we sweep into the younger day,
  Better fifty years of Europe than a cycle of Cathay."
                                        Locksley Hall.

ALTHOUGH the Orange River territory had been abandoned by the Imperial Government, the High Commissioner felt a deep interest in the welfare of its people. The process of disintegration, commenced by abandoning the Transvaal and then the Orange River sovereignty, found, as we have seen, no sympathiser in Sir George Grey.

In his opinion, as appeared afterwards in the case of Samoa, the United States occupied the position of the most prominent portion of the British Empire, which in truth meant the English-speaking peoples. No accident of Government or temporary method of rule could ever, as he believed, effect a severance in the ultimate unity and destiny of that great race to which he was proud to belong, and to whose work as the rulers of the world he devoted the constant energies of his busy life.

Nor was it the least merit of his people, nor their least claim to universal supremacy, that they were able to absorb and assimilate members of all other races, and to raise them in a higher and nobler sense than ever did ancient Rome, to the privileges and duties of a nationality unique and unexampled.

He was especially qualified to hold these views, both by personal character and by hereditary descent.

The respect with which the Boers, whether of the Transvaal or the Orange Free State, or in the Queen's dominions, regarded him, was warmed into affection by his conduct towards them on all occasions.

But Sir George Grey enjoyed a peculiar and personal claim to their regard which no other Governor possessed. On his mother's side he claimed descent from a Huguenot noble, who had, at the Revocation of the Edict of Nantes, by the side of Lord Ligonier, afterwards William's general of horse, cut his way, followed by armed retainers, to the sea coast, and thence escaped to England. When a youth Grey had gone to Normandy and visited all the scenes amongst which his mother's ancestors had lived. And now he could describe to these South African descendants of Dutch and French refugees the places where many of their fathers, as well as his, had lived and died. Blood is proverbially thicker than water, and when the Boers found that within Sir George Grey's veins there coursed a strain of Huguenot blood, their hearts warmed towards him in an unwonted fashion.

In his first visit to the Orange Free State the difficulties in the matter of education, with which this new community was forced to contend, presented themselves distinctly to his mind. Among the fathers and heads of families there were men of culture and refinement, but among the stalwart youths and the thousands of boys growing rapidly to manhood there was a lack of that higher education which in these days is necessary to enable men to take a useful position in public affairs, or to keep upon an equal rank with the men of other countries.

This impediment to progress was enlarged and intensified in the case of the Orange Free State by its sudden abandonment. It was, in a single day, thrown upon its own resources. Rude wealth and plenty, wide pastures, flocks and herds, great possibilities for future development were indeed possessed by the infant republic. But it had no form of government, no institutions. These it had to create for itself.

The first necessities of communal existence and safety demanded all that the republic and its leaders could give of time and thought. At a glance it became evident to Sir George Grey that higher education, upon which so much of the future happiness and prosperity of the country must depend, was, while absolutely necessary, yet likely to be overlooked. Indeed, situated 800 miles from Cape Town, and speaking a foreign tongue, the Free Staters seemed left to ignorance and barbarism in the midst of savage nations.

Gratified, even delighted at the genial hospitality and kindness shown to him by the people of the Free State, and anxious to find some method of expressing his gratitude, the means by which that feeling might be permanently expressed quickly suggested themselves. To found and establish a college for the higher branches of learning, which college, situated in the capital of the republic, should be immediately accessible to all its youth, would fitly embody that spirit of love and sympathy which Sir George Grey felt within him for the people. He resolved, therefore, to lay the foundations of a college at Bloemfontein.

As soon as his determination became known, he

received assurances of assistance and support from all quarters. The President, Mr. Boshoff, expressed his pleasure and willingness to co-operate. Communications were entered into with the leading people of the State, and also with the Transvaal Republic, with the view of extending also in the Transvaal the benefits of higher education.

Sir George drew the plans on which the new educational institution should be conducted. As the majority of the youth of the country spoke the Dutch language only, he advised that while English should not be neglected, the main current of teaching should be in Dutch. He knew that this would obtain for the young community substantial assistance from the Universities and people of Holland.

Endowments for the Bloemfontein College were readily procured. The Government also assisted. Correspondence was opened with the Universities of Holland. Professors were appointed who took the learning of the old world to South Africa. Temporary buildings were as soon as possible procured. And thus the cause of the higher knowledge was absolutely victorious, and its teaching established for ever in the Free State.

That college has never languished. Year by year its endowments have increased by the gifts of the living and bequests. The Government and the Volksraad have diligently nursed it. The number of students has grown with its accommodation. Some years after its opening a grateful people gave to it the name of its beloved founder, and the " Grey College " will, so far as human wisdom can foresee, last as long in Bloemfontein as human civilisation exists.

The progress of this institution has always been to Sir George Grey a matter of delight. In December, 1890, the railway, in continuation of that which he

had commenced in 1855, at length reached Bloemfontein. On its opening to the capital of the Free
State there were public rejoicings and festivities. The
English South African Governors were invited, and
the principal personages of all the civilised portions
of South Africa were gathered at Bloemfontein to
participate in the national holiday.

Among those who joined in this glad festival were
many of the leading men in the Free State, the
Transvaal Republic, Natal, and the Cape Colony, who
had received their education at the Grey College.
Some were men of mature age, fathers of families.
As they gathered together on this auspicious occasion,
beneath the shadow of the College halls, they did not
forget the man who, now laid aside by age and sickness from public duties, had thirty-five years before
planned the existence and constitution of their University.

On December 23rd, 1890, there appeared in the
New Zealand Herald in Auckland the following paragraph :—

SIR GEORGE GREY AND SOUTH AFRICA.

The other day, in mentioning the visit of Sir Henry Loch to
British Kaffraria, and the speeches made at the gatherings on
the occasion, we noted the fact that the memory of Sir George
Grey in South Africa remains as fresh as ever. A fresh illustration of that fact we give to-day. A cablegram has reached
Sir George Grey by the hands of Dr. Lemon, Superintendent of
Telegraphs, which he has received from Sir John Pender, Chairman of the Eastern Extension Telegraph Company, to whom it
had been sent by the Minister for Crown Lands, Cape Colony.
In sending the message to Sir John Pender, the Minister for
Crown Lands says :—" We are in the midst of very enthusiastic
festivities in connection with the opening of the Free State railway. At a most successful gathering I agreed to send to you the
following message, with a request that you would kindly see to
its reaching Sir George Grey." The following is the message

referred to, sent through the courtesy of Sir John Pender as a cablegram memo., as well as Sir George's reply :—

"BLOEMFONTEIN, December 18th.

"At a meeting of the Grey College past students, who assembled to celebrate the opening of the railway of Bloemfontein, they, there being present with them the President of the Free State, the Governors of Cape Colony and Natal, the representatives of the South African railway, the Administrators of Bechuanaland, the Administrators of the Basutos, and three members of the Cape Ministry, and a number of other visitors from the surrounding states, send their greetings to the founder of their Alma Mater."

To this Sir George sent the following reply :—

"Dr. Lemon, Wellington. Sir John Pender. Kindly forward the following to the Minister of Crown Lands, Cape Colony :— 'Greetings gratefully acknowledged. In thought I am often with you. All blessings attend South African States. May the College ever train noble citizens.'

"G. GREY."

The telegram reached Sir George on Sunday morning. The church bells had ceased to ring, and the worshippers were gathered through the length and breadth of New Zealand for their Sabbath devotions. Lonely and quiet, weak from illness, Sir George sat, thinking of the varied scenes of his strange life. Only the day before he had been speaking of the establishment of the Grey College at Bloemfontein, and expressing his gratitude to God for its success. His mind was running upon South African matters. Missionaries, whose memories were recalled to him by the presence in Auckland of Captain Hore, fresh from Lake Tanganyika; the Grey Hospital at King Williamstown, which had also been the subject of recent conversation, the Cape, Natal, and the surrounding districts, were crowding one upon the other through his memory.

In the midst of this train of thought the telegraph

messenger arrived, and Sir George read with feelings too deep for utterance, the pleasant message which had traversed the world to find him. A great traveller and philosopher, Baron von Hübner, in the description of his travels through the British Empire says :—

" Passing before the Public Library (in Cape Town) I stop sometimes before a stone statue, not on account of its artistic value, but because it represents a remarkable man. It is one of the rare examples of a monument erected in honour of a man during his lifetime."*

This refers to the statue of Sir George Grey.

The receipt of the telegram which showed that his memory was fresh and grateful to the people of the Free State, and that the remembrance of that which he had done was cherished there, was to Sir George Grey more gratifying than the erection of any monument of brass or marble. For it revealed the fact that he himself was remembered with affection, and had a place not merely given by the pencil of the artist or the chisel of the sculptor, but imperishably engraven by the loftiest human sentiments upon the hearts of men. And deeper still was his gratitude to the Almighty that he had been spared to see in his lifetime, such wonderful results following the thoughts and deeds of bygone years.

The influence exerted by the Grey College is evidently not restricted to Bloemfontein, nor to the Orange Free State.

"Directly Mr. Rhodes got back to South Africa after his recent trip to England, he hastened to Kimberley, where in a speech at the Africander Bond dinner, amongst other things he said: 'I have obtained enormous subscriptions in order to found a

* "Through the British Empire," vol. i., p. 40—Baron von Hübner.

teaching university in Cape Colony. I will own to you why I feel so strongly in favour of that project. I saw at Bloemfontein the immense feeling of friendship that all members had for the Grey Institute, where they had been educated, and from which they had gone out to the world. I said to myself, if we could get a teaching university founded in Cape Colony, taking the people from all parts at the ages of eighteen to twenty-one, they would go back tied to one another by the strongest feeling that can be created, because the period in one's life when you indulge in friendships which are seldom broken is from eighteen to twenty-one.' " *

* *Greater Britain*, May 15th, 1891.

CHAPTER XXXVI.

LETTERS FROM AFRICAN CHIEFS.

" Nature is fine in love, and when 'tis fine
It sends some precious instance of itself
After the thing it loves."

Hamlet.

DURING the whole of his residence at Cape Town, Sir George Grey often received letters from the heads of the native tribes under his rule. The affectionate dependence on their good Governor which these "children of a larger growth" expressed is at once touching and quaint. They looked upon him as both willing and able to satisfy all their desires. Appeals were made to Sir George when famine threatened them, when the injustice or depredation of neighbouring tribes called for punishment, when a new gun or saddle was eagerly desired, when their children needed education, or pestilence was destroying their people. Nothing was too great, nothing too small to be brought under the notice of the " King of the Cape," as Sir George was styled in some of these appeals.

And they were justified in this belief by the never-failing consideration to their requests, and the sincere interest in all that concerned his native subjects shown by the Governor. Ever busy, he had yet time to attend to the most trivial wishes of single individuals. He not only established hospitals for their

E 2

sick, but would undertake toilsome journeys into most remote parts of the country to visit one dying native; he founded great schools where their children might learn useful trades or fit themselves to teach and follow scientific pursuits, and at the same time he granted the childish wishes of many little students, writing to them, sending gifts, arranging for some of them to go to school in England, and encouraging all of them to write to him about anything which interested or concerned them.

Amongst the treasures of Sir George Grey's correspondence, the simple, heart-felt utterances of these little native children hold an honoured place. They are dearer to him than the eulogistic letters of the wise and the great of the earth.

George Macomo and Duke Ishatshur, amongst sons of the other principal chiefs, were sent to school in England, and wrote long letters from Nuneaton to their benefactor. They sent messages to their relations through the Governor, and asked him of their welfare. Everything they saw in England was compared (generally unfavourably) with what Sir George had at Government House. The boys went to a cattle show. They saw some fine horses—" but although they have not reached up to yours," writes George; he continued, " we are thankful to God for this mercy to hear our prayer, when we prayed for you, to send you back again because you did so please us. . . . I am sure it does make me feel to wish to be there."

A very touching little letter, from Emma Sandilli, deserves to be quoted at length. The writer was the only daughter of Sandilli, paramount chief of the Kafir tribes. She afterwards married the paramount chief of the Tambookie tribes. Sir George Grey had her placed at the Kafir School, which he founded and maintained at Zonnebloem, near Cape Town. No home-sick English school girl ever wrote to her parents with more perfect confidence that her request would meet with loving and indulgent consideration than Emma Sandilli to the Governor of Cape Colony.

Zonnebloem, November 2nd, 1860.

My Lord Governor,—I meant to ask you if you please, Sir, to let me go back to see my parents for a short time, and I will come back again. I will not stop any longer. It is because I do desire to see my own land, I beg you to let me go to see my parents, and if you do let me go I shall never forget your kindness. I should be so pleased to see my mother's face again. I beg you do let me go, my Lord Governor. Of your kindness I am quite sure that you will. I cannot do as I like now because you are in my father's place. If you do listen to my ask, I am sure I do not know what I shall do, because I cannot do anything for you, and you can do so much for me.

EMMA SANDILLI.

The sons of the chief Moroka were much attached to Sir George Grey. The Governor desired to give the elder of these lads an English education. His proposal to do so nearly sent Samuel Moroka wild with delight. How eagerly he grasped at the offer, and how anxious he was that his wishes might not be misinterpreted, may be gathered from the following expressive if rather incoherent letter :—

Cape Town.

To Sir George Grey,—I send this letter to you, Sir. I like to go to England, Sir. I like very much, Sir, and I want anything I must ask to you, Sir, and I was wrote to my Father. I tell him I shall ask to you, Sir, and he said it is good. He said if I want anything I must ask to you, Sir. I like very much, Sir, if I can go England, I shall be glad, Sir. Please Sir, I like to go, and I thought my Father he shall be glad, Sir, if he hear I go England to learning. He shall very glad Because you Promise my Father you said to him You shall Bring me England. Please Sir, I like very much, Sir, to go to England, Sir.—I am.

SAMUEL MOROKA.

George Moroka, a brother of the last writer, was at the Kafir College at Zonnebloem, when he received a letter from his father containing bad news. A rumour had reached Moroka's settlement that their good Governor was going to leave them. George wrote immediately to Sir George Grey. His letter, dated July 11th, 1861, contains the following passage :—

> He (Moroka) say he heard some people say you go away from the Cape. He say he don't know if it is true or not. . . . I tell my father, I say to him, if Sir George Grey go Home I will go with him, but he say very well; but I tell him if you go I shall go with you.—I am, your affectionate son,
>
> GEORGE MOROKA.

A letter written nearly twenty years after Sir George Grey left South Africa for the second time, by one of the former students at the Kafir College at Zonnebloem, says :—

> Vast changes took place since you left us, and we are unto this day like unto the children of Israel after the death of their kind Pharaoh. My heart aches when I remember the time you kept us, when you used to give us goodly dinners, and used to return to Zonnebloem each time with 5s. each boy, and all wishing for the morrow to buy sweets and marbles. In the year 1877 my native race broke into war with the colony. The consequence is the death of Sandilli, killed in a bush, and the capture of all his sons, Edmund and all who are in Robbin (or Seal)* Island unto this day.
>
> I do mourn for His Excellency, for I am sure I would not have been so poor if he were still with us.

Sir George Grey's indulgent kindness was not confined to the children alone, as is shown by many letters, like the following, which a missionary in the Nyati country wrote at the request and dictation of one of the greatest of all African chiefs :—

* Place where political prisoners were occasionally confined.

Moselekatse, the King of the Matabele,

To the King of the Cape,—Oh! King of the Cape, I send these words to you to inform you that the waggon with all the fine things it contained, which you gave me, was taken away by the Boers, and to beg of you to help me by giving me another waggon containing guns, powder, lead, beads, boiling-pots, and clothing.

That I long to see the way clear from here to the Cape, so that I may trade with the English, and that thus we may become one people.

With my kindest regards to you, and longing to hear your reply, and also to welcome messengers from you.

MOSELEKATSE.

The chief being determined that the " King of the Cape" should receive his actual handwriting, persisted, in spite of the arguments and opposition of the missionary, in adding a purposeless and complicated scrawl to this letter, which Mr. Thomas sent with many apologies to His Excellency.

The chief was obdurate, and to all the missionary's efforts to dissuade him simply remarked, "You are against me, for you will not send my words to the King. I know that the King will hear me; and, therefore, why do you refuse to send to him?"

The feelings of the coloured people of Lesseytown when Sir George Grey visited them in 1860, after his return from England, found expression in the following original address :—

To the Chief, that is, Sir George Grey,
    Governor of the Country.

Chief,—We greet you, because you have returned and come to our place. We thank thee because thou hast come, thou, who art so great, to us, the little lot of Lesseytown.

The thing we thank for is this: In time gone by in our sitting we had not the thought that a thing so great as thou could come to where we sit.

Another thing we thank thee for: it is the word you have spoken. We see the *House* to teach *Children* is standing by your word.

Another thing it is to thank : that we see our children, they begin to learn the trades ; it is by your kindness. May the *Lord of Heaven* put His blessing upon these works, that it may be a light to them, the many of our nation, they, who yet sit in darkness, that they may see the standing of righteousness, which is fastened among us.

Another thing also which we thank thee for : it is that we have sent a little lot of our children to go and learn at Salem.

Again we thank for your desire to help us, with a stone to grind. But we have got another thought of it : we have cut our lands, we have ploughed wheat to sell it to finish that thing.

Now then, Chief, we need your help ; we ask of you the trade of building waggons, that our children may learn it also.

We now greet the Chief. We pray for thy hearing to these words we have spoken. Go then, Chief of us, by safety, to those troubles you are going to. It is us, who would it may come right for you, by the help of God.

A letter from Moshesh, which is not dated but must have been written about the same time, conveys the pleasure of that chief at Sir George Grey's return. The following is a close translation :—

To the Governor,

My Lord,—I rejoice in that I am again given an opportunity to meet the Representative of the Queen in this part of Africa. I had longed that you could have come to separate us before this war had yet been fought, but those who made war upon me would not. To-day Boshof has sued (for peace), and we have placed our arms on the ground ; and I am glad, for war is not a thing which I have ever liked. But since you desire that peace should be built up between the Boers and me, I ought to tell you the secret of my heart.

The little matters of my nation are known to you. You know that when the whites had not yet crossed the Orange River, I was lord of the land, commencing from the junction of the Orange and Caledon, to the districts of Smithfield and of Bloemfontein and Thabanchie, and reaching to Winburg and to opposite Harrismith. You know that those who crossed the river first were people who asked me room to sit for a short time to pasture their flocks, and it happened that when they began to trouble me, Governor Napier scolded them. Afterwards other Governors even asked me for room to place whites on some farms, and I consented (to place them), but not after the manner of the whites, it was according to the laws of the Lesuti. Now with us the land is the chief's, and a *man* is not permitted to sell it. That which

I now say is that the Representatives of the Queen have borrowed farms from me and placed people on them, while some have only placed themselves (squatted). I had trusted that these people whom I received would have trusted me, whereas it is not so, but ever since I lent them a portion of my land there has been no peace, and there have been always disputes and quarrels. Now I say those who borrowed from me were the Representatives of the Queen, and whereas these loans have already given birth to wars, and will continue to give birth to them, I pray them to return me that which I lent them. There can be no real peace until this stumblingblock is removed. Yes, I lent to the Government of the Queen, and to no other, and the duty of the masters when they went away was to return to me that which they had borrowed from me. In questions of land I do not know the Boers, for it is not they who borrowed from me. The things I now tell you are things of truth, and I trust that the Government of the Queen will adjudicate righteously.

Moshesh next requested that firearms and powder might be given to his people. He said they were a quiet tribe, not given to war.

There is game in the land of the Lesuto, and we are without that with which to kill it.

I have other things, which I shall tell you with my mouth. Though, however, I have been telling you my little affairs, it is not that I would dictate how you ought to act, for you are greater than we. In short, I have placed my hope in you, and have confidence that you will adjudicate righteously.

Another letter from Moshesh, dated August 20th, 1861, commences thus :—

Sir,—I have learnt with sorrow that you are on the point of leaving Cape Colony to go to New Zealand. I wish you all sorts of prosperity in the new responsibility which is going to be confided to you, and I pray you to remember me and my people. I ask you also to speak of me, and of what concerns me, to your successor, so that he may have the same kindness for us which you have had for us.

In the month of July last I wrote to you to tell you that I was not bound to anybody to make war upon you, and that was the truth. To-day I learn that there are troubles among the Zulus at the place of Panda's son, and I think that Your Excellency is convinced that I have no part in that business. If, following the example of the kings of Medes and Persians, I could at my death leave laws to my people, I should tell them never to make war against the English people.

Strange rumours have reached me. They say, and I have reason to believe that it is true, that Pretorius went to Panda to ask him for help to make war against my people. I have also heard that Panda would have refused with indignation and anger, but his son would have accepted on condition that the booty taken in the war should be for him, and the country for the Government of the Free State. Great chief, you who receive news from all parts of this country, do you know anything of this plan of Pretorius ?

This was accompanied by another letter from the son of Moshesh, also written by the French missionary. It alluded to the warlike attitude of the Boers, and the rumour of their uniting with the Zulus to make war upon Moshesh and his people. It also spoke of another matter :—

I have been directed by my father, Moshesh, to thank you for the care bestowed on my brother, whom you have sent to England for his education. He has written to tell us of his arrival in Europe.

CHAPTER XXXVII.

REVIEW OF SIR GEORGE GREY'S ADMINISTRATION IN SOUTH AFRICA.

" Be useful where thou livest, that they may
    Both want and wish thy pleasing presence still;
Kindness, good parts, great plans, are the way
    To compass this; find out men's want and will,
And meet them there. All worldly joys go less
To the one joy of doing kindnesses."

Herbert.

WITHIN twelve months of Prince Alfred's visit to South Africa, Sir George Grey received an intimation from the Imperial Government that his presence was urgently needed once more in New Zealand. For the third time he was called away from the government of one colony which he had brought triumphantly out of great danger, to undertake fresh responsibilities in another. For more than twenty years he had occupied the position of Governor without intermission, and yet, during that time, his administration of the affairs of any colony had never once been terminated by the expiry of his term of office.

On the present occasion his prompt obedience to the call of duty was in direct opposition to his own interests. The Governor-Generalship of Canada had been promised him at the expiration of his government in South Africa. This would in all probability have led to the administration of India. Both these positions offered great possibilities of public usefulness, far more attractive to men like Sir George

Grey than the social distinction they confer are to the majority.   Yet, in going to New Zealand in 1861, he unhesitatingly renounced these hopes.

For eight years he had governed Cape Colony. With his coming representative institutions had been inaugurated.   The history of the colony in its present form dates from 1854.   On his arrival he had found diversity of interests, discontent, confusion everywhere—in government, in commerce, in Imperial directions, and local management.   The Governor had steadily reduced this anarchy to order.   He had fought ignorance, injustice, apathy, want of sympathy and indifference.   He had established schools, libraries, hospitals, and other institutions of a similar nature in many parts of the country.   Cape Town, Zonnebloem, Lovedale, King Williamstown, Port Elizabeth, Lesseytown, Smithfield, and Bloemfontein are amongst the towns in which such monuments recall the memory of a " good, great man."

Forms of government had been firmly established, great public works, like that of the breakwater in Table Bay, begun.   Roads had been made, and communication with the interior of the country rendered easier.   Just before his recall, Sir George Grey had commenced a work which he had long planned.   On the 31st March, 1859, he turned the first sod of the Cape Town and Wellington railway.   This was the first line constructed in South Africa.   Twenty-five years later the colony had 1,599 miles of rail open for traffic, and had spent nearly 13½ millions of money on their completion.   In 1855 the value of exports from Cape Colony amounted to £970,839.   When Sir George Grey left, this sum was nearly doubled.

One of the most important sources of South African wealth is ostrich-farming.   Previous to Sir George Grey's governorship no attempt had been made to domesticate these birds, and it was feared that they would be exterminated for the sake of their feathers. The Governor, however, believed it possible to tame them. His experiment succeeded so well that others followed his example. The average sales of ostrich feathers from Port Elizabeth alone now amount to over £50,000 a month.

But none of these undertakings seemed to Sir George Grey more important than the reforms he instituted among the natives. Their peace and well-being were his constant care. In dealing with them he obtained the counsel and assistance of experienced and competent advisers.

Several letters from Florence Nightingale on the subject of his native schools and hospital show the liveliest interest in his work, and a great desire to help with suggestions as to management and in any other way possible. The tone of the letters throughout is expressed by the concluding sentence of one of them dated 16th April, 1860 :—"God bless you for all you are doing for these fine races."

Sir George frequently applied to her for information as to the best means of treating these aborigines so as to lessen the perils from new and strange diseases so generally fatal to native races. Accordingly Miss Nightingale prepared a Form of Return for the native schools, which the Duke of Newcastle had printed. "If these could be filled up," wrote Miss Nightingale, "they would give us the information we want, in order to enable us to judge of the influences which deteriorate the children's health."

In Sir George Grey's farewell address to the Parliament at the Cape of Good Hope in August, 1861, he thus spoke of his aims, and of his feelings in leaving South Africa :—

Every effort has, therefore, been made to build up a system under which the various races in South Africa might with mutual advantage be brought into constant and open intercourse with each other, as the civilised portions of the population spread further and further from the parent colony in which themselves and their ancestors had been originally settled.

The necessary operation of such a system was that here, on the spot, would, at least in part, be trained the statesmen, the lawyers, the divines, and the leaders who would direct, lead, and control the tide of emigration which must year by year with ever-accumulating force pour forth from this colony and its offshoots.

.   .   .   .

Now that my own part on the scene of action has been played out, I look back with regret on some things done, at much that has been left undone, but with pleasure at some things which have been planted, some growing into life. But amidst these mingled feelings of sorrow and of hope, which must long live in my mind, there will ever survive a grateful remembrance of the sympathies and the assistance which have on so many occasions been given by this Parliament and the inhabitants of South Africa to the efforts I have made to conduct successfully the Queen's service, and to give effect to Her Majesty's ceaseless desire to promote the happiness and welfare of her subjects and of all the races to whom the influence of her very extended sway reaches.

The plan Sir G. Grey proposed was "to gain an influence over all the tribes inhabiting the borders of the colony, through British Kaffraria eastward to Natal, by employing them on public works, opening up the country, by establishing institutions for the education of their children and the relief of their sick, by introducing amongst them laws and regulations suited to their condition, and by these and other means gradually winning them to Christianity and civilisation, thus changing by degrees your apparently irreconcilable foes into friends, having common interests with yourselves."

With such an earnest desire to benefit and civilise the coloured population of South Africa, it was only natural that Sir George should be in frequent correspondence with the various missionaries there. He sympathised with and helped all missionary effort, untrammelled by any narrow sectarian prejudices. While forwarding their work, he was much assisted in his own plans by the information these heralds of Christianity were able to give him. By their labours he was able to make a splendid collection of vocabularies and other books in the different South African languages, as well as to learn thoroughly the condition, the wants, the character, and the best method of dealing with the various races. A few quotations from the letters he received from missionaries in South Africa will illustrate this, and show the mutual benefits conferred and received by the Governor and themselves.

A letter from Bishop Colenso, then at an industrial school in Maritzburg, Natal, dated 1859, relates the progress made by native pupils. It also tells of the difficulties the Bishop was experiencing in getting his Zulu grammar with appendix and abridgment printed. Sir George is thanked for his aid both in this work and towards the enlargement of the college buildings.

In June, 1859, the Bishop wrote to ask Sir G. Grey's advice on the subject of his resigning the Bishopric of Natal, and offering his services as Missionary Bishop of Zululand. There had not previously been such an officer, but it had been decided to send one, and no suitable person could be thought of.

Several very interesting letters from Mr. Wm. Govan to Sir George, written from Lovedale early in 1857, give detailed accounts of the progress of the native school at that place. At that time about twenty Kafir youths were received and taught trades as waggon makers, tailors, blacksmiths, carpenters, and masons. Frequent allusion is made to the deep interest taken by the Governor in the early Kafir literature, and his untiring efforts to make a complete collection of the earliest printed works.

Mr. Govan sent him a number of old and interesting copies. The following extract from one of his letters gives some idea of the hopes which filled the hearts of missionaries and others who wished for the welfare of the native people, and their rejoicing at the course of conduct adopted by Sir George Grey, so different to the cold judicial policy of most of the Governors:

" Allow me to say that it is to me and my brethren a cause of much satisfaction that Your Excellency has been led to take so deep an interest in Kafir literature and Kafir history. We anticipate under the Divine blessing most important results from Your Excellency's researches and measures."

Letters from the Bishop of Grahamstown go quite as fully into all details connected with mission work in the interior. The readiness of the Governor to provide funds for this object is shown by the frequency and expectancy with which demands for still further assistance are made.

A number of letters in 1858 from Robert Moffat (Matabele Mission) relate to specimens of the Bechuana language which he was indefatigable in procuring for Sir G. Grey, who on the other hand interested himself in sending lesson-books in Zulu to the missionary.

Exploration and discovery owed much to the Governor. It was he who started Speke on the expedition which ended in such an ovation on his discovery of the sources of the Nile. One of Speke's letters to Sir George Grey, after the return of the latter to New Zealand, tells its own story. It was written from that ill-fated town in Upper Egypt, where Gordon, deserted and friendless, met a hero's death :—

Khartoum, March 30th, 1863.

My dear Sir George,—As I have now joined the two hemispheres, traced the Nile down from the Victoria Nyanza, and know its length is equal to $\frac{1}{12}$ the circumference of the globe, I cannot refrain to express to you what I have ever felt at heart, the warm gratitude that pervades me for the many kindnesses you evinced in my behalf on the Fort and at the Cape. I have now accomplished my work, and I believe done it well, for I have mapped my route on foot the whole way, and am carrying home upwards of one thousand observations.

Sir George Grey's prudence and foresight in providing Captain Speke with a native guard were highly applauded by Livingstone, whose letters are perhaps the most interesting of any in this portion of Sir George's correspondence.

When Dr. Livingstone and his wife went to the Cape in 1858, they took letters of introduction to the Governor from Mr. Labouchere (Lord Taunton). From that time a deep and strong friendship subsisted between them.

Livingstone's letters date from May, 1858, to February, 1863. They are all in his own handwriting, cover sixty pages of foolscap, and are full of interest and information.

Writing in June, 1859, of the statement made by an English minister in 1857 that two black men with Portuguese names had been the first to traverse the African continent, Dr. Livingstone said that the ignorance of the Portuguese of the existence of Lake Shirwa, and other evidence, conclusively proved that they had only gone to Tette, not to Mozambique, about 400 miles further. The Portuguese, however, afterwards attempted to claim this honour and reap its advantages.

Another letter announces the discovery of the source of the River Shire in "the hitherto undiscovered Nyassa, one of those lakes with which South Africa is studded." Dr. Livingstone was much amused at the information conveyed by English papers about the region of his explorations. A great deal of it was new to him, and most interesting. "I wish our good friends would only tell us all about it beforehand. It would save us a good deal of trouble, and deliver us from the perplexity of guessing and grumbling. . . . Now, anything positive, if given beforehand, will be thankfully received, though it comes from the archives of Prester John." There is something delightfully calm and business-like in the following paragraph from the account of a visit to an island in Lake Nyassa : "Elephants and hippopotami very tame. Alligators seldom kill men, so we could bathe in the delicious cool waters when we liked."

The steamer they had on the Zambesi did not particularly arouse the explorer's enthusiasm, to judge by his description. The engines were so weak " as to be unable to help us in the difficulty. She was only one-sixteenth of an inch thick in the beginning, and is now like an old copper kettle, full of holes in one part." Alluding to future navigation he prudently adds : " if she will only stick together so long." In another place he says : "We have left Macgregor Laird's precious punt in a sinking state— funnel, furnace, deck and bottom all done simultaneously, after only twelve months' wear."

These letters deal with the navigation of South African rivers ; the discovery and exploration of wild country ; the derivation and grammatical structure of the various dialects ; the diagnosis and remedial measures for the treatment of the fatal African fever, which the explorer had had himself in severe forms twenty-seven times, and for which his cure was almost infallible; the capabilities of different districts; and the use of newly-discóvered plants, and directions for their cultivation. Accompanying these letters were maps, vocabularies, reports, seeds, plants, and innumerable interesting specimens in many different branches of science and research.

In Dr. Livingstone's letters there are also continual references to the pernicious influence of the slave trade, and plans for establishing English stations which would encourage commerce. About twenty thousand slaves annually pass through Quiloa on their way to the Coast from the Lakes. Portuguese trading had evil effects, and Dr. Livingstone writes:—" We must have English colonisation. I have no doubt as to its success had we a man like you to set it agoing."

When Sir George was recalled from the Cape, Livingstone begged his assistance in getting free navigation on the Zambesi. He said it was admitted by the Governor of Tette that he and his party were the first to reach that district by the Zambesi from the sea. The devoted explorer wrote that he would not mind owning the supremacy of the Portuguese over any part known or traded to by them; but his explorations and those of Speke and Burton had opened up widely-extended territories. Could these lands be utilized for English settlement and commerce it was but reasonable to suppose that a great trade in cotton would spring up, and a stop be put to the slave trade. If the Government did not help in these plans, Livingstone wrote, he would build a boat at his own expense to protect settlers and develop lawful trade. The Portuguese he knew would object to this, and had the power of placing great obstacles in the way, but he was firm in his opinion. " We ought to have free passage to our discoveries, and our success, without diminishing their territory an inch, would promote the prosperity of their establishments."

The censure of the Home Government when they recalled Sir George found no echo in Livingstone's mind. He seems scarcely to have been aware of it when he wrote, " I need scarcely say that I am as sorry as anyone on account of your departure from the Cape. But I hope it may be only to afford you wider scope for your energies." When the news of the Governor's return reached him he wrote, " Right good tidings they are, and I am extremely glad and thankful in consequence."

The missionaries had great cause for thankfulness at this event, as they realised still more fully after Sir George Grey left the Cape finally. Livingstone's letters illustrate this. One of February, 1863, begins : " We have been very much baffled in our work since you left, and our prospects now are far from bright." The concluding paragraph runs thus : " If you still wish to do us a good turn write a line, for a word from you is ever valuable and exhilarating."

CHAPTER XXXVIII.

THE GREY LIBRARY.

" For his bounty
There was no winter in't ; an autumn 'twas
That grew the more by reaping."
Antony and Cleopatra.

ALTHOUGH Sir George Grey did not present his magnificent library to the Cape during his residence there, yet an account of it will occur more appropriately here than in any other division of this work. A few months after the Governor had gone to his new duties, one of the members of the Ministry at the Cape of Good Hope received an interesting letter from him. Sir George Grey began by stating that throughout his life he had delighted in collecting manuscripts and early-printed books, with the idea of publishing fresh editions of many of them in the leisure of advancing age. This hope, he now found, was an illusion. Instead of lessening, the claims on his time grew more numerous and pressing each year; and his self-imposed task had now grown to such dimensions that it would require a lifetime to accomplish, however imperfectly. Anxious lest the collection, which had been made with so much care, should be dispersed in private hands, he had formed the design of bestowing it on the people of South Africa, not after his own death, but making the gift immediately to the colony, for which he felt much affection. A few cases of books accompanied this letter. The main part of the library was, however, in England. It was not till April, 1864, that the whole collection was housed in the building which Prince Alfred had opened four years earlier.

At the first annual meeting of subscribers to the Cape Town Public Library after Sir George Grey had made his noble present, the chairman, Mr. J. Fairbairn, M.L.A., in the course of an eloquent address, said :

This institution has been favoured with a gift of great value by our late excellent Governor, Sir George Grey. It consists partly of manuscript copies taken before the art of printing was known in Europe, and early printed editions of works that have shone like stars in the firmament of literature for many generations, and which, in their youthful dress with decorations significant of manners and fancies long vanished from life, are much esteemed by the philosophic historian as well as by the curious antiquary. . . .

The venerable libraries in the most famous abodes of learning would have acknowledged such a gift with gratitude as a priceless addition to their stores. . . .

But highly as we prize this rich gift as a possession and a trust for future ages, we experience a more profound and pleasing sentiment of regard towards the giver, who has selected us from all the world to be recipients and guardians of this treasure. . . .

In many of its aspects the Government of Sir George Grey in South Africa will be regarded as a remarkable era in our history. . . .

This considerable collection of books with free access to all who may wish to consult or peruse them, has ever had the praise of strangers. In their new abode, in union and communion with a Museum already rich and arranged with science and taste ; in a sweet and quiet garden, terminated in prospect by a college expanding into a university, this institution has now every quality to fix the affections of a man like Sir George Grey—one endowed with large discourse, looking before and after, discovering the fruit in the bud, and disposed by habit to view with complacency the early developments of society, to which a single mind may sometimes give a permanent direction towards truth and virtue.

After speaking of the foundation of the Library, exactly one hundred years previous to the date of Sir

George Grey's trust, by a bequest of books, manuscripts, paintings, and a sum of *£*200 by Joachim Nicholas Dessin, the chairman pointed out that it was founded by private liberality, that private individuals had since contributed largely to its stores and convenience, that Sir George Grey had now enriched it with a gift worth more than all the previous collection, and that the Government and the people as a whole had hitherto done very little towards its support.

When Sir George Grey first landed in South Africa, the Public Library at Cape Town was of considerable size and importance, but was very inadequately lodged in a side room of the Exchange Buildings. It was owing to the Governor's persistent and personal influence that the Cape Parliament voted the large sum of money spent in building the present handsome edifice. Afterwards the Cape people erected a statue of Sir G. Grey immediately in front of the Library.

The possession of Sir George's literary treasures (one of the finest private collections in the world) made the South African Library take a very high position. Mr. F. S. Lewis, M.A., Chief Librarian of the South African Public Library, who had long been connected with the " Bodleian," at Oxford, referring to the position which the South African Library occupies with regard to others, said it was the third in point of size of colonial libraries, but it was first in point of importance. If the Grey Collection were burnt or destroyed, the fact would be known all over the world and regretted by every man who loved learning. Other libraries might be destroyed and the loss would only be local, but if this collection, or indeed some particular books in it, were lost, there would be a cry throughout the whole world.

Glancing at the contents of the bookshelves, the visitor is first struck by the prominence given to philological works. Brought much into contact with the natives in all his governments, and holding very decidedly the opinion that to successfully govern uncivilised races an intimate knowledge of their characters, traditions, and manner of thought was necessary, Sir George diligently studied the languages of the various coloured populations under his rule.

The estimation in which leading authorities on philology held the service rendered to science by Sir George Grey's researches and collections is gathered from many letters. Space will only permit of quotations from two or three.

Professor Max Müller wrote in 1860, thanking Sir George Grey for a present of books, and particularly mentioning the catalogue of the Library at the Cape, about which he said : "I have but little doubt that it might form the subject of an article in the *Quarterly*, which would interest many readers in England and abroad. If the editor of the *Quarterly* would offer the article to me I should do my best to make it interesting, though one could hardly avoid entering into some questions connected with the science of language, which would necessarily require a somewhat minute treatment. However, an account of your own services and of the services rendered by missionaries to the cause of philology and ethnology, might give to the article a certain variety and relief, and I should hope to be able to turn it into an appeal to the public for granting a more active and permanent support to a science which I believe will rise in time to be the most important of all sciences, the science of language and of man."

Another interesting letter is from Baron de Bunsen. It is dated the 2nd of October, 1860, and runs thus :

"You have heaped upon all scholars of African ethnology, and upon all friends of comparative philology such rich treasures of new and of true facts that we are really, all of us, and particularly those of the school to which I glory to belong, the historical, forced by you to make the *first* step in knowledge, which is that of knowing the full extent of our ignorance as to what we wish to know and to understand. As to myself, I hope to have made, and most willingly, at the head of those precious linguistic documents, the *second* step, viz., that of convincing myself of the abundance of matter which is in store for us, thanks to your enlightened and indefatigable researches and collections. They have surpassed my fondest expectations."

The letter goes on to say that what Sir George Grey had already done in the cause of science had raised everywhere the expectation that he would succeed in his project of establishing a permanent African University, or, at least, a South African Ethnological Museum, thus leading to more complete and certain knowledge concerning the origin and descent of the various native tribes by the collection of facts concerning their languages, dialects, and idioms.

Remarkably similar to Bunsen's expression is the following passage from one of Ch. Lassen's letters, written from Bonn in August, 1859 :—"All students of general philology will for ever remain deeply grateful to your Excellency for making known to them such a rare and complete collection of works on the languages and ethnology of Africa and Polynesia."

In the collection thus alluded to, now in the South African Public Library, there are publications and manuscripts in, or relating to, seventy-eight African languages and dialects, comprising 815 books in all. There are specimens of over twenty Australian dialects given in forty books. Sir G. Grey's researches, as published in his "Journal of Two Expeditions," first proved that all South Australian languages were related to each other. Many works on the structure and grammar of these dialects were written by Captain Grey himself, whilst a large proportion of the others were prepared at his request or published at his expense.

Nearly 40 books and manuscripts relate to the Papuan languages.

In the Fijian language, the different dialects of five islands, there are 42 works.

Rotuma or Granville Island contributes 4 works.

In the Maori language, spoken by the native inhabitants of New Zealand, the Chatham and Auckland Islands, there are 524 books and manuscripts. Many of these volumes contain a great collection of different poems, legends, letters, vocabularies, etc., each complete in itself. The entire number of leaves represented by the 524 Maori books is 13,216. There are also 8 books in the Dayak language spoken in Borneo.

As soon as Sir George Grey presented his library to Cape Town, Dr. Bleek was engaged to classify, arrange, translate, compare, and comment on the vast collection of manuscripts and printed works in the various African dialects. His heart was in the work, and his letters for several years to Sir George Grey show how efficient his services were.

On the death of Dr. Bleek, Professor Max Müller and Mr. A. H. Sayce wrote to Sir Bartle Frere, High Commissioner for the Cape Colony, testifying to the great importance of the work that had been done by Dr. Bleek, and hoping that a fit successor would be found to carry on his devoted labours, " who, besides being entrusted by Government with the continuation of Dr. Bleek's philological labours, should have charge of the valuable collection of philological books and manuscripts entrusted by Sir George Grey to the safe keeping of the Cape Colony, and maintain it, if possible, in that state of completeness and efficiency in which it was left by its munificent donor."

Of more general interest to the visiting public than these books, in strange tongues, from barbarous lands, are the costly illuminated manuscripts and missals, and early black letter printed works. They are in many languages indeed, but the history of the times from which they date is, at least in part, known to us.

The manuscripts number 120, and range from the tenth to the fifteenth centuries. Many of them are on vellum, and most of them are magnificently illuminated. They are written, not in Latin alone, but also in French, German, Italian, Dutch, English, Greek and Hebrew.

Amongst them are two valuable Dante manuscripts, several of Petrarch's, one of the earliest manuscript copies of the "Roman de la Rose," and an old Flemish manuscript of Sir John Mandeville's travels.

The early printed books are classed under two heads, Continental and English. There are a great number in the first division, of which no less than one hundred were published within fifty years of the invention of printing. In the second class there are 316 books, whose quaint titles, peculiar spelling, strange expressions, and old-world beliefs are irresistibly attractive. Many of these are priceless, some so rare that they could not possibly be replaced, while in the case of others the loss of a leaf might detract £100 or £200 from their value.

It would be impossible to enumerate these books.

It is equally impossible to pass them over without special mention of any. To begin with, there is a very valuable English translation of Polychronicon, dated 1482, printed by Caxton, the only production of his press bearing the date of that year. This is a complete copy. Latterly an incomplete copy, with at least two leaves missing, was sold for £500.

The historical books range from the creation, through Roman history to the affairs of England, Ireland, and Scotland at the time of their publication. The contemporary history and political literature are treated of in books with such titles as the following :— " Sir Walter Rawleigh's Ghost, or England's Fore-warner—Discovering a Secret Consultation newly holden in the Court of Spaine, Together with his Tor-menting of Count de Gondomar, and his strange affrightment, Confession, and publique Recantation, laying open many treacheries for the subversion of England." A quaint old newspaper, without title-page, printer's name or place, is headed thus—" Mercurius Pragmaticus — Communicating Intelligence from all Parts, touching all Affaires, Designes, Humors, and Conditions throughout the Kingdom, Especially from Westminster and the Head-quarters. From Tuesday, August 8, to Tuesday, August 15, 1648." Then there is " A true narrative of the Horrid Plot and Conspiracy of the Popish Party against the Life of His Sacred Majesty, the Government, and the Protestant Religion."

What a contrast to the short titles of modern books is the following, but what modern title could so whet our curiosity, or prove so suggestive of interest and amusement?—" The discoverie of Witchcraft, Wherein the lewde dealing of witches and witch-mongers is notablie detected, the knavrie of conjurors, the impietie of inchantors, the follie of soothsaiers, the impudent falshood of consenors, the infidelitie of atheists, the pestilent practices of Pythonists, the curiositie of figure casters, the vanitie of dreamers, the beggerlie art of Alcumystrie, The abhomination of idolatrie, the horrible art of poisoning, the vertue and power of naturall magike, and all the connivances of Legierdemaine and iuggling are deciphered. . . . . Hereunto is added a treatise upon the nature and substance of spirits and divels, etc." First edition. Many copies of this edition were burnt by order of James I. This copy is in fine preservation, and bears date 1584.

The true story of a rich man's avarice and its tragic requital, attended with much blue flame and other suggestive and unnatural appearance in broad daylight, is contained in *The Mowing Devil ; or, Strange News out of Hartfortshire*, published in 1678.

Delightful reading, too, are many of those "most famous, pleasant, and delectable" adventures of heroes, knights, and paladins. Fifty chap-books deal with the sorrows, the joys, the loves and hates, the virtues and the vices of the forerunners of the heroes and heroines found in modern fiction.

Forty-two volumes represent original editions of works published by Daniel Defoe, or attributed to him. In this collection also may be found the first complete edition of Chaucer's works, dated 1532, "Probably the only book with a printed date issued from the press of Godfray. It is also the FIRST EDITION of the ENTIRE *Works of Chaucer*, with the exception of the *Ploughman's Tale*, which latter was first printed by Bonham or Reynes in 1542." *

The only complete copy of the First Folio Edition of Shakespeare's plays existing out of Europe is in the South African Library. It is dated 1623. There

* Dibdin.

is also a copy of the Second Edition of the same work. One copy of this edition was sold in 1864 for £148.

Amongst other valuable early editions are *Paradise Lost*, printed in 1669, which is precisely the same as the first edition of 1667, with the exception of the prefixes; the first original edition of Young's *Night Thoughts*, 1743, a very rare book; and the first edition of Burton's *Anatomy of Melancholy*, 1621, a complete copy.

A copy of a work which is regarded by some of the highest authorities as "the most curious and elaborate of all the books printed in England in the fifteenth century" is found in the Grey Collection. It bears the title, *Bartholomew Glanvile de Proprietatibus Rerum*, and was printed by Wynkyn de Wirde, in 1494. It is a complete compendium of mediæval science, and the copy in the South African Library is in excellent preservation.

The bestowal of such a princely gift upon the people of South Africa fitly crowned the noble work performed during eight years by Sir George Grey. If his achievements in New Zealand entitled him to the unbounded praise bestowed by Earl Grey, Sir Frederick Peel, and the Duke of Newcastle, those which he accomplished in South Africa may fairly challenge comparison with the record of any Government in any age during the history of the world.

Description is unnecessary, for the simple records of history are themselves a vivid description. Comparison is impossible, for no such scene of chaos in every department of a State was ever before reduced into such perfect order. The most unerring evidence which can possibly be given as to the merit and value of Gray's work in South Africa is found in the unanimous and concurrent testimony of all classes and diverse races of its people, and the universal affection yet borne to his memory.

𝔅ook the 𝔖ixth.

SECOND GOVERNORSHIP OF NEW ZEALAND, 1861-1867.

CHAPTER XXXIX.

NEW ZEALAND AFFAIRS FROM 1853 TO 1861.

" When sorrows come, they come not single spies
    But in battalions."

Hamlet.

SIR GEORGE GREY landed in Auckland on the 26th September, 1861. The history of New Zealand for the eight years which had elapsed since the Constitution was brought into force, had been one of singular expansion and misfortune.

The Maoris viewed the introduction of the new Government at first with suspicion, and at last with open enmity. They understood the Government of the Queen as administered through her representative. When the swift campaign of Ruapekapeka had been brought to a close, and Sir George Grey, by mingled firmness and conciliation, had subdued and disarmed all opposition, they submitted willingly to the rule of a firm, a vigorous, and a friendly hand.

The Governor was indeed a great chief. He could call for assistance and advice upon his council; but in himself rested the powers of legislation so far as they were concerned, and his hand wielded the rod of sovereignty. If they were injured or wronged by Europeans or other natives, the Governor's ear was open to their cries for assistance. His arm was equally strong to punish and to protect. If they needed advice, the Council Chamber of the Governor was always accessible. If they desired aid for schools, for churches, for flour-mills, for farming implements and stock, they appealed to the Governor, and not in vain.

With their plaintive farewells to Governor Grey, and the pathetic songs which followed him as he left the shores of New Zealand, the old order of things closed and passed away.

When the first Parliament met in Auckland under the Constitution, many Maori chiefs gathered on the spot now occupied by the Supreme Court, and watched with anxiety and forebodings the installation of the new system of government. They could not understand its meaning. Some of the leading chiefs determined to test both the power and disposition of this new authority.

They sent a request to the Government for assistance to build a flour-mill in the Waikato. They soon found that the old direct and personal rule of the Governor had gone for ever.

The system of responsible and party government in New Zealand was inaugurated by a party struggle. In the heat of this political conflict the Maori request was slighted, and the chiefs retired to the Waikato, convinced that a dark day had dawned for the native people.

Gradually the separation between the two races widened, until in 1859, only five years after Sir George Grey had left the colony in perfect peace, the conflict at the Waitara again lit up the flames of war, which burned fiercely, though intermittently, for over ten years.

Nor had the introduction of local self-government been more fortunate in its aspect towards and influence upon the European colonists. As soon as the strong hand of Sir George Grey was removed from the reins of power, the aggressive and acquisitive spirit of a large section of the early colonists asserted itself strongly. The wise and beneficent laws concerning the acquisition of land, and its taxation, were set aside. In provinces where there were valuable waste lands of the Crown available for settlement, laws were speedily passed which enabled those who had political power or official position to monopolise great territories, and stop the expansion of that system of settlement which Sir George Grey had fondly believed to be permanently established. Thus in the Wellington and Canterbury provinces especially, and in Nelson and Marlborough also, wide tracts of valuable land were seized upon by those who subordinated their public position to their private ends.

The number of the European population had greatly swollen, not only by natural growth, but by the constant influx of fresh colonists. The infant settlements cf Otago and Canterbury had expanded into populous and thriving communities. Commerce, manufactures, agriculture, as well as flocks and herds—all had increased.

There was an utter want of sympathy between the settlers and the Maoris in New Zealand. Jealousy, distrust, and suspicion existed on both sides. A very slight breath of air was needed to fan the smouldering embers of discontent into the destroying flames of war. Such a state of affairs could not last long. The events which led to the actual outbreak were these.

The European colonists in New Plymouth (which had been originally founded by the New Zealand Company) clamoured for land upon which to settle.

The Government, under Colonel Gore-Browne, proceeded to purchase from the natives such tracts as they were willing to sell. At the Waitara near New Plymouth, a large area of fertile soil offered many advantages for occupation, and was much coveted by the Europeans. On a part of this land a native chief, Wi Kingi, who with his people had been for many years converted to Christianity, had built a township, where almost in European fashion his people dwelt. Their cottages were surrounded by fields and cultivations. The school house was regularly filled with children. Morning and night the church bell called the people to their simple worship. It would have been difficult in any land owned by a savage race, or in any country suddenly brought under the dominion of an alien people, to find a community more peaceful or more happy than Wi Kingi and his tribe at Waitara by the sea.

Of all the spots in New Zealand, filled as the islands are with places of surpassing beauty, no locality possessed more natural attractions than the district surrounding this native village. Journeying from Auckland to Wellington by the West Coast, the eye of the traveller rested with unalloyed pleasure upon the Maori township, surrounded by its pleasant fields, backed by the lofty glories of Mount Egmont. Peaceful and sequestered, the very last thought to be suggested in the human mind would be that this spot was to become the theatre where should be waged the first conflict of a bloody and expensive war.

Conflicts had taken place between the followers of Ihaia and Wi Kingi at the Waitara, in which blood had been freely shed; and the people at Taranaki became restless and alarmed. Peace was, however, made between the contending natives in June, 1858.

In March, 1859, Governor Browne went to New

Plymouth. He was welcomed by both Europeans and natives. The European settlers were pressing and persistent in their applications for land on which to make homes. The Governor held a meeting with the Maoris, and caused it to be made known that he desired to purchase land for the Europeans. At the meeting Teira rose, and offered to sell to the Government the territory on the south bank of the Waitara. The Governor agreed to purchase if the title were found to be in Teira and his people. Teira thereupon laid a mat at the feet of the Governor as a testimony that the sale was completed.

Wi Kingi, who was present, immediately rose. He called upon the Governor to listen to his words. He would not permit Waitara to be sold. Waitara was his. He would not give it up. Never! Never! Never!

Immediately after the repetition of his immutable purpose, Wi Kingi called upon his people, and followed by them all, withdrew from the meeting.

The Government then proceeded to purchase the Waitara from Teira. Wi Kingi protested against their action, and still declared the land was his. He affirmed that this had been admitted by Governor Grey, and that upon the original map of the district would be found the surveyor's line marking the boundary between his land and that which Teira or Ihaia or any other chief had power to sell. No such plan was, however, found; and Commissioners were sent by the Government to inquire as to the title.

Before these Commissioners Wi Kingi refused to appear. He alleged that they were servants of the Government, and would therefore be influenced against him. He demanded that a proper tribunal should be appointed—a Judge of the Supreme Court, or some other impartial and independent authority. This was refused. Wi Kingi gave no evidence, and the Commissioners reported in Teira's favour. The Government thereupon bought from him and gave notice to Wi Kingi and his people to leave the land.

Surveyors sent by the Government were removed from the land by the women belonging to Wi Kingi's tribe. Soldiers, volunteers, and militia, in their turn, drove the Maoris off the disputed territory with great carnage, and the whole coast became involved in a war which, during the next two years, became general.

Teira's object in selling was not so much the desire to assert title, as to be revenged on Wi Kingi and his people. A Maori girl had deserted Teira's son, to whom she was engaged, and transferred her affections to a favourite nephew of Wi Kingi. The latter acknowledging the indignity which, according to native custom, had been offered to Teira, sent thirty sovereigns and a valuable horse as a peace offering to the offended chief.

Teira brooded over the insult. The money and the horse were not a sufficient atonement. The savage passions of his ancestors, dominant in him, demanded a more serious payment. "Utu" could only be satisfied by blood. To embroil the proud and high-spirited chief with the Queen's Government would wash away in reddened streams all traces of the insult which had been offered to him and to his hapu. Thus, as in other lands and other times, disappointed love, treacherous revenge, and war, went hand in hand.

Many years afterwards, when thousands of lives and millions of treasure had been expended, a competent tribunal did take evidence and hear the case, which showed without the shadow of a doubt that the land belonged to Wi Kingi. Teira himself admitted Wi Kingi's superior right. Wi Kingi and his witnesses did not appear, but the evidence adduced by his antagonists was so conclusive in his favour that the Judges of the Native Land Court were convinced that they were bound to give judgment for him. Startled by the peculiar position of the case, and remembering that the title to the Waitara had been the cause of a dreadful war, the judges adjourned the court to deliberate upon the course they should pursue. Wi Kingi was not only not before the court. He had not applied for the exercise of its jurisdiction. It was, however, evident that a verdict must be given against the applicants then appearing. Such a verdict, openly pronounced, would involve momentous results. It was, indeed, not only of Colonial, but Imperial importance.

With the concurrence of his brother judges, Mr. Fenton, the Chief Judge of the Native Lands Court, sent a memorandum to the Government of the day requesting that a Minister might come to New Plymouth and decide upon the step which the Government would deem it necessary to take.

His request was complied with. One of the Ministers—said to be Colonel Russell—visited the town where the Court was sitting, and took upon himself the conduct of the proceedings. What arrangement was made with the native applicants it is impossible to say. But when the Court again opened, no one appeared in support of the application; the case was indefinitely adjourned for want of prosecution; and to this day the title to the Waitara has never been determined.

The blood, the treasure, the national good faith which we so freely wasted in that terrible conflict must be placed to the account of the Colonial and English Governments in the pages of history.

The unhappy dispute between Wi Kingi and the

Government was aggravated by appeals made to a new authority, which had meanwhile come into existence in the person of the Maori King, who was none other than Sir George Grey's old and trusted friend Te Whero-Whero. After Grey's departure, and the establishment of responsible government in New Zealand, the Maoris, believing themselves to be injured and rendered practically helpless by the new system, had determined to make a king among themselves.

On the 14th of July, 1857, Te Whero-Whero, under the name of Potatau, formally accepted the Kingship, and sent a message to that effect to the different Maori tribes. The restrictions which Sir George Grey had placed upon the sale of ammunition and firearms to the natives had been removed by his successor, acting on the advice of his responsible advisers. The remonstrances of those who foresaw the evil effects of such a course were overruled. The Maoris became eager purchasers of firearms, powder and lead. Their old weapons were also repaired to an extent which was not permitted by Sir George Grey.

Thus, while on the one hand the Colonial Government was alienating the affections and arousing the fears of the Maoris, it was, on the other, permitting, almost inviting the tribes to arm themselves for war.

CHAPTER XL.

THE WAIKATO WAR.

" But who, if he be called upon to face
 Some awful moment to which Heaven has joined
 Great issues, good or bad for human kind,
 Is happy as a lover."

Wordsworth.

SIR GEORGE GREY'S reception in New Zealand was
enthusiastic. All traces of the bitterness which had
been felt towards him by many of the early settlers
had disappeared. Time had removed many unfavourable impressions and justified many of his actions
hitherto misconstrued. The clamours which for many
years had echoed against him had died away, and the
old colonists lost their memories of fancied slights
and arbitrary rule, and remembered only the courage,
the skill, and wisdom which had been so signally displayed in the nine years of his former government.
Public meetings were held, and congratulatory addresses largely signed before his arrival. The address
presented in Wellington was written by Dr. Feather-
stone, and the following passage is taken from it :—

"Remembering the warm interest which during
your former administration you ever took in the
advancement of these provinces, and the many and
important benefits you then conferred upon us, we
cannot refrain from availing ourselves of the opportunity afforded by your arrival amongst us to give
you a hearty welcome, and to renew the expressions

of our personal esteem and respect, and of our most fervent wishes for the success of the policy you have inaugurated, and for your own health and happiness."

The loyal chiefs welcomed him back to their country, and presented addresses equal in depth and fire to those which his departure from the colony in 1853 had drawn forth. These Sir George enclosed to the Secretary of State, for the Queen's perusal.

Her Majesty was so much pleased with them, that at her suggestion the Duke of Newcastle sent a copy of one to the *Times* for publication. In a letter from the Duke to Sir George, dated November 26th, 1862, he wrote:—

"The Queen was greatly gratified and touched by the feeling and poetic address of the New Zealand chiefs, and desired me to tell you so. It was at Her Majesty's suggestion that I sent a copy of it to the *Times*, so that it might be read and admired by all her subjects."

On the Governor's arrival in New Zealand, six thousand soldiers were placed by the War Office at his disposal. Without loss of time he met the Ministry then in power, obtained possession of all the information available, and with characteristic energy proceeded to concert his plans to terminate the present disastrous state of affairs, and to restore peace and tranquillity to the colony. He resolved to employ the troops in road-making, especially in those directions and localities where roads were indispensable for military purposes.

Governor Browne's manifesto was set aside, and the Maoris were informed that military operations against them would only be resorted to in the last extremity. Various reforms among the natives themselves were also initiated. The Maori tribes which had not become actual participators in warlike operations eagerly accepted the institutions framed by the Governor. But the great Waikato tribes, among whom William King was an honoured guest, were still silent and sullen.

The military roads which the soldiers, under Sir George Grey's instructions, were making into the Waikato, steadily advanced. The Maoris declared that so long as the road was in the Queen's country they would take no notice. If, however, it were carried across the Maungatawhiri River into the land nominally rendering allegiance to the Maori king they would take it as a declaration of war.

At that time Mr. John Gorst (since Sir John Gorst, Under-Secretary for India) exercised official duties as magistrate in that district. He established a school and printing press at Te Awamutu. The Maoris had a newspaper at Ngaruawahia, a few miles distant, and Mr. Gorst also published one at Te Awamutu. In the columns of Mr. Gorst's paper the king question was discussed without hesitation. The Waikato chiefs were offended at his plain speech.

One morning a Ngatimaniapoto chief, named Patane, accompanied by thirty armed men, visited Te Awamutu, and requested Mr. Gorst at once to depart. He refused. Patane argued, some of his principal followers joining in. Gorst was obdurate. The Maori school children clambered on the fence around the school, and, with bright eyes and laughing brown faces, clapped their hands and enjoyed the fun.

After a time Patane, discomfited, and doubtful of his own authority, withdrew. His reward was a censure from the King's Government, and a request to the great chief Rewi that he would keep his subordinate chiefs in better order. A law was issued, however, from the King's Council, prohibiting all Maoris from

seeking redress in Mr. Gorst's court, which was there-
after abandoned by the natives.

On New Year's Day, 1863, the Governor paid his
last friendly visit to the Waikato. The canoe in
which he travelled upon the river was manned by
some of the late King's personal friends, for Te
Whero-Whero had paid the last debt, and gone to
his fathers. He had died in 1860, and his son Matu-
taera, commonly known as Tawhiao, was elected to
succeed him. He was buried at Ngaruawahia.

On the 3rd of January the Governor, leaving his
large Maori escort, rode alone to Ngaruawahia. Dis-
mounting at Te Whero-Whero's grave, he stood for a
time thinking of the scenes through which in the days
gone by he and the Maori King had passed together.

As he meditated, a crowd of Maoris, attracted by
the sight of the solitary pakeha standing by the King's
last resting-place, drew near. He was suddenly recognised by some of the older chiefs. With shouts of
joy which might almost have waked the dead, the
Maori cry of welcome, "Haeremai! Haeremai!"
echoed far and wide.

Tawhiao was not at Ngaruawahia, but Te Paea, the
King's sister, and some chiefs were there. Messengers mounted upon fleet horses were at once sent to
the King and to his principal chiefs. Immediately
upon receiving the news of the Governor's visit,
Tawhiao mounted and rode hard to see him. But he
was stout and not strong, and suffered so much that
he was obliged to stay at a place called Rangiaohia.
Anxious lest Sir George Grey should misconstrue his
absence, Tawhiao sent a certificate, signed by the
Maori missionary and the Maori catechist, testifying
to his condition, and stating that he could go no
further.

The great chief, Tamehana, with a number of other

heads of the different tribes, had a long consultation with the Governor. It was upon thiš occasion that a statement was made by Sir George Grey which has always been imperfectly interpreted and misconstrued. Tamehana asked the Governor if he was opposed to the King. To this Sir George replied, " I shall not fight against him with the sword, but shall dig round him with good deeds till he falls of his own accord."

In all the reports which have been made of this celebrated speech of the Governor, the words " with good deeds " are invariably omitted. This omission alters its meaning altogether, and changes a friendly and benevolent intention into a direct threat.

The chiefs desired to have a longer interview with the Governor, Tamehana and many others being most anxious to avoid war. A great meeting was decided on, to which the Governor was to be invited. That meeting was never held, for Sir George, tired and unwell, had been called to Auckland on urgent business.

The hostile attitude of the natives, for a short time allayed by the Governor's visit, was gradually resumed. On the 24th of March, 1863, Rewi, with a large force of armed men, visited Te Awamutu, and finally told Mr. Gorst that he must leave. All next day the discussion continued. Rewi was determined. If Mr. Gorst remained at Te Awamutu he would be put to death. Mr. Gorst refused absolutely to leave without the Governor's orders. An armistice was agreed upon, giving the European magistrate time to write to Auckland. Gorst's letter speaks for itself;—

Awamutu, March 25th, 1863.

My dear Sir George Grey,—The natives have utterly beaten me at last, broken the press and taken away the pieces, and effected a lodgment on the ground, from which they refused to

stir until I left the place. At last, by dint of great obstinacy, I have got an armistice to communicate with you, and if you allow me to remove I am to retire with the honours of war, *i.e.*, all the property. . . . Rewi allows three weeks in which to receive your answer, but he says if you leave me, you leave me to death.—
Your faithful servant,

J. E. GORST.

Upon receiving this letter the Governor immediately issued his instructions to Mr. Gorst to retire. He knew Rewi too well to doubt his iron inflexibility. He was well assured that if one hour beyond the three weeks elapsed, and Mr. Gorst still remained at Te Awamutu without orders to leave, he would no longer be in the land of the living. It is not given to every Secretary for India in peaceful England to be able to look back upon a time when in very deed and truth his days were numbered.

Nor had Mr. Gorst himself a shadow of a doubt of the reality of his own peril. He, too, knew Rewi. He knew that dogged resolution which was so strong a feature in the old chief's character. When, during the war that followed, the name of Rewi became immortalised by the stern heroism of the defence of Orakau, neither the Governor nor the magistrate felt surprised. The type and other metal taken by the natives was cast by them into bullets, and used in the war which followed.

During the next eventful three weeks the fate of New Zealand was being decided, not at Te Awamutu between Rewi and Mr. Gorst, but at Taranaki and Waitara. The inquiries which Sir George Grey had made regarding the ownership of the land at Waitara convinced him that Wi Kingi's contention was correct, and that in truth he and his people were the real owners, according to native custom, of the disputed territory.

The Governor made personal inquiries for an old

plan which he belived that he had himself seen, on which appeared a line showing Wi Kĭngi's boundary, and effectually settling the question. He was assured by his Ministers that there was no such plan, and that although Wi Kingi himself had appealed to it, the conception of its existence was a mistake.

The Governor was uneasy and disturbed. He proceeded to New Plymouth, and personally examined officers and documents. Especially important evidence was afforded by Mr. Bates, a lieutenant in the Sixty-fifth, who occupied the position of Native Interpreter to the Forces. It became evident that there had been such a plan, and that upon it the boundary line as stated had been drawn. Mr. Bell (now Sir Dillon Bell, recently Agent-General for New Zealand) was in attendance upon the Governor during the investigations. Mr. Bell still insisted that the idea of the plan and the boundary line was a mistake. Before advising Governor Browne to assume military possession of the land at Waitara Ministers had taken every precaution to assure themselves and His Excellency that they were right. They still adhered to this statement. In regard to the plan alluded to, the only thing of that nature of which Ministers were aware was an old tracing recently found in the office at New Plymouth.

Sir George desired that this tracing or plan might be sent for. On this being done, and the plan produced, the Governor detected the very boundary line the existence of which was denied.

Mr. Bell was overcome with astonishment. Impulsive and impressionable, the sudden disclosure of a fact which threw such lurid light upon the whole conduct of the Government in the matter confounded him. Amid the silence which followed the Governor's discovery Mr. Bell requested permission to withdraw.

Sir George Grey was left alone with the map on the table before him.

The Governor's mind was immediately made up as to the course to be pursued. He determined that the land should be publicly given back to Wi Kingi, that the purchase from Teira should be rescinded, and that all the reparation now possible should be made.

Calling his Ministers together, he laid the facts fully before them. A great wrong had been done, in which Ministers, Parliament, and the Crown had all participated. The loss of life had been lamentable, and the expenditure of treasure great. It was indeed humiliating to the last degree to confess that the Government was wrong and the natives right, but the demand made by justice was inexorable. The only course consistent with honour was to acknowledge frankly the wrong that had been done and offer reparation.

The Cabinet, at last convinced, were yet unwilling to humble themselves and, as they thought, the colony in the way and to the extent insisted upon by the Governor. For a considerable time, stretching over several weeks, they hesitated to adopt a course which to them was exceedingly bitter.

Their hesitation and the delay consequent upon it were fatal to all hopes of a speedy reconciliation between the races. The Maoris, ignorant of Sir George Grey's plans regarding the Waitara, and alarmed by certain movements of the troops, laid an ambuscade on the 4th of May, which destroyed a party of the 57th Regiment on their way from the camp to New Plymouth. Four days afterwards, on the 8th of May, Ministers tardily published the proclamation in the *Gazette*.

It was too late. Had the Ministry, when convinced of the wrong which had been done, honourably admitted the error and allowed the Governor at once to issue his proclamation, the ambuscàde in which the party of the 57th fell would never have been laid, and peace might well have been restored.

As the Maoris said in relation to this matter, "The fire had been put to the fern," and the flames swept in a short time over all the centre of the North Island.

From this time forward the conflict continued. Nearly twenty thousand men were put in the field. The story of the New Zealand war, with its long catalogue of sufferings and incapacity, and of gallant deeds on both sides, is a matter of history—affecting more the history of New Zealand than the biography of its Governor.

Well established as the foregoing facts are, many of Sir George Grey's political opponents attempted to throw the responsibility of the Waikato war upon him, and not upon his Ministers. Mr. C. F. Hursthouse, in his pamphlet, *The Case of New Zealand*, says : "Just or unjust, necessary or unnecessary, the war was the Governor's, and not the colonists'." Rather more than eighteen months after the ambuscade at the Waitara, on the 25th of January, 1865, a letter from Mr. Fitzgerald appeared in the *Times*, containing the serious charge that "Sir G. Grey, although he had many months before promised to investigate the Waitara case, and to do justice in it, proceeded early in 1863 to march an army into the Tataraimaka to recover it, *before having made any inquiry into the facts of the Waitara.*"

This letter called forth a prompt reply from another New Zealander. The writer of this answer is believed to have been Colonel (now General Sir George) Whitmore. He emphatically denied Mr. Fitzgerald's statement, and added—

"It is difficult to imagine how Mr. Fitzgerald, who

is a member of the Assembly, and who shows himself well up in some parts of the colonial blue-books, can make the statement that the Tataraimaka was occupied before 'having made any inquiry at all into the facts of the Waitara.' Before troops moved to the Tataraimaka the two principal colonial Ministers, Messrs. Domett and Bell, who were at New Plymouth, had settled with Sir G. Grey that the Waitara was to be given up, and it was the openly avowed intention of the Governor and Ministers to occupy the Tataraimaka and evacuate the Waitara on the same day.

"When the day fixed (the 4th of April) came, the troops marched out, but the Ministers had not yet prepared the proclamation giving effect to their decision on the Waitara question, and it was solely owing to their not having done so that the one block of land was occupied before the other was evacuated. I know that few, if any, of the events which have taken place in New Zealand since that have caused Sir G. Grey or Sir Duncan Cameron so much annoyance as the delay of the Ministers in issuing their proclamation,—a delay to which it is entirely attributable that we are placed in the false position of appearing to give up the Waitara from fear, because it was not done until after the murders were committed. These facts are patent to all who were there at the time, and I can further state that several of the friendly chiefs were told, before the murders were committed, that the Waitara was to be given up ; but as day after day passed and no proclamation came forth they began to disbelieve it, and when a month passed and still no proclamation appeared, is it to be wondered at that the natives came to the conclusion that we did not mean to keep our word about the Waitara, because we had been allowed to occupy the

Tataraimaka in peace—a conclusion to which some of our own party were also brought by the unaccountable delay ï " *

Seeing that this matter is of momentous importance, and that the whole facts of the Waitara case, with the concluding evidence given by Mr. Fenton, the Chief Judge, is now placed upon record, it is absolutely certain that the whole responsibility for that terrible conflict rests not upon the shoulders of Sir George Grey, but upon those of the Ministry of the day.

The difficulties by which Sir George Grey was surrounded prevented him from calling into requisition his own peculiar aptitude for dealing with savage races under such circumstances as those which now existed in New Zealand. Fettered in one direction by Parliament and a responsible Ministry, he was precluded in the other from taking a controlling part in the conduct of the campaign. The troops were under the orders of the General in command, who was not responsible to the Governor, but to the Ministry in England.

General Cameron, though skilled in European campaigning, was inexperienced in bush warfare. He held too lightly both the courage and capacity of the Maoris, and received during the two or three years of his command in New Zealand several severe repulses, which created dissatisfaction and anger among his troops, and tended to prolong the strife. Had Sir George Grey possessed absolute command, it is probable that six months would have seen the end of the war. A few sharp lessons would have taught the Maoris that the forces of the Crown, properly led and guided, were not to be resisted.

That this is no exaggerated idea may be justly

* *Times*, January 31st, 1865.

inferred, not only from Sir George Grey's former experience and exploits in New Zealand and South Africa, but from circumstances which happened during the war itself.

Between New Plymouth and Wanganui the Maoris had built a pah at Te Wereroa. From this pah they issued from time to time in marauding parties. The reduction of Wereroa became an absolute necessity. Representations were made to the Governor, and through the Governor to the General. Sir George Grey himself expressed his desire that the Wereroa pah should be destroyed.

General Cameron refused to undertake the duty. He said it would require at least two thousand (in all 6,000) more troops than he had under his orders available for the task. When further urged, the General accused the New Zealand Government of indifference as to the lives of Her Majesty's soldiers. He also refused permission to Colonel Waddy to march a regiment towards the pah to act, not as a reserve, but as a support for the Colonial forces.

For some time the natives within the pah had expressed a desire to agree to terms of capitulation. While these overtures were under consideration fresh supplies and reinforcements found their way into the Wereroa. Major Rookes and Captain McDonnell spent some days at a pah belonging to the chief stronghold, while the natives debated whether it should be peace or war. Eventually the white men were told to go, as the defenders had resolved to hold the place.

Meanwhile several friendly chiefs had hastened to Wellington to ask the Governor himself for assistance in subduing the Hauhaus who had mustered behind the strong defences of Wereroa. When these Maoris arrived at Government House it was late at night, and Sir George Grey was asleep. Knowing the character of the Governor, they demanded and obtained immediate admittance. Sitting on the floor or standing round the bed they traced diagrams describing the position and construction of the pah, and told of the distress which the settlers and loyal natives suffered from its occupation by the rebels.

As Major Rookes retired from the Perikamo pah, after learning the final decision of its garrison to fight and not to yield, he met the Governor on his way to the Wereroa, and turned back with him. Sir George Grey was quite convinced in his own mind " that all intention of giving the pah up had been abandoned by the mass of the people in it, and that they would not do it, and were only pretending in order to gain time."

No trace of this distrust appeared in his conduct. He accepted the invitation to go up and take possession of the fortress, two of the chiefs who had ridden out to meet him returning to the pah in order to make preparation for his reception.

They advanced to within one hundred and twenty yards of the palisading, and then were stopped by natives who came out of the pah, and asked the various conditions of the terms which would be granted if they gave up the fortress. What followed is concisely told in the Governor's memorandum on the subject :—

" They then said it was all satisfactory, and Aperahama, the principal chief of the pah, came out and requested that Hori Kingi and myself alone would at once go into the pah. Hori Kingi came to my side (we were on horseback), and said, ' Oh, Governor, do not let us go in ; ride up and touch the fence with your hand,* and let that satisfy you : do not let us go in.'

"I saw he was in great fear of treachery. Several of the natives earnestly begged me not to go on, saying the people in the pah were fanatics, given up to old customs.

"I told Hori Kingi that he must come on. He gave way, and Mr. Parris, myself, Hori Kingi, and Hori Kerei, rode on towards the pah. When we arrived within about thirty or forty yards of the pah, the priest of the fanatics came out, and ordered the natives not to allow us to come farther, that they would not give up the pah, and Hori Kingi said that he saw their guns prepared, and that we should be fired on if we moved on ; and the friendly chiefs of the Wereroa pah, who stood between us and the pah, seeing what was intended, prayed us not to go on."

Although alluded to so quietly, the danger in which the little party stood was most imminent. Colonel Rookes says that the palisading before them bristled with *tuparas* (double-barrelled guns) levelled at the Governor, while the clicking of the guns being cocked was distinctly heard.

One of the old chiefs rushed from the pah, and, holding up a blanket before Sir George Grey, implored him to turn back. Standing between the guns and those whom they menaced he brought them a temporary protection. But he assured the Governor that the Maoris were in grim earnest, and that any attempt to advance closer to the gateway of the pah would inevitably bring death upon the whole party.

Even then Sir George hesitated to withdraw. For a few minutes he endeavoured to reason with the

* A sign to the native mind of the establishment of authority.

excited natives, calling upon his "children" to reflect, and not to break their word or behave so badly. At last, convinced of the uselessness of further argument, he slowly gave the order to retire—an order which was welcomed and obeyed without loss of time by those in attendance upon him.

The next day the Governor received a letter from the occupants of Wereroa, saying that if he would send away the forces, then they would come to terms. His reply was characteristic :—

O Sons,—I will not cause my men to return to Wanganui. I have but one word, that your words to me be fulfilled, that I come into the pah ; then will I fulfil my words to you, and in every way I will treat you well.—Your friend,

18th July, 1865.   G. GREY, Governor.

When it was hopeless any longer to expect a peaceful surrender of the stronghold, Sir George Grey undertook the responsibility of an assault. He mustered a few hundred men (friendly natives and Forest Rangers), assumed personal command, and in three days had taken the dreaded pah, holding its garrison as prisoners of war, without the loss of a single man.

What a contrast was this to the disastrous and bloody scenes of Rangiriri, the Gate Pah, and other places.

Another instance of the disagreements between the Governor and the General in command involved not merely the safety of the people of Taranaki, but the reputation of Sir George Grey and Colonel Warre.

About four miles from New Plymouth, a spur of the range running towards the sea from Mount Egmont falls rapidly to the South Road, and forces that road down nearly to the sea level. A celebrated pah, once held by Bob-e-Rangi, had been built there. Upon the crest of the spur, some distance on its upward course, an old chief had built a pah, from which he and his people descending, had from time to time committed robberies and murders upon the people of New Plymouth.

Moved by the complaints of the Taranaki people, and by his own knowledge of the circumstances, the Governor invited the General to accompany him to reconnoitre the position of the enemy. From the road by the seashore they perceived distinctly the earthworks and palisading of the Maori stronghold. Sir George directed the attention of General Cameron to the fact that the interior of the pah, especially that portion of it which dominated the ascent from below, was opened to and commanded by the upper portions of the same spur, and suggested that a body of picked marksmen should take possession of the hills above the pah, and then, an attack being made in front, it would be impossible for the Maoris to approach the palisading to defend it.

General Cameron refused to take the advice tendered, using at the same time words as to the Quixotic character of the Governor, which in reality amounted to an insult.

Shortly after this, Sir George Grey and General Cameron both proceeded to Auckland. Grey was determined that something should be done to rid the people of the West Coast from the danger by which they were continually menaced. While laying his plans, the matter was summarily ended from another quarter.

Colonel Warre, a very able and energetic officer, had been left in command in Taranaki. Moved by the evident military necessity and by the representations of the settlers there, and being ignorant of the refusal already given by his commanding officer, he proceeded to drive out the obnoxious garrison. After careful inspection of the stronghold, he took the very steps which Sir George Grey had urged upon the General. Throwing a strong force of riflemen along the range above the pah, he attacked it in front.

When the old chief and his people rushed to the palisading to repel the attacking force, they were paralysed by the firing from the hills above them. After having suffered some loss in killed and wounded, they fled from the pah by the sides which led into the dense forests and escaped. The troops suffered no loss.

General Cameron immediately concluded that there was a conspiracy against him existing between the Governor and Colonel Warre. He wrote to the Horse Guards, accusing Sir George Grey and the Colonel of this supposed conspiracy. Both were called upon by the Duke of Cambridge to explain. Both denied emphatically that any correspondence, direct or indirect, verbal or written, had ever passed between them on the subject, Sir George Grey stating that he had never received any letter from Colonel Warre but one enclosing some sketches of scenery which the Colonel, who was an artist, had forwarded to him ; and the only letter that he had written to that officer was one thanking him for his kindness and praising the pictures themselves.

He added that he was not surprised at Colonel Warre's action, because it was evidently induced by proper military considerations, and was such as should have suggested itself to any officer in command.

The Duke of Cambridge afterwards told Sir George Grey that in spite of his emphatic denial and that of Colonel Warre, he found himself bound to accept the statement of General Cameron, his own immediate subordinate. To Sir George Grey this mattered nothing, but Colonel Warre for years afterwards found that this unjust and untruthful accusation was a constant bar to his promotion in the service.

The war was virtually at an end in 1866. A few skirmishes and casual encounters did indeed take place during the last six months of that year, but in the beginning of 1867 the troops were gradually withdrawn from New Plymouth, the last leaving in July.

One incident, not of this war, but of a conflict between two native tribes, deserves to be recorded, as it illustrates the character of the Governor and the position he held in the eyes of the Maori people.

Sir George Grey had forbidden all tribal wars. Sometimes the old nature of the Maori would overcome the new system of things, and instead of referring to the arbitration of the Governor or the tedious process of the law, an appeal to arms was made as an easy and speedy method of settlement.

On an occasion of this nature, word was brought to the Governor at Auckland that two tribes to the northward had commenced hostilities. A well-known chief named Tirirau had marched his people on to the territory of an old enemy, and was laying deliberate siege to his principal pah.

The Governor was determined to put a stop to all such proceedings. Instantly embarking in a man-of-war then in Auckland harbour he proceeded to Whangarei. Landing there in the early dawn with a half-caste guide, he obtained horses and proceeded over the ranges toward the scene of conflict. During several hours he rode as fast as the track would permit, till at length the pace and difficulty of the way told upon the horses.

By making a slight deviation he was able to call at a farm owned by a gentleman he knew. There, hastily eating breakfast—it was now high noon—he procured fresh cattle, and rapidly cleared the remaining distance, accompanied only by the guide. Upon his arrival at the pah he found the battle already begun. The besiegers had brought with them an old ship's cannon, and he could hear far off the sound of the solitary piece of ordnance. Drawing nearer, the cracking of rifles and gunshots told the fight was fast and furious. At last he came in sight of the pah, and the stockades and rifle pits of the attacking party. Putting spurs to his horse, he dashed into the line of fire and threw up his right hand, shouting at the same time to both parties to cease firing. As he rode by, the brother of Tirirau fell shot through the neck.

The person of the Governor was at once recognised. In a moment all was silent. Sir George Grey, still sitting on his panting horse, commanded both parties to come out and range themselves on either side of him without their arms. His word was law. In a few minutes several hundreds of fighting men stood drawn up in two bodies, only separated by the Governor and his orderly.

In a severe tone Sir George Grey reminded the chiefs on both sides that as the Queen's representative he had forbidden all fighting, whether for land or in revenge for any injury or insult. He bade both sides depart at once for their ordinary homes, and he would himself decide their disputes. A few of the chiefs and common men were to stay to look after the dead and wounded, the rest were to depart.

To the Maoris the voice of " Te Kuwana " was as the voice of God. To hear was to obey. Without remonstrance the defenders left the pah, the besiegers left their pits and whares. Shouldering arms, they marched away contentedly to their various kaingas. The wounded were looked to, the dead were buried, and the Governor, having examined into the dispute —which was, as such disputes usually were, about land—settled it satisfactorily to both sides.

Personal intervention like this, regardless of danger or fatigue, challenged the admiration of the chivalrous Maoris, while the constant kindness and justice exercised towards them won their confidence and love.

CHAPTER XLI.

" Striving to better, oft we mar what's well."
King Lear.

ON his return to New Zealand, although but a few years had passed since he had left it, Sir George Grey thus found the natives and Europeans in deadly conflict, and he found also his liberal and democratic land administration practically destroyed.

Nor was he able under these adverse circumstances, to use the powers with which he had been invested on his first arrival in the colony. He was hampered and tied down in many ways. There was a large military force in the North Island, but not under his immediate command. General Cameron was utterly unfit to cope with the difficulties presented by the forest warfare, increased by the skill and bravery of the warlike Maoris.

Sir George found his advice slighted, his warnings laughed at. He was bitterly mortified at the sight of brave men led on to certain death, and at the spectacle presented by the humiliating repulse of British troops by a handful of half-armed savages.

Nor could he control the civil government. The Parliament of the colony had replaced his former Council and his semi-autocratic power. His exercise of authority was not limited only by the existence of a Parliament. As the Governor of New Zealand under the Constitution, he could only act by the advice of his Ministers. He found himself impeded and harassed, thwarted and defeated, sometimes by the stiff and formal rule of the General, at others by the divided counsels and incompetence of some of his Ministers; though he was often cheered and aided by a spirit of loyalty and true friendship amongst those he called to his assistance.

From the commencement of his second period of office in New Zealand, it was evident that complications which had not before presented themselves must inevitably arise. The Home Government had for many years declared their purpose of withdrawing the Imperial forces from the distant colonies. It is not necessary here to enter into a consideration of the motives which actuated successive Ministries upon this point. Conservatives and Liberals agreed that the expense of maintaining armies in distant lands was too great to be borne, and that the scattering of different portions of the small army which England could call its own in widely sundered localities tended to weaken the nation in the Councils of Europe, and render it helpless in the event of war.

The colonists on the other hand had not yet made up their minds to rely upon themselves. And as by the Constitution they had the power of legislating for themselves, dissensions were almost sure to follow between the Government in England and the Government in New Zealand.

Between the Imperial and Colonial Governments the Governor held a most unhappy position. It was indeed impossible to conduct the affairs of the Colony at that time without giving dire offence either to the Ministers in London or to the Ministers and people in the Colony. It was highly improbable that the Governor could escape offending both parties, and this improbability was deepened by the fact that Sir George Grey was a man of original ideas and resolute character.

On the whole, during the six years between 1861 and 1867, he worked more in harmony with the Colonial Government than with Downing Street and Pall Mall. This was not owing to any predilection of his own, but rather because the Colonial Ministry generally took the most reasonable view of matters, and acted conscientiously in the performance of their duties ; while the Colonial Office and the War Office pursued their usual erratic and arbitrary course.

Sir George Grey was fully alive to the probable consequences which would follow a continued opposition to Ministers at home. But he did not permit the fear of official displeasure to distract his attention or to divert his purpose. Unforeseen contingencies also arose to add to his anxiety and trouble. One of these, typical of others, but in itself of considerable importance, and leading to grave results, took place in the following manner.

The Governor received from Mr. Cardwell, then Secretary for War, enclosed in official despatches, a communication marked "Private and Confidential." This despatch contained a statement which had been made in confidence to Mr. Cardwell, accusing the Governor of having caused certain Maori prisoners taken in battle to be put to death. Mr. Cardwell stated that the facts had been given to him from such reliable sources that he could not but believe them to be correct ; that he was deeply grieved at the occurrence, and trusted that the Governor would be able to explain so serious an accusation, although he feared that explanation was impossible. He had marked

his letters " Private and Confidential," lest the records
of proceedings certain to bring discredit upon the
name of England should become matters of public
comment.

Sir George Grey, more accustomed than Mr. Cardwell to face dangers, recognised at the first glance the
false position in which the New Zealand Government,
and especially himself personally, were placed by
the conduct of the Secretary for War. He felt that
to conceal charges so serious behind the veil of
privacy and confidence was to hide fire in the midst
of combustible materials.

Without hesitation he summoned a meeting of the
Cabinet, and laid the " Private and Confidential"
despatch before his Ministers. In explaining his
conduct to them, he urged that they were accused of
a very heinous crime; that he especially was singled
out by some unknown enemies, and an offence equally
grave in the eyes of nations and of individuals alleged
against him. If this charge were true,—if by any
means it could be sheeted home,—he was no longer
fitted to be a Representative of the Queen, nor even
to remain in her service. If on the contrary it were
proved to be false, punishment of equal weight should
be meted out to those by whom he had been falsely
accused. If it were true, no Minister and no Representative of the Queen could properly consider it as
a private and confidential matter. If it were untrue,
it should be publicly exposed and refuted. And he
asserted his own opinion that no unsolicited communication, although marked " Private and Confidential,"
which contained serious accusations against great
officers of state ought to be treated in any other way
than that accorded to ordinary official despatches.

The Ministers sided entirely with the Governor.
Neither Governor nor Ministers knew anything of the

occurrences which were alluded to. After considerable deliberation it was resolved that rewards should
be offered in the *Gazette* to anyone who could give
information upon the matters contained in Mr. Cardwell's letter. It was decided to institute the strictest
inquiries, and to leave no stone unturned in the
search for the whole truth regarding this remarkable
accusation.

The efforts of the Ministry were but scantily
rewarded. They ascertained that there had been a
military execution without the knowledge or consent
of the Governor; that the officers of one or two of the
regiments had made strong representations regarding
the manner in which the victims had met their death;
and that to appease their anger against a proceeding
which they deemed to be disgraceful to the service,
it had been in some way conveyed to them that the
Governor was responsible. Some of these officers
had thereupon written to their friends in England,
who had in their turn communicated with the Secretary for War. Thus had arisen the grave scandal
which he had desired the Governor, if possible, to
explain.

Without loss of time, Sir George Grey advised Mr.
Cardwell of what had been done, and transmitted a
full official memorandum. The Secretary for War
was grievously offended. He considered that his
confidence had been abused, and his kind intentions
rewarded with insult. He complained very bitterly
to his colleagues of Sir George Grey's conduct, and
the matter was discussed at some length by the
English Cabinet.

To add to Mr. Cardwell's annoyance he found that
his fellow Ministers approved of the course adopted
by the Governor of New Zealand. They endorsed
his opinion that the reputation of no public man

would be safe if any serious indictment could thus be brought against him under the shield of privilege.

They were not, however, inclined actively to support Sir George Grey's contention that they should enforce the regulations which provided that no man after a court-martial should be put to death in a British colony without the assent and signature of Her Majesty's representative. As we shall see, this point of contention was one of the final causes of disagreement at a later date between Sir George Grey and Earl Granville.

General Chute succeeded General Cameron, and brought to the conduct of the campaign far more energy and knowledge of bush warfare than his predecessor had displayed.

Gradually the war waned. Although the Maoris had been successful in defending many of their fortresses, their losses had been very great. The troops were gradually withdrawn, and by 1867 only one or two regiments remained in the colony.

Sir George Grey had written in very strong terms to the English Government regarding General Cameron and the Secretary of State for War. Lord Carnarvon had requested Sir George to withdraw this letter, but he declined to do so, stating that he considered it as due to his Ministers and the colony that their vindication should remain on record side by side with the accusations which had called it forth.

When Lord Carnarvon resigned his position as Secretary for the Colonies, the Duke of Buckingham took the seals of that office.

Within three months of his appointment the new Secretary, influenced, it may be presumed, by the long and growing bitterness of feeling against Sir George Grey, closed a despatch mainly upon military subjects by regretting that such serious controversies had existed between the Governor and the officers in command of Her Majesty's forces. The noble Duke concluded by saying:—"I shall again address you upon this matter. I shall then be able to inform you of the appointment of your successor, and of the time at which he may be expected to arrive in the colony."

No notice whatever had been given by Her Majesty's Government to Sir George Grey of his intended recall. After such great achievements in peace and war, an illustrious public servant was thus summarily notified of the cessation of his duties in a paragraph that would not have been courteous if dispensing with the services of a temporary clerk in a merchant's office.

Thus were ended Sir George Grey's connection with the Colonial Office and his career as a Colonial Governor. When, fifteen years before, he had left New Zealand, the native population of the country was overwhelmed with grief. On this occasion, also, spite of war and troublous times, many of the Maori chiefs regarded with sorrow the removal of that Governor in which they recognised a sincere friend as well as an inflexible ruler. But it was from the European subjects of the Queen that Grey now received the most cordial and earnest sympathy.

Addresses, resolutions from public meetings, correspondence from many quarters, the universal consensus of praise and admiration in the colonial press, all testified to the admiration and gratitude of the New Zealand colonists for one who, during nearly twenty-five years, had been the hope, the guide, and the shield of the community.

Both Houses of Parliament in Wellington passed votes of sympathy and appreciation with an enthusiasm and unanimity rarely manifested. Colonists recognised the fact that it was in defence of their Constitutional rights and the vindication of their liberties that Sir G. Grey had drawn upon himself this last and final blow from Ministers of the Crown in England.

The address voted by the Wesleyan Methodists was fairly typical of the general feeling towards the departing Governor. It was as follows:

To His Excellency Sir George Grey, K.C.B.,
        Governor of New Zealand, etc.

We, the ministers of the Wesleyan Methodist Church in the Northern Island of the colony of New Zealand, desire, on the occasion of Your Excellency's departure from us, to acknowledge the readiness with which you have always encouraged our missionary work.

From the time of Your Excellency's first arrival in this country you took a deep interest in the educational progress and religious welfare of both races of Her Majesty's subjects in New Zealand. But particularly in our efforts for the evangelisation and civilisation of the Maori tribes, so hopefully prosecuted up to the date of the late calamitous war, the Wesleyan Mission was greatly indebted to your hearty co-operation. We shall ever remember with gratitude the personal attentions with which many of us were cheered and honoured by Your Excellency during the earlier struggles with the difficulties incidental to a new country. And now that you are about to retire from the administration of the government of this colony, we beg most respectfully to offer our cordial wishes for your future happiness; and with our earnest prayers that the blessing of the Almighty may be with you, we bid Your Excellency an affectionate farewell.

Signed for and on behalf of all the Wesleyan ministry in this Island,

                            JAMES BULLER, Chairman.
Auckland, December 16, 1867.

To this Sir George Grey made the following reply :—

Reverend Gentlemen,—I thank you most sincerely for this address.

I can assure you that I have for years watched with interest and gratitude the zealous efforts you have made to promote the religious and secular welfare of both races of the Queen's subjects in New Zealand, and especially have I felt grateful to you for the noble and self-denying efforts you have made for the evangelisation and civilisation of the people of the Maori race. You are good enough to allude to the assistance I have given you in the prosecution of these works ; but I can assure you it was to me rather a pleasure than a duty, to co-operate with you in the efforts to attain such great and important objects.

I am much obliged to you for the affectionate farewell which you bid me on my removal from office, and for your prayers and wishes for my future happiness. I shall carry the remembrance of these with me into my retirement, and shall always desire to hear of your welfare, and, if possible, to aid those for whom so many years of friendly intercourse have made me feel no ordinary esteem and regard.

Government House, Auckland,   G. GREY.
      28th December, 1867.

CHAPTER XLII.

" Thou teachest me to deem
  More sacredly of every human heart,
  Since each reflects in joy some gleam
  Of heaven, and could some wondrous secret show
  Did we but pay the love we owe,
  And with a child's undoubting wisdom look
  On all these living pages of God's book."
Lowell.

THE colony was once more at peace. Spite of war and devastation, the opening of the goldfields and the flowing tide of immigration had expanded its resources and increased its wealth. The European population, acknowledging the great services which Sir George Grey had rendered to the country, joined together in expressions of gratitude and of respect. Limited as his powers had been, beset with innumerable obstructions, he had, nevertheless, succeeded in steering the colony safely through another great crisis. He had preserved intact their privileges. He had vindicated their constitutional rights against the encroachments of his superiors.

Their regrets were bitter, but unavailing. He had been appointed by the Crown, and by the Crown he had been superseded. All that the colonists could do was to express their sense of his worth and of the generous and liberal conduct which, both in public and private life, had marked his career in New Zealand.

The whole attention of Sir George Grey had not been engrossed by his political and military cares. Among his correspondence during this period is a letter from Florence Nightingale, dated July, 1863, written on hearing that Sir George Grey was building a hospital, in which she said that every spare moment for two years past had been devoted to working up and reducing to a report statistics obtained from the Colonial Office as to the mortality of native races. Her sincere sympathy with and appreciation of his efforts were expressed in the words, " God bless you! I wish I could have helped you more. You will do a noble work in New Zealand."

In another paragraph she wrote, " You are nearly the only Governor, except the great Sir John Lawrence, who has condescended to qualify yourself by learning the languages, the physical habits, and the ethnological peculiarities of the races you had to govern."

She also prepared some exhaustive notes on the New Zealand depopulation question. " The introduction of *pigs* as an article of food, has been certainly one cause of evil. . . The pig is, of all animals, the decivilizer. Ireland and New Zealand both suffer under the incubus of pigs and potatoes." Summarising the diseases to which New Zealanders were peculiarly subject, Florence Nightingale dealt with each, showing that sanitary dwellings, proper clothing, wholesome food, active exercise, and more regard for personal cleanliness were needed to improve the health of the natives. In paragraph vii. she treated of education :—

" Uncivilized man cannot be dealt with in the same way as civilized man. Even here, education means keeping a certain number of children a great part of each day in a close room—cramming them and exciting them with formulæ.

"Clever bread-winning, stunted growth, high mortality, are what *we* produce.

"But this system would be fatal to a race subjected to it for the first time.

"In their children it produces bad health, scrofula, consumption, and is, in reality, death with slow torture.

"At home we find that as much (*or more*) is taught in three days as in six (or in six *half-days* as in six whole days), *the physical system being developed by exercise or work* in the other three days (or six half-days).

"This is the clue to all proper school management, especially among the uncivilized.

"If a child's brain is forced, whose father's brain has been free, the child dies : children are killed by school discipline.

"In an aboriginal school there should be ample space, free ventilation, cheerfulness, half-time *at least* given to out-door work or play." She goes on to say that greater care still must be taken when a change of religion is added to all the other great changes. "Without bodily activity, the best man among the converts will fall under disease, and thus become lost to the cause of Christianity."

With all Sir George Grey's genius for great plans and public reforms his influence was still more attributable to his rare power of individual sympathy. Without this a man may be a great leader and a successful ruler, but he can never awaken in the hearts of thousands of his fellow-men the affection of children for a father.

With children he was ever a favourite ; but it must

be admitted that he was too indulgent to them.   The little tyrants soon found out their power, and the ruler of great colonies, the man who had issued his commands in opposition to the Imperial Government and been obeyed, was often a slave to a child's whims, and helpless when confronted by a lisping "I don't want to."

The Governor had a soft spot in his heart for the little brown-skinned native children.   For their sake he established schools, and gave special treats and privileges.   He delighted to see them in hearty enjoyment of their sports.   When it was impossible to benefit them on a large scale, he chose the most promising as recipients of his gifts.

In this way he selected three boys from Norfolk Island, and had them educated and trained as missionaries under the direction of the wise and good Bishop Patteson, who a few years later bravely met the death of a martyr.   The following letter from the Bishop relates to his protégés :—

Kohimarama, March 6th, 1863.

My dear Sir George Grey,—I enclose three short notes from your three adopted Melanesian boys.   They are lads in whom I am sure you will take a great interest, and I am equally sure that they understand your kindness to them, and the object you have in view in helping them.   I need not say how much I thank you. This is precisely the way in which help can be most usefully given to us, and your example may be followed by others.

All struggling authors, poets, and artists wrote to Sir George Grey asking his advice and assistance. He was never too busy to help and encourage real merit.   To foster literature was one of his chief aims. The standard work on New Zealand, writen by Dr. Hochstetter, owes its origin indirectly to Governor Grey.   The author had been the guest of Sir George for some time in the colony, and was ever ready to declare his grateful sense of the kindness and assistance which he had received. The following simple letter gives utterance in Hochstetter's own words to the feelings by which he was influenced :—

To Sir George Grey,

Your Excellency,—After five years of labour I have now finished my publications of New Zealand to which your Excellency gave me the first instigation. . . .

May your Excellency accept my works with indulgence, and see in them only the effort to do my best towards extending the scientific knowledge of an English colony, whose population greeted me with the greatest hospitality, and by this to pay the tribute of gratitude which I not only owe to the English colonists but to England in general.

Believe me to remain with greatest esteem,

Your Excellency's obedient servant,

PROF. DR. F. V. HOCHSTETTER.*

Dr. Ferd. Mueller, Curator of the Melbourne Botanical Gardens, carried on a long correspondence with Sir George Grey, evincing in all his letters the greatest admiration for the latter's varied achievements. In one he enclosed a letter from Prof. Rafn, Secretary of the Royal Society of Northern Antiquarians, written from Copenhagen in November, 1862, asking him to forward to Sir George Grey various interesting papers connected with the founding, history, and proceedings of the Society, and intimating that they should consider it an honour to elect Sir George as one of the Fellows of the R.S.N.A. Society. Sir Henry Barkly wished to propose Sir George " as pre-eminent for rank and learning " to this position. The friendship between Dr. Mueller

* Letter from Dr. Ferdinand von Hochstetter, Vienna, Sept. 20th, 1865.

and Sir George Grey was marked by a continuous interchange of plants and animals, and of information concerning them.   Sir George having sent him a sample of New Zealand flax, Dr. Mueller manufactured it into paper, which he sent to Sir George on Christmas Day, 1866.   The letter accompanying this specimen was published for public information by the New Zealand Government.

After the arrival of Sir George Bowen, and his assumption of the Government on the 9th of February, 1868, Sir George Grey retired to the island of Kawau. He resided there for several months, and then returned to England in the New Zealand spring and English autumn.

Book the Seventh.

SIR GEORGE GREY ENGAGES IN ENGLISH POLITICS. CRITICISM OF THE COLONIAL DEPARTMENT, 1868-1870.

CHAPTER XLIII.

NEW PRINCIPLE OF APPOINTING COLONIAL GOVERNORS.

> "His head
> Not yet by time completely silvered o'er
> Bespeaks him past the bounds of freakish youth,
> But strong for service still, and unimpaired."
>
> *Cowper.*

THE curt letter, in which the Duke of Buckingham in fact dismissed Sir George Grey from the public service, was well calculated to wound its receiver sorely. No regret was expressed, no approval of long and faithful service, no sympathy with the suffering which such a deliberate insult must inevitably cause.

The Governor was not greatly surprised. For more than twenty years he had refused to truckle to Downing Street and Pall Mall. Minister after Minister, both Liberal and Conservative, had chafed at his inflexible opposition and independent judgment. He had been threatened often—accused times without number. To his other faults this was added that the threats could never be fulfilled, the accusations were always refuted.

The time was come, as the Colonial Office thought, when they could do without Grey. The transition period, as they believed, had passed. The colonies were fairly launched upon a safe course, and henceforth Governors might be found who depended not on strength of character, on wisdom and judgment, but whose claims to preferment rested on social rank and courtly manners.

There seems little doubt that Lord Carnarvon held Sir George Grey's despatch, so strongly animadverting on the position taken by Mr. Cardwell and General Cameron, as a direct act of mutiny. It was the bad fortune of Lord Carnarvon always to be drawn into antagonism to Sir George, and always to be compelled to feel that he was "a dangerous man."

Before proceeding to extreme steps Lord Carnarvon requested the Governor of New Zealand to withdraw this document. To this request Sir George gave an emphatic refusal. While the refusal was on its way to England Lord Carnarvon resigned, and the Colonial Office was handed over to the Duke of Buckingham. In May, 1869, His Grace acknowledged Sir George's letter. Correspondence most probably passed between the Duke and Lord Carnarvon, and the result was that in June the Duke informed the Governor that in a further despatch he would inform the Governor of the appointment of his successor, and the time of his arrival in the colony.

There was another reason which probably influenced the Imperial Government in their conduct at this time. Mr. Disraeli, in his ultra-aristocratic proclivities, had determined to confine the governorships of the great colonies to peers or the sons of peers. Henceforth the right to represent the Crown in the great dependencies was to be a birthright. It was indispensable that a man chosen as governor should be "born in the purple." One exception only was to exist. To marry a peer's daughter was in some cases to confer the same right as noble birth. It was indeed urged by Mr. Disraeli and his friends that the colonists themselves desired this new departure.

One of the ills which colonies are heirs to arises from the success which attends so many of their early leaders. In new countries riches are oftentimes swiftly amassed. The sudden development of fresh sources of wealth, the opening of mines, the discovery and utilisation of pastoral countries and wide agricultural areas, with their attendant commerce, finance, and increased land values, have specially during this century raised a large class of colonial monied aristocracy. Of these considerable numbers return to the old country, and make strenuous efforts to penetrate the sacred circles of what is called "society." It thus happens that there is always in London an army of colonists, formidable both in numbers and financial power. Many of these are men who have occupied prominent positions in the political and social world in Australia, Canada, South Africa, or New Zealand. They have united to form associations, partly social, partly intellectual, and indirectly political in character. They are always present to the English public, and are certainly sufficiently self-assertive. But in reality they do not represent the public feeling of the colonies, nor are their views at all to be taken as an index of the state of public opinion there. Among them are men of undoubted ability, of unostentatious liberality, and high character; but there are also many who are vulgarly anxious to be—or at any rate to appear to be—on familiar terms with people of high position. Snobbishness is as much a weakness

among wealthy colonials as among fortunate trades-
men and the parvenu wealthy of the Mother Country.
It is through such channels that, too often, English
public men obtain distorted and contemptible ideas
of colonial character.

It was probably from such sources that Mr. Disraeli
received the impression that, in the sarcastic words
of the *Saturday Review*, "the colonists particularly
desire to be governed by the Porphyrogeniti."

In 1867 a new batch of Governors was appointed.
Lord Belmore was sent to New South Wales, the
Marquis of Normanby to Queensland, Sir George
Bowen being sent to New Zealand from that colony,
as he had not completed his term, and Lord Canterbury to Victoria. On the appointment of Lord Belmore, the new rule was openly canvassed. The
Saturday Review, in a caustic article on that appointment, remarked, "Indeed it seems absurd to be called
upon to notice the cool proposition that unless a man
is born in the purple he is disqualified from representing the Sovereign in her colonial dependencies.
This is an evidence of the intrepidity which presumes
on the ignorance of the multitude." To this day,
although some noticeable exceptions have from time
to time occurred, the rule then established has been
acted on, at least by the Conservative party. The
most recent appointments carry it out fully. Lord
Carrington and the Earls of Hopetoun, Onslow, Kin-
tore, and Jersey have had the Australasian Colonies
committed to their charge.

It is said that Lord Knutsford alleged that the
colonies cared little or nothing for ability in their
Governors, but regarded it as due to themselves that
gentlemen of rank, wealth, and social qualifications
should be appointed to represent the Queen, at any
rate in the more important colonial possessions.

In the practical dismissal of the Governor of New Zealand, the Colonial Office accomplished two objects. It severed the connection with a Governor whom it cordially disliked, and it opened a place for some titled protégé under the new colonial regulations. Both reasons were understood and appreciated by Sir George. As regarded himself he felt that he was treated discourteously. As regarded the new rule for the qualification of future Governors, he felt that the efficiency of the public service would be impaired, a laudable ambition would be taken from a large number of men eager to serve their Queen and country, and an altogether false idea would henceforth govern the relations between Great Britain and her colonies, which might possibly lead to evil results. Sir George had long since arrived at the belief that complete freedom in self-government, to the full extent of selecting their own Governors, alone could enable the colonies to achieve the greatest results in happiness and usefulness.

Sir George Grey had, as we have seen, been promised by the Duke of Newcastle the government of Canada when his term had expired at the Cape of Good Hope, but he relinquished that expectation with the government of the latter colony as soon as it was fully determined that he should assume the government of New Zealand, at a time when the difficulties of administration called in an imperative manner for the ability and administrative capacity which he possessed. On his return to England, Grey applied to be reinstated at the Cape, and received answer from Lord Granville that his application had been noted. For twelve months he was kept in uncertainty and suspense, and when, urged by his friends, he applied for a pension, Lord Granville replied that it was not possible to give a pension to any person who was not either sixty years old or incapable of discharging the duties' of any public office.

Sir George then allowed the matter to drop, but writing in 1869 he said: "My situation has, however, been rendered by Lord Granville a hard one. I am as capable as I ever was of serving Her Majesty in a good climate, and I am liable at any moment until I am past sixty to be called on by the Secretary of State to serve Her Majesty until I am sixty-six. If I decline to do so, or do so negligently in the opinion of the Secretary of State, I forfeit all claim to pension. Until, therefore, I am past sixty, it is difficult for me to determine on any future plan of life. After a career of great activity I am thus plunged into a life of uncertainty, and without an object of any kind before me. . . . I feel that after thirty-three years of unusually severe service in the colonial department, and after the sacrifices, personal and pecuniary, which I have on several occasions made to meet the views of the Government, it was hard to condemn me to doubt and uncertainty of this kind, and the expense and discomfort which necessarily followed from it. Twenty-six years' service as Governor, and an intimate acquaintance with the customs of the colonial service, enable me to say that the course pursued towards me is in several respects harsh and unusual."

For a long period Sir George Grey waited and hoped for employment. His enforced idleness while he was waiting the pleasure of Lord Granville did not, in the opinion of many eminent men, evince much wisdom on the part of Ministers. Thus General Napier, an old college chum at Sandhurst, wrote to Sir George Grey in February, 1869: "What a pity they did not send you out to India, instead of Lord Mayo, where your talents would soon have had ample

scope, for matters appear to be coming to a crisis
there on our north-western frontier." In December
of the same year he wrote that Sir George was wanted
again at the Cape, "as you are in two or three other
colonies, to set things to rights." He then went
on to say that he thought Ireland would be all the
better for a share of Sir George Grey's government.

Patiently the great pro-Consul waited upon the
pleasure of Lord Granville, refusing to believe that
his proffered services would be declined. He was in
full possession of mental and physical powers such
as few men in a generation are permitted to enjoy.
The quick activity of youth was indeed gone, but the
ripe judgment of mature age, the enduring powers of
a sound manhood, the vast experience of an eventful
life, far more than made up for the bounding step or
the enthusiastic hopes of bygone days. Not yet sixty
years of age, unequalled in his power over savage
races, and in his knowledge of practical colonization,
he stood alone in the greatness of his views and plans,
as well as in his boundless hopes for the future of the
English people, and through them, for the nations of
the earth. His mind, enriched by a thousand streams
of knowledge and reason, instinct with masculine
vigour, and guided by the noblest principles, was
capable of great, almost unbounded usefulness. To
him the Queen, her Ministers, Parliaments, and
people had been often indebted. The lives of colonists, their property and safety had been by him
conserved. The honour of the Empire had times
without number been vindicated by him. No possible
opportunity had ever presented itself in vain in which
the glory of the Crown or the welfare of the subject
could be increased; always successful in the field,
always wise in the Council chamber; a leader in
every good and worthy enterprise; a patron of

learning and the fine arts ; a passionate devotee and teacher of science; a born ruler of nations, he was the very first of England's sons who claimed at once the gratitude of his country for foreign work well done, and the proofs of a solitary greatness in colonial government.

South Africa was then and for years after crying out for one hand and brain to guide her. That hand and brain were ready and anxious to take up a work so grateful, but the calm self-sufficiency of Lord Granville, and the prejudice and dislike of Lord Carnarvon, passed by, and relegated to the obscurity of private life, the one man who could have saved the Cape from the terrible disaster which threatened it. No greater political blunder was ever committed than that of which Lord Granville was here guilty, afterwards followed by Lord Carnarvon, in relation to Sir George Grey and the colonies of South Africa.

CHAPTER XLIV.

PROPOSED APPOINTMENT OF GENERAL GORDON AS
MILITARY DICTATOR IN NEW ZEALAND.

> "Whatever day
> Makes man a slave, takes half his worth away."
>
> *Pope's Odyssey.*

THE news of the Maori outbreak, and especially of
Te Kooti's massacre at Poverty Bay, alarmed and
confounded the English Ministers. It seemed to
them that all the expense and loss already suffered in
New Zealand had been useless. The Horse Guards
shared with the Colonial Office in the depression and
anger excited by these unhappy tidings. So many
brave men had been sacrificed by divided councils,
so much irritation had been felt and such decided
friction aroused between the Imperial and Colonial
Governments through the exercise of dual authority,
that Ministers contemplated the possible propriety
of taking steps to suspend the Constitution of the
Colony, and appoint a military Dictator with absolute power, in the hope of ending the Maori difficulty
forthwith.

Sir Bartle Frere, then and afterwards a valued
adviser, strongly pressed this plan upon them. He
proposed that a large number of the Indian Police
Force should be shipped to New Zealand, that the

Constitution should be temporarily suspended, and the ablest man obtainable placed in supreme power. Gordon, now lovingly remembered as " Khartoum Gordon," was, it was understood, to be invested with plenary powers of government. The Dictator was to make laws, to raise taxes, to call out the people as an armed militia, and generally to act as in the possession of despotic authority. Frere's suggestions were favourably considered. The propositions were reduced to writing, and the matter submitted to Ministers.

Before anything final was done it was decided to obtain Sir George Grey's advice and, if possible, his assent ; it being understood that if that assent was refused, the plan should not be persevered in. It was felt that the step contemplated was of a most serious nature. A military officer in the confidence of Government was sent to acquaint the ex-Governor of New Zealand with the nature of the plan which was under consideration, and to obtain a full expression of his mind upon its merits, and his recommendation that it should be carried out. This gentleman bore with him a printed copy of the proposals. When he and Sir George Grey met, the project was fully explained.

The memorandum to be submitted to the Cabinet was produced and handed to Sir George. With his ample knowledge of the character and feelings of the New Zealand colonists and their high spirit, he saw at once that such a proceeding would be fatal to the good feeling existing between the mother country and the colony ; and beyond the immediate effect of such an unprecedented course in the colony more immediately affected, Sir George felt certain that this arbitrary act would do more in one day to sever the colonies from England than all the efforts of the

economists could accomplish in twenty years. Their
Constitution would be seen to be valueless, and held
upon an absolutely uncertain tenure, terminable at
the sudden caprice or mistaken judgment of any
Minister. From the moment when he fully understood what it was the Government intended his mind
was made up.

After discussion, Sir George pointed out that the
matter was one of very grave moment, and that he
was asked to take upon himself a responsibility which
demanded serious consideration. Ultimately he opposed it on every ground. The alarm felt in London
was unwarranted. The colonists were well able to
deal with the disaffected natives if moderate assistance were afforded by the Imperial authorities. The
New Zealanders were a bold and resolute community.
They would resent such a sudden and uncalled for
interference. Willing as they were to pay taxes
levied, and engage in active service ordered by their
own Parliament, they would object to both if exacted
by a military Dictator. General Gordon's fitness for
the position was freely admitted. If such a task were
to be accomplished, no man would be so likely to do
it successfully as Gordon. The colonists, however,
would lose sight of the personal merits of the man in
the contemplation of the gross wrong which they were
compelled to suffer.

The results would be disadvantageous to England
also. The colony would be irreparably offended.
Public money would be spent without the authority
of the Colonial Parliament, and New Zealand would
not only hold England responsible for any loss which
might be suffered by the settlers, but they would
possibly refuse to pay the great charges to which the
military chest would certainly be subjected. Finally
he distinctly refused to sanction a course of conduct

which he believed to be a blunder, and which might
possibly be called a crime.

Thus the negotiations closed. The Ministerial
envoy went away disappointed. In the face of Sir
George Grey's strong protest the matter dropped.

A copy of the paper containing the propositions for
the Cabinet was left with Sir George Grey. It is stil
in existence.

CHAPTER XLV.

THE DISMEMBERMENT CRAZE.

"A thousand years scarce serve to form a State :
An hour may lay it in the dust."

Byron.

SIR GEORGE GREY landed in England just prior to
the elections. Within a few days of his arrival the
Duke of Buckingham called upon him and apologised
for the substance and manner of his despatch. The
Duke's words as well as his demeanour convinced the
ex-Governor that the regrets expressed were sincere
and cordial. As Lord Derby had ten years before
doubted the wisdom of his recall from the Cape, so
now the Duke of Buckingham spared no pains to
assure him of the high esteem felt by Ministers for
himself personally, and their admiration for his services to the Crown. His Grace supplemented the
interview with a most kind and courteous letter.

To show the reality of their esteem Mr. Disraeli
proposed to put Sir George into the House of Commons for Nottingham, and a formal offer of that seat
was made to him. Without hesitation the offer was
courteously declined. Many years before, Disraeli,
at the commencement of his political life, had asked
O'Connell for a seat, even if for a Radical consti-
tuency. The great agitator refused, and the seed
of hatred was sown between them which bore such

bitter fruit in after years. No like result happened between Disraeli and Grey, although the refusal on Grey's part conveyed a clear intimation to the Conservative leaders that he would oppose them in politics.

Lord Granville succeeded the Duke of Buckingham as Secretary for the Colonies, when the Liberals came into power on December 10, 1868, Mr. Disraeli having resigned on the 9th. Sir George Grey was staying on a visit to the Queen at Windsor at the time when Mr. Disraeli came there to resign. Between the new Secretary and Sir George there were not the most friendly feelings: probably Grey's resolute action against Mr. Cardwell may have influenced Mr. Cardwell's colleague. In a short time other and more serious matters of dispute arose.

During his Governorship of the Cape Sir George had ventured to draw up a series of rules to regulate the respective administrative positions of the civil and military authorities. These had been adopted by the Imperial Government, and were found to work well. In New Zealand Sir George found that General Cameron had disregarded several instructions from the War Office, which directed him, as the officer commanding the forces, to obtain under certain circumstances the assistance and consent of the Governor. On one point especially the mind of the Governor was strongly moved.

In all military matters which form the subject of a general court-martial, especially where the penalty for crime is death, the Judge-Advocate-General has to advise the Crown before any sentence is carried into execution. In such cases the Crown looks for assistance, not to any of the principal Secretaries of State, but to the Judge-Advocate-General.

When troops are upon foreign or colonial service

in distant parts of the world it would be at once useless and impracticable to transmit the proceedings to England. The custom, therefore, grew up of carrying out, on the authority of the officer commanding, sentence of death when recorded by a competent Court of General Court-Martial. In this way in a colony prisoners were put to death without the Queen's intervention, and without the knowledge of her representative.

To this plan Sir George Grey stoutly demurred. His remonstrances were attended to. Orders were issued from the War Office that in all such cases the papers were to be transmitted to the Governor, and in the absence of the Queen her representative was to authorise the punishment. To Sir George's surprise and dismay he found that this order among others had been disobeyed. He again complained, and requested that as Sir Trevor Chute, who succeeded General Cameron, had broken the rule laid down, it should be formally republished, and strictly enforced, so as to attract the attention of military commanders. The Home Government refused. In England Sir George waited upon Lord Granville, and repeated his request. His lordship again refused. The discussion led to a serious difference between them.

Sir Boyle Roche is reported to have said on one occasion, "Single misfortunes never come alone, and the greatest of all possible human disasters is usually followed by a much greater." Without impeaching or indorsing the logic of the Irish legislator's "bull" it is certainly true that frequently one difficulty seems to prepare the way for another. It was so between Lord Granville and Sir George Grey.

In the ten years which had elapsed since his recall by Sir E. B. Lytton, the dismemberment craze had spread far and wide. Some indeed among the leading intellects of England were awaking to the danger which threatened her greatness from this direction, but Mr. Goldwin Smith and his friends and admirers, who comprised most of the leaders of the Liberal party, had persuaded a large portion of the talking and writing public that it would be far better for England to cast off the colonies altogether.

The idea was to keep a powerful navy in the narrow seas, to form a strong and elastic military force within the four shores of Britain, to isolate England from all outward interests and complications, and then to turn the once " Merrie England" into a vast workshop, from whose looms and forges the markets of the world might be supplied. For this result the greatness of Britain was to be bartered, her diadem broken, her influence for good among the nations of the earth for ever lost. For this ignoble end the manifest destiny of the English race, so far as England was concerned, was to fail in its accomplishment, and her light was to go out for ever. In twenty years the dream would have been rudely dissipated. Foreign competition would have pressed far more heavily than it now does upon English manufactures ; the colonial markets ever expanding, the colonial lands ever open to the great stream of British immigrants, would have been the heritage of alien nations. Discontent and want coming like an armed man ; hopelessness within, and contempt and insolence without, would have been the fruit of this gospel of greed. All was to be abandoned, even India.

" It is difficult to believe that any sane man, not utterly ignorant, could meditate the abandonment of those mighty territories, that world-wide empire, which is England's present glory, and the guarantee of her future greatness and safety. The next generation will scarcely credit the statement that the influence of the

teachers of a selfish political economy was so great
in the United Kingdom that they had obtained the
tacit consent of all political parties to the disruption
and desertion of the whole outside Empire. They
had no mercy. From the ancient kingdom of the
Moguls to New Zealand, from Canada to Hongkong,
all were to be abandoned. Lands won by the sword,
lands ceded by treaty, lands obtained by occupation,
all were to share the same fate. The fruits of a hundred victories, in which on land and sea the blood of
our best and bravest had been shed like water, were
to be given up and sacrificed at the shrine of mammon.
The labours and sufferings of centuries were to be
forgotten or only remembered as a dream. The graves
of sainted martyrs and of gallant warriors were to be
deserted. Cities as great as the capitals of Europe ;
a commerce vaster in extent as it was greater in value
than that of any nation, ancient or modern, save of
the United Empire of which it formed a part—all were
to be voluntarily abandoned. The red cross of Britain
was no longer to float proudly in widely-sundered
lands. A sentence of eternal banishment was decreed
against the millions of colonists who, going forth in
full love and allegiance to the Queen of their people
and the country of their birth, had crossed the sea or
the trackless desert, and made their dwelling in the
wilderness, carrying with them to their new homes
the boon of freedom, race, and country which is the
heritage of every Briton. The beat of the morning
drum around the world was to be silenced. The sun
was to set upon Britain's Empire. No such act of
national suicide was ever contemplated by the leaders
of any people. Had they succeeded—and it is beyond
question that they had arrived, to use Mr. Gladstone's
phrase, within 'measurable distance' of success, and
already in South Africa commenced to dismember the

British Empire—to what a future of misery and peril
would they have doomed the British Crown and the
British people!   It is impossible to contemplate their
purpose without indignation or their plans without
contempt.   ' The colonies cost England money.'   This
was their cry.   Cut off the colonies.   Let them shift
for themselves.   Everything is to the economists and
the Manchester school to be measured by money.
Even to the day of his death Mr. Bright ridiculed the
idea of a federated Empire." *

Against this policy of national suicide Sir George
Grey took an immediate and absolute stand.   He
spoke, he wrote, he held public meetings, and framed
petitions to the Crown.   He knew that by so doing
he would forfeit assistance from the Liberal party,
but he did not for a moment hesitate.   His vigour
and determination in this direction could hardly fail
to impress Lord Granville with a sense of personal
antagonism.

Scarcely inferior in importance in Sir George Grey's
mind to the retention of the colonies was the question
of emigration.   The population of Great Britain was
rapidly increasing.   Her agricultural labourers were
leaving the fields of the country and flocking into
towns, or engaging in mining or other industries.   To
provide a safe and sufficient outlet for the increasing
multitudes in the Colonial Empire was, in his opinion,
an absolute necessity if a revolution of hunger and
want was to be avoided.   This also ran counter to the
ideas of the Liberals.   Only a few years before, when
the American civil war had shut up the cotton mills,
and thrown hundreds of thousands out of employment, the merchants and manufacturers of Cotton-
opolis had protested against a system of State-aided

* " From Poverty to Plenty."   W. L. Rees, 1st edition, p. 159.
Wyman and Sons, 1888.

emigration. The employers of labour could not spare so many "human machines." To this question Sir George directed his eloquence and zeal. He strove with all his might to rouse a public feeling in favour of colonisation, for he saw in this the only safety for the future of England, and the only avenue to happiness for her innumerable children.

In his writings and speeches he pointed out that the course of British colonisation and acquisition of new territory had flowed in many channels. In the early dáys it had assumed the form of charters and monopolies granted to individual subjects or to companies of so-called "adventurers," entitling them to great territories of unoccupied lands beyond the seas. Then it had taken the form of the transportation of political prisoners and criminals to the American plantations and finally to Australia. Then it had shaped itself into a method of endowing the State Church with vast areas of waste lands in all the great dependencies of the Empire. Then the bestowal of whole regions upon associations of the wealthy and the offshoots of noble families, on such terms as would enable them to raise a landed aristocracy in these new worlds, and provide them with cheap labour. Then it had conquered and acquired whole regions in order to advance and stimulate commerce so that merchant princes and manufacturers might build up huge fortunes. Thus the aid of the Government had been given to the aristocracy, to the Church, and merchants, manufacturers, financiers, monopolists and the middle classes generally.

Even the wretched convicts had received to some extent the assistance of the State, although no doubt the primary intention was to rid the United Kingdom of the danger and expense attendant upon the existence of a race of criminals within its boundaries. To one class only had the Government afforded no assistance. But that was the most numerous class of all. In the whole record of colonisation no effort had ever been made to help the industrious poor, the labouring classes, to settle upon the waste lands of the Crown beyond the seas.

It was to this that Sir George Grey now wished to draw attention and assistance. Reason, humanity, expediency, righteousness, all lent their aid to increase the force of his arguments.

He proposed that the counties and parishes should become owners of large tracts of territory in the different colonies, that they should settle upon these great estates the redundant labouring population from their respective localities, advancing all monies necessary, and making such monies charges upon the properties of the various emigrants so assisted. By this process not only would the poor rates be lessened by reason of the stoppage of the streams which fed the workhouses, and in some instances the gaols; but waste lands of great extent belonging to the local bodies at home would yearly increase in value by the settlement of population, and would ultimately not merely provide an outlet for the surplus numbers, especially the youth of both sexes, but would yield a revenue and harvests of various commodities sufficient to maintain within Great Britain the weak, the feeble, and the aged, without their being a burden upon the local funds.

Had his proposal been favourably entertained and become the subject of legislation, the people of Great Britain would have been in a different state to-day to that which they now occupy.

Upon these two kindred subjects he travelled through England, holding public meetings and addressing crowded audiences. A monster meeting was held at the Lambeth Baths, in London, and petitions were signed by over one hundred thousand people in favour of colonisation and against the abandonment of the colonies. Nor was he alone in this noble and patriotic movement. A number of influential men formed themselves into a committee to watch and guard against the disruption of the Empire. The following letter from Mr. Froude to Sir George Grey tells its own tale :—

My dear Sir,—Lord Salisbury tells me that Lord Carnarvon means to take up the subject in the approaching session. Lord S. himself, however, is desponding, and confirms the impression which I have received from other quarters that the Conservative party in the House of Commons is not to be relied on.

The hope is that on both sides of the House there is still a patriotic section. Enough may be done now to keep the Economists in check. Hereafter we may see a fresh organisation, and the old Imperial temper revive.

If mischief can be prevented meanwhile, this will be the happiest result. The Tories, if they moved now, would do it only as a party dodge, and rather discredit than further a nobler line of policy.

Lord R. has remonstrated earnestly with the Government *in private*. You will have seen Mr. Forster's speech at Bradford.—Faithfully yours,

J. A. FROUDE.

CHAPTER XLVI.

THE NEWARK ELECTION.

" His was no common party race
Jostling by dark intrigue for place." '
Marmion.

"Who in his mightiest hour
A bauble held the lust of power,
Spurned at the sordid lust of pelf,
And served his Albion for herself."
Ibid.

UPON another subject then attracting considerable attention in England Sir George Grey felt deeply. The elections of 1868 had been decided by a large majority in Mr. Gladstone's favour on his famous declaration that "the time was come for the disestablishment of the Irish Church." The need for reform in Ireland had made itself felt throughout Great Britain, and when Parliament met on December 10th under the ministry of Mr. Gladstone, they had a majority in the Commons of over one hundred.

Sir George Grey had never forgotten the misery which he beheld in that unhappy land nearly fifty years before. He had never relinquished the purpose then formed of attempting to relieve that misery and to induce such government and circumstances as would gradually heal the wounds which had been inflicted during many centuries of misgovernment, and give to the impulsive children of the Emerald

Isle a fair opportunity for a happy and brilliant
future.

With these great principles prompting him to
action, and being unable to obtain employment in
the colonies from Earl Granville, he determined, if
possible, to enter Parliament, and there gather around
him a party which should be pledged to carry out
these plans.

In March, 1870, a writ was issued for Newark, which
seat had been rendered vacant by the lamented death
of the good and gentle Denison. He entered vigor-
ously upon his electoral campaign. Sir Henry Storks
was contesting the seat, backed by all the force and
influence which Mr. Gladstone could bring to bear.
Sir George remonstrated strongly with Mr. Gladstone,
as he himself was a strong supporter of the Liberal
party. His remonstrances were unavailing. The
great Liberal leader sent a letter to Sir George Grey
by Mr. Stanhope full of eulogiums of his opponent,
and stating the unqualified hope that the Liberals
would vote for Sir Henry Storks in the coming
election. This strange letter closed with the following remarkable paragraph: "I have sent a copy of
this letter to Sir Henry Storks, with permission to him
to make use of it in any way."

In truth, matters between Sir George Grey and the
Liberal leaders had by this time come to a crisis. On
March 27th of the previous year he had published a
letter in the *Daily News* on the position of the agricultural labourers in Ireland, and the influence of that
condition upon the welfare of the poor in England,
which had created a painful sensation. In this letter,
after commenting upon the history of the estate of
Farney, in the county of Monaghan, and showing
from it the terrible condition to which the Irish people
had been reduced, and the successive steps by which

that condition had been brought out, he urged that, in the interests of the nation and of humanity, it was the duty of Parliament at once to institute remedial measures of a drastic character. This letter, in conjunction with Sir George Grey's other utterances, alarmed Ministers, who were already well aware of his extreme views upon the consolidation of the Empire and the importance of emigration.

On the 7th of October, 1869, Earl Granville, as Secretary for the Colonies, wrote a despatch upon the subject of the withdrawal of troops from New Zealand, which drew a further expression of opinion from Sir George Grey. As this matter is of the very greatest importance, not merely as giving evidence of the relations between Sir George Grey and Lord Granville, but as the practical commencement of the Home Rule movement, it is proper to place it in full before the public. It is headed "The Irish Land Question." The following is its text :—

A despatch from Earl Granville, dated the 7th inst, which raises very grave questions, has induced me to re-publish a letter I wrote upon the state of Ireland, which was printed in the *Daily News* of the 27th of last month.

Earl Granville has in that despatch stated in telling language some general views of the highest possible importance, and capable of the widest application. Although he there applies them solely to the case of New Zealand, their utter inapplicability to the state of that country, and other causes, must insure the ulterior object being gained of ascertaining with what degree of favour the opinions expressed will be regarded by the public of Great Britain, and to what extent they will desire to see them applied in Ireland, and in other parts of these islands.

The general principles laid down by Lord Granville as the basis for his subsequent arguments may be stated as follows :—

That there is a part of the Queen's dominions in which it is manifest that the deep and wide-spread discontent which there exists arises mainly from the lands of the original owners having been confiscated. That it is the opinion of the Government that

in such a country the larger and more generally operating incite-
ment to rebellion is the hope of recovering land and status, while
it finds that the restoration of the large extent of land originally
confiscated is often unequivocally put forward by the inhabitants
of such a country as a condition necessary to ensure their pacification.

The Government has further remarked that an independent
people very unwillingly see their nationality pass from them, and not
unnaturally long for some recognition of their national authority.

Lord Granville then observes that the causes above alluded to
being the real sources of great dangers to which the country he
alludes to is exposed from its inhabitants, it is evident to Her
Majesty's Government that the task of continually keeping down
the people of such a country by military force is beyond the
strength of the Empire. This is conclusively shown by the experience of many years past, during which time, in the island spoken
of, a strong local force has always had the assistance of a large
body of regular troops, yet such is its present state that the
discontented amongst its inhabitants suffice to impose a ruinous
insecurity on a large number of landholders, and a ruinous expenditure on the local and British treasury.

In such a case large concessions are, from the causes above
stated, unavoidable to appease a pervading discontent with which
it is otherwise difficult to cope, and still larger concessions will
be necessary to insure the respect of the inhabitants of the country
when the large reductions contemplated in our military expenditure
have been carried out.

It is then stated that in the case of the island alluded to the
abandonment of the confiscated lands to its people, the recognition
of a national Government, and the maintenance of larger and
expensive local forces, however indispensable some or all of them
may be, are remedies which would be distasteful to many people,
and which will not be resorted to so long as they continue to
expect assistance from British troops. A decision, therefore, to
maintain the past and present policy would be injurious to the
people of the country, as tending to delay the adoption of those
prudent counsels on which its restoration depends.

These remarks are not made in any spirit of controversy. Lord
Granville would not gratuitously have criticised the proceedings
of another Government, but a case has arisen in which Her
Majesty's present Government is asked for assistance—it is asked
for assistance to sustain a policy which it does not choose to
assist, and is not able to foresee.

Upon such a state of facts many questions arise, and among them it becomes material to enquire whether the assistance expected by a portion of the people is for the real advantage of those who seek it. Earl Granville, in judging from the best materials at his command, is satisfied that it is not so, and that it is not the part of a true friend of the inhabitants, by continuing a delusive support, to divert their attention from that course in which their safety lies—the course of deliberately measuring their own resources, and, at whatever immediate sacrifice, adjusting their policy to them.

It is not without a full sense of the responsibility which attaches to Her Majesty's Government in deciding on such an important question, nor without a firm belief that they are discharging that responsibility in a manner most conducive to the interests of the country, that they have determined to carry out the line of policy pointed out in Earl Granville's despatch.

Such are the undoubted general truths which had been put forward by Earl Granville in reference to New Zealand alone. I cannot but hope that in writing them he must have thought of Ireland, that country which at the present moment engages so largely the attention of Her Majesty's Government and of all thoughtful minds, for it is hardly possible for language more truly and accurately to describe the state of Ireland than the language used by Lord Granville, yet it could easily be shown that his language has little or no true reference to the state of New Zealand.

The measures and principles inculcated by such high authority may, therefore, be probably meant for the wide scope which they legitimately embrace. Are they intended, then, to be bounded in their application to Ireland ? or are they intended to be extended also to England, where such vast tracts of Church land, once the undoubted heritage of the poor of this country, and so great an extent of public land, once the heritage of the entire nation, have been confiscated for the use of private persons ? In both these countries it has been seen that from the confiscations made a small number of persons have been constantly, yet rapidly, growing into inordinate wealth, whilst the number of landholders has been rapidly diminishing, and the mass of the nation is sinking into helpless and indescribable misery, which the heart sickens in contemplating, and the eye grows sad and weary in looking on.

Lord Granville truly states that the content of a people and the strength of an empire would be vastly augmented by large concessions in the direction which he has traced out, and that still larger concessions would insure the respect of a people, even if very great reductions in the military expenditure were carried out.

It is possible that the Government, carrying one degree farther the ideas they have expressed in reference to the more distant colonial possessions of Great Britain, may have thought that in the case of Ireland it is wrong that the miseries and poverty of the productive classes in England should be augmented by their being heavily taxed, to pay for the maintenance of a large military force in Ireland, to prolong the wretchedness of that country. The people of England and Ireland have all interests in common. It is only those who have self-interested views to advance who strive to make them enemies. In Lord Granville's words: "It is not the part of a true friend of the inhabitants of such countries, by continuing a delusive shadow of support, to divert their attention from that course in which their true safety lies—the course of deliberately measuring their own resources, and, at whatever immediate sacrifice, adjusting their policy to them."

To show how truly Lord Granville's description applies to the state of Ireland, I now proceed to reprint my letter on the 27th of March last.

Then followed a transcript of the letter on the agricultural labourers in Ireland already alluded to as having been published in the *Daily News* of March 27th. At the conclusion of the letter, Sir George added the following remarks :—

In conclusion, I would now say, let Her Majesty's Ministers fairly apply, so far as they are applicable, their own principles to Ireland, to a country close to them, regarding which they have complete knowledge, instead of a distant dependency of the Crown regarding which they know nothing. Here, before them, in their presence, they have a misery, a wretchedness, which is a disgrace to mankind and to civilisation. All future times will look with wonder on statesmen who could speak as some of the present Government have spoken, or who could write as Earl Granville has written, if whilst in the very presence of want, and woe, and ignorance, exceeding, in some respects, the want, and woe, and ignorance of barbarism, they hesitate to act; or who, whilst looking at a deep and wide-spread discontent, frequently almost approaching to revolt, and who, seeing under such circumstances that in one island the discontented amongst its inhabitants suffice to impose a ruinous insecurity on a large number of landholders, and a ruinous expenditure on the public treasury, should yet hesitate to use the powers they hold to put an end to such a state of things.

I would suggest one mode in which I believe they might most beneficially apply in part their own principles to Ireland without delay.   Let them at once give to that country a State Legislature, sitting in Dublin, composed of two elective Houses—a House of Representatives and a Senate, and having the same legislative powers as a State Legislature in the United States of America. Let them leave in the British Parliament the Irish members as at present, but without power to speak or vote upon any such question as the State Legislature sitting in Dublin is competent to legislate upon.   In this manner the Parliament of Great Britain and Ireland sitting in London would have the power of settling all Imperial questions, such as the strength of the army and navy, customs duties, postal service, etc., etc.   The State Legislature sitting in Dublin would have the power of dealing with all local questions, such as the Land Question, Education, etc., etc.

Many advantages would spring from such an arrangement, such as Irish members no longer interfering in English domestic affairs, and English members no longer interfering in Irish domestic affairs.   The domestic affairs of each of the two countries would then be conducted far more with a view to the welfare of the inhabitants of each than to the passions of party warfare and to the desire of making or pulling down Ministries.

It should also be remembered that the union of several Parliaments in one, charged with the duty of minute special legislation upon so many points in different countries, has thrown upon that one Parliament an amount of labour which it cannot perform. Hence its attention is distracted from its really important duties. Each determined party can force its own job through a distracted and bewildered Assembly.   Matters of the highest interest are neglected.   All legislation is crude and unsatisfactory, and little or no explanation can be asked or afforded regarding the expenditure of the public funds, which are often squandered at the caprice of the party in power for the time.   Whilst confused Ministers frequently, indeed generally, new to their different offices, occupied with their duties in the Cabinet, in leading the two Houses of the Legislature, and torn and worn by the enormous mass of duties of every kind thrown upon them in their respective offices, from the most important to the most trifling, in their efforts to attend to all, are forced to neglect all, and the Government of the country has fallen into the hands of irresponsible clerks in the different offices, who care nothing for ruining Ministries, or individual statesmen, if they promote views of their own, or advance the interests of their relations or friends. Hence is arising a disorder and an insubordination in the Empire such as has never before been seen.

Mr. Disraeli must have felt the necessity of some such arrangement for Ireland as I have proposed when he made his speech on returning thanks at his last election. He then said :—

" I admit that there is a certain degree of morbid discontent permanently in Ireland. But you must look a little to the race, and probably that will account for it. The Irishman is a very imaginative being, and he lives in an island with a damp climate, and contiguous to a melancholy ocean. With extraordinary talents he has no variety of pursuits open to him. There is no nation in the world leading such monotonous lives as the Irish, because they have only the cultivation of the soil before them. Men are discontented when they are not occupied. But put an Irishman in a country where there is a fair field for his talents in a variety of occupations, and you will see the Irishman not only equal, but superior to most races."

In the latter half of this quotation lies its main truth. Give to Ireland a State Legislature and a State Executive in Dublin ; secure thereby the residence of its ablest men in the country. Open a fair field, as ministers, legislators, orators, to its best and wisest men. Afford from the same source, as would necessarily and certainly be done, occupation to Irish architects, sculptors, painters, and secure a resident aristocracy, of worth, talent, and wisdom, and you will at the same time restore the wealth, trade, and commerce of Dublin and Ireland. Dumb Ireland will then speak again. Half inanimate Ireland will again awaken to national life, and breathe the breath of hope and freedom ; whilst by again accustoming the Irish people to the management of their own affairs, and to administrative duties of the highest order, a willing people will be educated in that political knowledge which will enable them to put an end to the ills which afflict them, the causes and cure of which none can understand so well as themselves.

Only those who have lived in populations accustomed to manage their own affairs can realise the dignity under such circumstances imparted to the mass of the people. The highest education in earthly matters that can be given to man is that education which trains him to consider his duties, position, and rights as a citizen of a corporate community ; to reflect on his duties to others, and their corresponding duties to himself ; upon the effect which every existing law or new measure may have upon the community of which he is a member, and upon his own interests ; to exercise that self-restraint and generous courtesy even to the meanest, which is necessary to secure the affection and regard of those who have not only a free voice in the choice of men who are to direct affairs, but who, from knowledge and position, have gained the political knowledge necessary to form a sound opinion upon the value or worthlessness of measures proposed to them.   To give such power and consequently such knowledge to a people is a really conservative step in the right direction.

All this can be done for Ireland without taking from England any power she wants, or which can be of the least use to her ; and if Her Majesty's Government really hold to the principles laid down, and so earnestly insisted upon, by Earl Granville, there is reason to hope that they will at once do something in this direction for suffering Ireland.

And what they do for Ireland will be equally done for the trade and commerce of England.   It is impossible to benefit one country without benefiting at the same time the other.   The miseries of Ireland now hang like a millstone round the neck of England. Restore Ireland to contentment, prosperity, political knowledge, hope in the future, and England will receive an impetus which will impel her onwards to a course of commerce, greatness, and happiness far surpassing anything which she has yet been able to achieve.   Raise the condition of the Irish labourer, render necessary to him the food, the clothing, the dwellings, the comforts which the very lowest order of civilisation requires, and you will save the English labourer and the English working man from that cruel competition which is ruining and deteriorating the nation.

The wonderful skill with which Sir George had applied the whole reasoning used by Earl Granville in the case of New Zealand to the case of Ireland appears in every paragraph.   His arguments are luminous, complete, and conclusive.   No illustration more apposite, no logic more convincing, is to be found in the whole range of literature upon this much-disputed subject than are contained in the few pages of this pamphlet.

At the end of the pamphlet Sir George gives a draft of a proposed enactment—

AN ACT TO GRANT A PROVINCIAL PARLIAMENT TO THE KINGDOM OF IRELAND.

Whereas, large numbers of Her Majesty's subjects, natives of the Kingdom of Ireland, have from time to time rendered most important military and naval services to the Crown and Empire, and have shown their capacity for Government by administering with great ability the Governments, or conducting the affairs of the Legislatures of many of Her Majesty's Colonial possessions, and whereas it is desirable to foster and restore the commerce and trade of the said Kingdom, and to encourage the residence therein of proprietors of land and others, and to open a field for the development of the talent, and patriotism of its inhabitants which does not now exist, and to restore contentment and prosperity to its people, by allowing them to exercise that control over the management of their local affairs, without the possession of which no nation can be either contented, prudent, or prosperous.

Be it therefore enacted, by the Queen's Most Excellent Majesty, by and with the advice and consent of the Lords Spiritual and Temporal, and Commons in this present Parliament assembled, and by the authority of the same as follows :—

There shall be within the Kingdom of Ireland a Provincial Parliament to consist of a Viceroy, a Senate, and a House of Representatives.

The pamphlet closes with the following words :—" I have here suggested this one mode in which immediate effect could be given in part to the principles put forth by Lord Granville ; but it is evident that other and most important modes of giving speedy relief to Ireland could be also suggested. Into some of these I hope to inquire at a future time."

The pamphlet was published about the end of October, 1869. It is the first definite and practicable proposition ever made for the local self-government of Ireland.

No form so simple has ever since been submitted to

the public. No plan so efficacious has been elaborated through the long course of the argument. Perhaps no mind in the world had thought out the question of local self-government so deeply as that of Sir George Grey. He had devoted years of study to the subject, which he believed to be of primary importance. His Constitution for New Zealand had been admitted by thinking men to be well-nigh perfect ; and though shorn of its fair dimensions in its application to that colony, had been almost completely adopted upon the vast theatre of the Dominion of Canada.

He was convinced that that which proved so great a boon to Antipodean nations would be equally full of blessing to the unhappy land which lay, as it were, within rifle-shot of Westminster. Like many of his other plans, this was far in advance of the intelligence of the time. Twenty years of strife and sorrow and oppression have not been sufficient to bring public opinion to the plane from which Sir George Grey then viewed the Irish question.

His two friends, Carlyle and Froude, equally differed from him in opinion on this subject at the first. Both wrote against it. The arguments used by Grey converted Carlyle completely, but Mr. Froude to this day seems to retain his old opinion.

The effect upon Lord Granville of this sudden demand of " Home Rule for Ireland " was instantaneous and remarkable. He attacked Sir George Grey violently in a speech in the House of Lords, and made no secret of the angry feelings aroused within him by this last act of his seemingly determined antagonist. Nor were Mr. Gladstone and Mr. Bright far behind their colleagues in their feelings of hostility to Sir George Grey. He became to them what Lord Carnarvon had long since pronounced him to be, in his opinion, " a dangerous man."

It was therefore felt that the contest at Newark was a contest, not between Liberals and Conservatives, but a contest between Sir George Grey—representing the extremest views upon the questions of the Colonial Empire, of Emigration, of Home Rule for Ireland, and the cause of the English poor—against all other political parties and all other political shibboleths huddled together.

The following manifesto was issued by Sir George Grey to the electors of Newark :—

To the Independent Electors of the Borough of Newark.

Gentlemen,—I offer myself as a candidate for the honour of being your representative in Parliament. I appear before you, not as the nominee of any section or party, but as an independent Liberal candidate. I promise to support, not merely a Liberal Government, but Liberalism in its truest, widest, and noblest sense. I desire to obtain the distinction which you can confer, from a wish to serve my country, by promoting measures calculated to foster and advance the morality, welfare, and commerce of this vast empire. As one to whom Her Majesty has repeatedly confided the important task of governing great dependencies, I take a great interest in Imperial questions. I am opposed to the views of those who advocate the severance of the colonies from Great Britain, believing that they add to her strength, wealth, and glory. In accordance with these opinions, I have striven to initiate a policy of emigration, by which, if conducted under proper conditions, our colonies would be regarded as the natural outlet for our excessive population, and instead of being looked upon as places of exile would be considered—what in truth they are—a home and heritage for the people of England. Equitable measures can also be adopted for reclaiming the waste lands of this country, thus establishing throughout the Empire the great remedial principle of "waste labour to waste lands." So strongly do I feel upon the question of the introduction of the ballot, that I should strive to prevent any further postponement of its adoption. I am in favour of a system of free education for the people, so devised as assuredly to reach every home in the country. I may point to many public efforts which I have made to promote the welfare of the working men of Great Britain as a proof that their interests will never be neglected by me. Should I have the good fortune to be chosen as your representative, I shall always remember that it is my duty, irrespective of class or party, to labour for the good of the borough of Newark, and of each of its inhabitants.—I have the honour to be, gentlemen, your faithful servant,

G. GREY.

Saracen's Head, Newark, March 25th, 1870.

The triangular duel was watched with extreme interest by the keenest intellects and the warmest hearts in the kingdom. On March 25th, 1870, Carlyle wrote as follows:—

Chelsea, March 25th, 1870.

Dear Sir George,—The day before yesterday I fell in accidentally with Lord Derby, and talked a few minutes (all the time we had) about emigration and you, with pleasure to both parties as seemed to me.

His Lordship, who is by no means an adherent of the hidebound political economist-system—rather a despiser of it, I should think—desired warmly that colonies and Mother Country should be kept together by every rational and feasible method : objects strongly to the notion of shovelling out paupers and other unfit *canaille* upon the colonies, but is "clear for emigration," could the great difficulties be overcome.

In short he seemed to me a man well worth your attending to and investigating further ; and when I proposed sending you to him for a little conversation, he at once, and with evident pleasure, assented, and I really believe *desires* to hear you explain yourself.

How important the help or countenance of such a personage might be at this stage of the affair I need not suggest : a man of such position, a man of sense, too, of quietly independent judgment, and not suspected of disloyalty of mind or character by anybody. I decidedly think it might be worth your while to go. Here accordingly is my card enclosed, which please do not take for an impertinence (though probably you know nearly as much of Lord Derby as I), but for a piece of punctuality and sign of willingness on my part, to be used or not used as you yourself judge fittest.—Believe me, yours always truly,

T. CARLYLE.

On the 29th of March, Sir George Grey received, among others, the following two letters. The polling was rapidly approaching, and the interest of those who had sufficient knowledge and discernment to understand the meaning of the struggle was becoming intense :—

> 5, Cheyne Row, Chelsea,
> 29th March, 1870.
>
> Dear Sir George,—My uncle bids me say that he has received your telegram ; and you yourself know how heartily he wishes you success in the object you have in view by getting into Parliament. For he considers *emigration* by far the most important question now on foot in England, and you of all Englishmen the most likely to bring it to a useful result. But for many years he has been resolved "neither to vote nor be voted for, nor in any way to concern himself" with any Parliament that can now be in England. But I am copying the parts out of his books in which he speaks of emigration, and shall forward them to you to-morrow. Perhaps you may be able to make some use of them instead of a letter from him, for the thoughts there expressed have in no way changed except always to grow more strong and decided.—I am, yours very truly,
>
> MARY CARLYLE AITKEN.

> March 29th.
>
> My Dear Sir,—I hear with the greatest pleasure that you are standing for Newark. I only wish I had a vote there or could in any way forward your return. The question with which you have identified yourself is incommeasurably greater than any other at present before Parliament. The Irish land affair is a mere puddle by the roadside in comparison with it. The leaders of this great Liberal party are either blind or worse if they send down a candidate to oppose you. I trust for once that the electors will use their own judgment, and that Radicals and Conservatives alike will recollect that they are Englishmen. I shall regard your success as a declaration on the part of this people that their eyes are open and that they will not be made fools of any longer.— Believe me, with most hearty good wishes, faithfully yours,
>
> J. A. FROUDE

On the day following Mr. Stanhope, who, as before stated, had been sent down specially by Mr. Gladstone, brought with him from a valued friend and relative of Sir George, the following letter :—

Charing Cross,
March 28th, 1870.

Dear Sir George,—The bearer of this is Mr. Stanhope, a Herefordshire man and a friend of mine. He wants a letter of introduction to you. The Government are, of course, anxious to get Storks into the House, so I hope you will not let in a Tory between you. Believe me, very truly yours,

M. BIDDULPH.

The next day Carlyle wrote to him thus :—

5, Cheyne Row, Chelsea,
March 30th, 1870.

Dear Sir George,—Having had for the last half-century these notions about emigration, and believing now, in the days which have come upon us, both that the question of emigration is the most important of all others for this nation, and that you of all men are the man to urge and guide it towards a successful issue, I need not say whether or not I wish you success at Newark against all comers.—Yours sincerely,

T. CARLYLE.

As the day of decision had now come, the excitement among the few initiated reached its height. Carlyle, unable to conceal the earnestness of his hope, sent the following as a last and final message :—

Chelsea, April 1st, 1870.

Dear Sir George,—Send me with your first moment of leisure, one word of tidings ; as soon as the result comes, do at least let me have that at once. I see no *newspapers* almost never, and am more interested in this one membership (as matters have come to stand) than in all the other 657.—Hoping *good* news, yours very truly,

T. CARLYLE.

To this note might be applied Longfellow's verse :—

> " This was the peasant's last good night,
> A voice replied far up the height,
> Excelsior ! "

The election, so far as Sir George Grey was concerned, never took place. Determined that Sir George Grey should not succeed in Newark, although, if he persevered, Sir Henry Storks was certain to be beaten, the Government kept their man upon the lists. Pressed upon many quarters not to sacrifice a Liberal seat, and seeing that with the Liberal votes divided, both must fail, Sir George agreed to an arrangement. Sir Henry Storks and he himself both withdrew, and another Liberal was put forward. The plan succeeded, and the Government candidate was returned.

CHAPTER XLVII.

FAREWELL TO ENGLAND.

" Farewell ! a word that must be, and hath been—
A sound that makes us linger: yet—Farewell ! "
Byron.

THE Newark election convinced Sir George Grey that his plans were distasteful to the Liberal leaders. His own health was affected, and the worry and strain of the last eighteen months, combined with the rigour of the English climate, had affected him considerably. He began to long for the clear skies and the balmy atmosphere of his island home in the Pacific. He believed also that reforms in Britain might be accomplished from the Colonies as readily as from the centre of England itself. He was strengthened in this belief by the fact that the New Zealand Constitution had been obtained by pressure from without, and he saw that it had borne good fruit in Canada.

The pamphlet which he had written upon the subject of Home Rule for Ireland had been discussed by a mutual friend with Mr. Gladstone. Afterwards his friend conveyed to him the fact that Mr. Gladstone, and indeed the leaders of the Liberal party generally, were disturbed by his persistence, and disposed to treat his efforts as embarrassing to the Liberal party and inimical to its interests. It was represented to

him that Mr. Gladstone pointed out that, in addition
to the disestablishment of the Irish Church, he was,
in conjunction with Mr. Bright, preparing a large
and liberal measure in relation to Irish land, which
would effectually dispose of the difficulties of Irish
government, and meet the first demand of the Irish
people.

Considering these facts, some members of the
Liberal party urged that the extreme measures proposed by Sir George Grey would be likely to disturb
and harass the Liberals, and might possibly cause
division amongst their ranks, and delay or defeat the
successful carrying out of the measures which that
Government proposed, by raising hopes of still more
liberal plans.   If Sir George Grey was not disposed
to rely altogether upon Mr. Gladstone's own opinion,
he was to be assured that Mr. Bright, whose sound
and critical judgment was scarcely equalled in the
Kingdom, fully concurred in the wisdom of the steps
being taken, their absolute suitability for the wants of
Ireland, and their entire sufficiency to achieve all that
was necessary to be done.

Sir George's mind was soon made up.   He was
determined that he would give no cause of accusation
by his own conduct.   If the Liberal party, speaking
through its leaders, was determined not to assist him
in the great measure he proposed, he would return to
New Zealand.   He had at any rate seen the tide turn
in regard to the dismemberment of the Empire.   He
had obtained the sympathy of many in his advocacy
of a true policy of emigration, and he had left on
record a common-sense and just proposal for the local
self-government of Ireland.

Indeed, though he knew it not, the great principles
for which he had striven were all made certain of
accomplishment.   The power of the economists to

dismember the Empire was shattered. The ground was broken for the inauguration of 'a future system of State colonisation, and with the publication of his short "Act for the Parliament of the Kingdom of Ireland," the future consummation of that also was probably assured.

Around all these questions the angry storms and passions of party strife might rage. The selfishness of human nature, the lust of power, the pride of hereditary superiority, would indeed delay the fulfilment, but the seed was sown. That seed was life-bearing and must germinate. No man would now dare, openly and seriously, to advocate the disruption of the Empire; and though well nigh fourscore years of age, Sir George Grey yet trusts to see the initiation of a wise system of Imperial colonisation, and a provincial Parliament sitting in College Green.

In 1870 he left the shores of England to return to New Zealand.

Although saddened and dispirited at seeing no visible fruits of his labours in England, Sir George Grey was yet able to look back with pleasure on many meetings with old friends, on much pleasant social and scientific intercourse with the leaders of thought, and on many new and enduring friendships made.

His presence in England had been early utilised by the devotees of science and literature. Thus, on March 15th, 1869, Professor Huxley wrote :

My dear Sir George Grey,—Our first Ethnological meeting here the other night went off so well that we are disposed to add to the three which we had already arranged to hold a fourth on the Ethnology of Polynesia. We propose to hold the meeting on the 11th of May, and my present purpose in writing to you is to beg to be allowed to announce a communication from you, short or long, but the longer the better.

"Maori Sagas" would be a splendid subject, and one which would be abundantly illustrated by the mere crumbs from your table.—Ever yours, very faithfully,

T. H. HUXLEY.

In continuance of the same subject came the following:

April 28th, 1869.

My dear Sir George,—I am particularly obliged to you for sending me the title of your paper in time to enable me to announce it last night. The topic you have chosen is profoundly interesting, and I have no doubt there will be a great attendance to hear you.

.   .   .   The Council wish me to precede you with a few remarks about Polynesia generally; and the Bishop of Wellington will follow you. You will represent the "secular arm" between science and religion.—Ever yours, very truly,

T. H. HUXLEY.

Grey's ardent devotion to scientific research was singularly illustrated immediately prior to his departure from England. Among other subjects of study to which he had paid much attention was that of the nature and composition of ether and its connection with and relation to electricity. He became convinced of the laminiferous structure of ether, and the positive and negative qualities of alternate strata.

If he was right in this, gravitation did not exist. It was an unnecessary conception, called into existence when the qualities of the ether were unknown. The theory of gravitation declared that every body in the universe attracts every other body with a force which varies inversely as the square of the distance. This was but half the truth. The theory of electricity, based on a compound ether, declares that the force, whether attraction or repulsion, varies inversely as the square of the distance. This is the whole truth.

The first half is gravity being incessantly exercised by suns, planets, and smaller celestial bodies, all of which by their rapid revolutions as they travel through space, continually by friction create electricity and give rise to vast electrical discharges, from which emanate light, heat, and other phenomena.

The influence of electricity upon the germination and development of life became in his mind intimately connected with this ether discovery which he believed he had made.

Both in England and on his return to New Zealand he discoursed with several scientific friends upon these subjects, and mentioned to them the arguments which had suggested themselves to his mind, and the results at which he had arrived. One of the first persons to hear Sir George speak of his theory was the great astronomer, Proctor. Several gentlemen now living remember conversations with Sir G. Grey on the subject in the years 1875 and 1876.

In 1889, one of these, upon reading Mr. Lodge's work in the *Nature Series* on " Modern Views of Electricity," was so struck by the verification of Grey's ideas, communicated to him fifteen years before, that he noted the passages and sent the book to Sir George in Auckland. Other friends, also, on seeing Mr. Lodge's book, remembered Sir George's conversations with them at that time, and wrote reminding him of their occurrence.

The value of this discovery, which has been variously and partially attributed to Mr. G. F. Fitzgerald, Mr. Hicks, and Sir William Thomson, is alleged by scientists to be beyond calculation. Mr. Lodge, at the conclusion of the preface to his elaborate and clever book, after speaking of this " Theory of Free Ether," thus writes :

M 2

The Theory of bound Ether and of Matter must next follow, and thereby, in addition to all optical and electrical phenomena, gravitation and cohesion must be explained too. Then must be attacked the specific differences between various kinds of matter and the nature of what we call their " combinations."

When this is accomplished, the complex facts of chemistry will have been brought under a comprehensive law. The next fifty years may witness these tremendous victories in great part won.

While leading the agitation against the abandon-ment of the colonies, and in favour of a national system of colonisation, Sir George, besides address-ing great meetings in different parts of England and Scotland, spoke also to very large assemblages in the metropolis. It was after one of these addresses at the Lambeth Baths that the late Governor of New Zealand met an old friend under peculiar but pleasant circumstances.

One among several speakers for the evening, his speech being ended and having another appointment, Sir George Grey left the hall, and wandering through some intricate passages, found himself at length in a narrow street, the name and situation of which were entirely unknown to him.

A stranger in that part of London, he did not know in which direction lay his path. He could see no policeman of whom to make enquiries, and he did not like to ask any chance passer-by. While thus hesi-tating, his attention was attracted by the opening of a door, and the sudden darting of a somewhat bright light from within across the roadway. The clatter of many feet and the sound of many voices drew his attention still more strongly.

Involuntarily he walked to the half-open door, and for the purpose of enquiring his way, entered the room. It contained a number of young men—clerks, shopmen, and respectable artisans—each with his

bundle of books; evidently an evening class composed
of youths who, unable to pursue their studies in the
day time, thus gathered together in the evenings, in
a sort of advanced school or college.   The intelligence
and good humour dwelling upon their countenances
pleased their self-invited visitor greatly.

Before he had time to make known the intention
with which he had thus suddenly intruded upon them,
Sir George was still more pleased, for in the tutor of
this class, standing at the head of the table, he recognised none other than his old New Zealand friend,
Mr. J. E. Gorst.

As in New Zealand this gentleman had given his
time and attention to the performance of public
duties and the training of the young without payment
or any pecuniary reward, so in London he had
unselfishly devoted one or two evenings a week to
the instruction of these young men, his only reward.
being the consciousness of duty performed.

As Sir George and Mr. Gorst met and clasped each
other's hands, the students, with looks of surprise,
departed.   Sir George's memory flew back to that
time when Rewi had issued the death warrant against
his present companion, and he rejoiced to find that in
London, as truly as in the Waikato, his friend pursued
the same quiet path of unostentatious and self-denying
usefulness.

Living at Kensington, and absorbed in his Parliamentary duties, Mr. Gorst yet came up regularly one
or two evenings every week to conduct the studies of
this class.

Throughout Sir George's election contest, Mr.
Edward Jenkins, the author of "Ginx's Baby," was
his warm supporter and most active worker. . An
extract from one or two of his letters will show the
feelings with which he regarded Sir George Grey.

A letter dated May 17th, 1870, was accompanied by a copy of "Ginx's Baby," which he told Sir George in great jubilation had been pronounced by Dr. Kingsley, "next to 'Lothair,' the greatest book out for many a day." The author went on to give an idea of a new book he was contemplating, "Ex Cathedra." In another letter, written on May 19th, Mr. Jenkins said :—"I cannot thank you enough for your delicate kindnesses, which give me proof that the old Christian chivalrousness of strong to weak is not everywhere extinct, though fast becoming fossil to this generation." In a later letter he wrote of a friend who showed him great hospitality on Sir George's introduction :— " He did not think 'Ginx's Baby' worth reading, but he treated the author with great consideration. That lucky book has reached a fifth edition, and will shortly reach a sixth. I was astonished on my return to find your early prognostications verified, and the book in every man's mouth. Tennyson, Arthur Helps, Sir Henry Holland, Laurence Oliphant, and a host of others, have testified their admiration in an unmistakable way. If it will only wake men's minds to the necessity of acting, I shall be happy." When he heard that Sir George Grey had determined to leave England, he wrote that no one would ever know how many hopes for England had perished in his heart at the news.

CHAPTER XLVIII.

SOUTH AFRICA AND ENGLAND: A CHAPTER OF DISASTERS.

> "In dim eclipse disastrous twilight sheds
> On half the nations, and with fear of change
> Perplexes monarchs."
> *Paradise Lost.*

THE years 1869 and 1870 may be looked upon as forming the exact period in which the tide began to turn. The projected breaking up of the Empire proposed by the Economists and Manchester school, and tacitly agreed to by all political parties, had carried England down in its ebbing waters almost to the brink of ruin. Sir George Clerk's abandonment of the Orange River Sovereignty, followed soon by his suggestions (which, endorsed by the English Government, were sent to Sir George Grey in 1855-6) had led to the withdrawal of troops from all the colonies. The remonstrances of Sir George Grey had saved the further breaking-up of Africa, although his efforts at confederation had been made the pretext for his recall.

In 1858-9, when Sir G. Grey had been recalled, Lord Carnarvon was, as we have seen, Political Under-Secretary for the Colonies, and he fully shared the ideas of his chief, Sir E. B. Lytton, in the condemnation of the proposed confederation of South

Africa. In 1866 the Earl of Carnarvon joined Lord Derby's third Ministry as Secretary for the Colonies. Lord Carnarvon's opinions had been changing during the seven years which had passed. He began to perceive that the colonies were not only useful to Great Britain at the present, but were likely to be still more useful to her in the future.

Twenty years before, Earl Grey had started upon that course of promoting representative and responsible government which had by 1856 raised into existence in North America, Australasia, New Zealand, and South Africa many young English nations —bold, prosperous, and self-reliant. The other strange and wayward effort, made with all the patient pertinacity for which the noble Earl was famous—the reintroduction of a system of convict settlements in the different colonies — had been abandoned and finally closed in 1854 by the authoritative memorandum of the Duke of Newcastle.

As Earl Grey had conferred upon the great colonies the rights of self-government, under which they grew and prospered, Lord Carnarvon determined that he would aid them in forming confederated States in their different locations, and in lieu of detaching them from the Empire, extend their territories and bind them more closely to the destinies of Britain. The project of confederating the British North American provinces offered to him a favourable opportunity for the practical inauguration of so great a work.

On the 17th of February, 1867, in a speech of great power and earnestness, Lord Carnarvon in the House of Lords moved the second reading of the Bill for confederating British North America, which practically created a second series of United States upon the Western Continent. This was almost his last appearance as a member of that Ministry, as he, with two of his colleagues, resigned in less than a fortnight on the question of the Reform Bill.

The ideas of colonial federation were slowly making way until the beginning of 1874, when Lord Carnarvon again took office as Secretary for the Colonies under Mr. Disraeli. By this time the tone of public opinion had changed. The efforts made by Sir George Grey, and the public and private utterances of many leading men, equally with the general tendency of the press throughout the Three Kingdoms, had borne fruit.

The well-nigh fatal apathy which the greedy spirit of the ultra-competitive school of economists had caused in relation to the colonies, had given place to a much sounder and more wakeful condition. To get rid of the colonies was no longer deemed desirable. The day had at last arrived when, in Mr. Froude's words, "The old Imperial temper of the nation had revived." From that time forward no party would dare to advocate the dismemberment of the Empire. Indeed there was now a danger of the pendulum swinging to the opposite extreme.

It was at such a time, and under such circumstances, that Lord Carnarvon returned to office. His cousin, Sir Robert Herbert, was permanent Under-Secretary. The political conditions of the great groups of dependencies were peculiar. In the west the provinces of British North America had fairly started upon their career as a confederated dominion. In the east, the long-sundered nations of Southern Asia had been welded into a vaster Indian Empire than Alexander or Genghis Khan imagined. In New Zealand the native question had been settled; and Australasian statesmen, while working out the destinies of their own particular colonies, were rising to the consideration of matters in which all were interested. Defence from foreign aggression on sea and on land, intercolonial tariffs, and other questions which pressed forward for thoughtful discussion were silently and in the order of nature raising an Australasian tendency towards federation, which the Mother Country and the Ministers of the Crown could aid forward without appearing to meddle with high-spirited communities unwilling to brook interference.

But in South Africa all was confusion. For nearly twenty years the South African States had felt little of the burdens and sufferings which in former days had afflicted them. Sore as were the settlers of the Orange Free State at their abandonment, bitter as was the feeling in the Transvaal against England and the English, yet the generous treatment and wise counsels of Sir George Grey during the eight years 1854 to 1861, and the abiding effect produced by his reforms, had helped to maintain a state of peace and of safety throughout South Africa generally till the year 1871.

In that year Sir Benjamin Pine had been appointed to the Governorship of Natal, and Mr. Theophilus Shepstone was still in office, having control of the Native Department. The unfortunate co-operation of these two minds, which in 1854 had so nearly created an independent kingdom for Mr. Shepstone, was again fated to produce a disturbing influence upon the African States. By a series of blunders and false alarms, a war was raised between Natal and Langabilalele. The followers of the native chief were shot and he himself captured. One man alone had the moral courage to protest against wrongdoing in high places, and to carry his complaints to London. That man was Bishop Colenso.

In response to this appeal for justice, the Secretary for the Colonies, after due investigation, emphatically denounced the conduct of the Government of Natal. Sir Benjamin Pine sent Mr. Shepstone to London in order that his astuteness and knowledge might counterbalance the zeal and earnestness of the Bishop. That object, however, was not accomplished. The facts were too plain, and the injustice and cruelty too great to permit of any valid defence. Sir Benjamin Pine was recalled. Mr. Shepstone was kept in London in attendance upon the Colonial Office, for reasons and purposes which are only to be explained by other events which transpired in relation to South African matters.

In the four years between 1871 and 1875, everything in connection with the colonies and states of South Africa drifted into confusion. On every hand, causes of quarrel and of contention presented themselves. Diamond fields of immense value were discovered in land which certainly belonged to the Orange Free State; but it was annexed by the Governor of the Cape.

This glaring violation of a solemn treaty exasperated the whole Boer population of the Cape, Natal, the Transvaal, and the Free State. Mr. Southey caused to be sold to the Kafirs and native workmen at these mines, great quantities of arms and ammunition. It is said that the almost incredible number of 500,000 stand of arms with ammunition, were so sold. This increased the bitterness in the minds of the Boers, as they believed these arms would be used by the natives against them.

The Secretary for the Colonies took it upon himself to advise the Cape Colony to enter upon that plan of confederation for proposing which he had helped to dismiss Sir George Grey fifteen years ago. At this interference, which the Colony considered both tyrannical and improper, the Cape people became frantic.

Resolutions were passed in Parliament, and the Colonial Secretary and his despatch held up to ridicule and opprobrium.

Mr. J. A. Froude, always a trusted friend and adviser of Lord Carnarvon, was requested by His Lordship to proceed to the Cape to mediate and explain. Sir Garnet Wolseley with a brilliant staff was sent to Natal. All was vain. The people, both of European and native descent, were becoming roused to a dangerous pitch. Lord Carnarvon was sorely troubled; but yet, with tenacity of purpose, adhered to his policy of confederation, and cast about for advisers and assistants whose aid would enable him to calm the troubled sea of South African politics, and effect a permanent union among its discordant peoples.

In furtherance of an idea thrown out by Mr. Froude, a conference was called and held in London on August 3rd, 1876, at which representatives appeared, and which was presided over by Sir Garnet Wolseley.

During the two years in which Mr. Shepstone had been detained in England, his advice and knowledge had been laid under requisition by Lord Carnarvon in relation to the tangled web which presented itself at the Cape of Good Hope.

To this conference Lord Carnarvon appointed Mr. Shepstone as a representative.

Up to this time the influence of Mr. Froude's advice and friendly intervention may have lasted. His counsel might be summed up in the three words, "Conciliation and Patience." Happy would it have been for England and for South Africa had that sage advice been followed.

The conference broke up without doing anything towards confederation. The South African members returned to the Cape, but Mr. Shepstone still remained in London, in continual attendance at the Colonial Office.

Two years and a half had now passed since Lord Carnarvon had taken office, and the South African matters were still unsettled.

Nearly every course possible had been tried, but failure had attended every effort. Mr. Froude's mission and Sir Garnet Wolseley's appointment had both been fruitless. His own despatches had been slighted, the conference had done nothing, and the intervention of foreign powers had been requested by the Transvaal Republic.

There were at this time two courses open to Lord Carnarvon. One was to ask Sir George Grey, then in the New Zealand Parliament, to take charge of South Africa and complete the task which he had commenced in 1859. The other was to take entire personal control and compel the acceptance of his plans without appearing to use either violence or unfair means.

Every successive despatch revealed more clearly the necessity for action. So rapidly was confusion overshadowing the frontiers of the colonies that to hesitate was to be lost. The first alternative, if ever seriously contemplated, was soon dismissed. It was bitter enough to confess that Grey was right and Downing Street wrong, without having to appeal to him for help. They had adopted his plans after repeated condemnations. To acknowledge that they could not carry those plans into execution without his assistance would have been an additional degradation. Doubtless Mr. Froude advised this course, for his mind was always stedfastly fixed upon this question. To him Sir George Grey was the only man capable of working out the desperate and tangled problem waiting to be solved in South Africa. In that belief

Froude never faltered.   Years afterwards, in the pages
of that "Oceana" which delighted multitudes, he
gave utterance to the same belief; and at a date still
later he approached the Colonial Office, hoping that
Grey might even yet be asked to undertake the task,
though bordering upon fourscore years.   When in
1880-1 Sir Bartle Frere, heartbroken by the difficulties
which defeated all his plans, left the Cape, he pointed
out the fact that Sir George Grey alone knew how to
deal successfully with the varied races and contending
interests of South Africa.   And in conversation with
Carlyle Lord Carnarvon had heard from the lips
of that great man a verdict upon the character of
Grey which deserves to be recorded:—"He is born
of the Tetragonidæ, built four-square, solid, as one
fitted to strongly meet the winds of heaven and the
waves of fate."

Driven back upon himself, the Earl of Carnarvon
determined to accept the responsibility.   No Secretary
for the Colonies had enjoyed greater facilities for
learning how to govern the Colonial Empire.   His
political career had been devoted to this portion of
the Imperial field.   Moreover he considered himself
fortunate in having been able for two years to consult
an adviser who was able, as he thought, to disclose
the whole truth in all its different lights upon every
matter apertaining to the Boers and the savage
tribes.

By what process of reasoning and counsel the final
result was achieved, it is impossible to say.   No
record of the interviews between Sir Robert Herbert,
Lord Carnarvon, and Mr. Shepstone now exists.
Probably the proceedings were never reduced to
writing, but gradually, through conversations and
interviews, suggestions and proposals, the plan which
was ultimately adopted was worked out.

Mr. Froude at this time seems absolutely to have lost, not only the influence which he had hitherto exercised over Lord Carnarvon's mind, but also the knowledge of what was passing and the intentions which were shaping themselves in the brain of the Secretary for the Colonies. In several lectures and publications given and issued by Mr. Froude this abundantly appears. No one was more surprised at the ultimate action of Lord Carnarvon than his friend and adviser, Mr. Froude.

Immediately after the conference, and without any notice to the Cape of Good Hope, or to any of the States or people interested, Lord Carnarvon determined upon a course of procedure, the stupidity of which was only equalled by its injustice. The triumvirate—the Earl of Carnarvon, Sir Robert Herbert (the Permanent Under-Secretary), and Mr. Theophilus Shepstone—decided to accomplish a confederation of the South African States, if possible by peaceful means, but if necessary by force. For this purpose a commission in the name of the Queen was, on the 5th day of October, 1876, issued to Mr. Shepstone (now created Sir Theophilus Shepstone, K.C.M.G.) appointing him a Special Commissioner, and giving him full power and authority to annex any territories bordering the British colonies in South Africa, and to incorporate them in the British dominions.

It was under this unconstitutional, oppressive and unrighteous commission that Sir Theophilus Shepstone annexed the South African Republic, brought on the Zulu war, caused the loss of thirty thousand lives, the expenditure of millions of treasure, and brought more reverses and disgrace to the British flag than were caused by any number of the Queen's subjects under any other document ever penned.

No such commission was ever before issued by the

Crown, probably none such will ever again be issued. The powers and jurisdiction which the Crown possesses, and for the enforcement of which it is able to issue commissions, are of two classes. The first class includes all those functions which belong to it by prerogative; the second those which are conferred upon it by the law of the land. Thus the Crown can of its own inherent right pardon criminals, bestow peerages, declare war, and make peace; but it can take no man's property, or life, or liberty, without the authority of the law—either the common law of the country, acting through its recognised tribunals, or by Act of Parliament.

Under which of these categories did the Minister of the Crown advise his Sovereign to sign this commission? It falls under neither. It purports to bestow authority upon Sir Theophilus Shepstone to annex all the territories, districts, and states adjacent to the British colonies in South Africa, and it commands all the officers and subjects of the Crown, both civil and military, to aid him in so doing. The Orange Free State, the South African Republic, the warlike Zulu nation, all the territories of the free natives, the Portuguese settlements at Delagoa Bay—all are to be annexed to the British Empire at the pleasure of Sir Theophilus Shepstone! There is actually no limit, no condition whatever but his own will. He himself was to be the judge of the facts by which his action was to be determined.

Nearly all these states or territories were in solemn treaty with us at this very time. To the South African Republic and the Orange Free State we had solemnly guaranteed the inviolability—so far as we were concerned—of their territories, and promised to annex no native territories beyond the Orange River. To the Orange Free State we had only three months before paid £90,000 because we had broken our treaty in this respect. No feature of atrocity is absent from this specimen of Imperial buccaneering. With the States intended to be affected we were at peace. The Imperial Government was at this very time loud in its expressions of desire for a friendly confederation under which their independence was to be secured. We were bound by treaties of the most solemn nature not to interfere. No words could be stronger than those used at the Sand River Convention. "The Assistant Commissioners guarantee in the fullest manner on the part of the British Government to the emigrant farmers beyond the Vaal River the right to manage their own affairs, and to govern themselves according to their own laws, without any interference on the part of the British Government, and that no encroachment shall be made by the said Government on the territory beyond to the north of the Vaal River." As to the Orange Free State, that we had abandoned against the wishes and prayers of the people, both Ministers and Parliament turning a deaf ear to the delegates who went to England in 1854. Not only was this commission a breach of the most solemnly pledged faith of the nation; it was absolutely un-righteous. What right had we to annex these States against their will? The ridiculous condition that Sir Theophilus Shepstone was "to be satisfied that a sufficient number of the inhabitants desired to become our subjects," was of course fulfilled. The experienced "Somtseu" easily satisfied himself, although President, Executive, Legislature, and public meetings were all against him. To add to the iniquity of the transaction, the commission was kept secret. It was given to Shepstone privately, and by him taken to Natal and Pretoria, no one but a few privileged persons knowing of its existence.

The subsequent steps taken under this Commission are too recent to need a full recapitulation. In April, 1877, Sir Theophilus Shepstone annexed the Transvaal. President Burgérs, in a memorandum full of dignity and constitutional learning, solemnly protested against the annexation. The Executive Council of the Transvaal endorsed this protest. On the 12th of April, Sir T. Shepstone issued a proclamation annexing the South African Republic. In the course of a speech made by him to the burghers, he said :—" Do you know what has recently happened in Turkey ? Because no civilised Government was carried on there, the great Powers interfered, and said, Thus far and no further. And if this is done to an empire, will a little republic be excused when it misbehaves ? Complain to other powers and seek justice there ? Yes, thank God! justice is *still to be found even for the most insignificant: but it is precisely this justice which will convict us. If we want justice, we must be in a position to ask it with unsullied hands."*

Prophetic words ! Surely the Power which opened the mouth and directed the words of the prophet Balaam, as well as of Balaam's ass, was present with Her Majesty's Commissioner on this momentous occasion.

The following agreement was signed at Wonderfontein, and published in a Dutch newspaper, the *Suid Afrikaan*, at Capetown, 15th February, 1878 :—
" In the presence of Almighty God, the searcher of all hearts, and prayerfully waiting on His gracious help and pity, we, the burghers of the South African Republic, have solemnly agreed, and we do hereby agree, to make a holy covenant for us and for our children, which we confirm with a solemn oath. Fully forty years ago our fathers fled from the Cape

Colony in order to become a free and independent people. Those forty years were forty years of pain and suffering. We established Natal, the Orange Free State, and the South African Republic, and three times the English Government has trampled our liberty and dragged to the ground our flag which our fathers had baptized with their blood and tears. As by a thief in the night has our Republic been stolen from us. We neither may nor can endure this. It is God's will, and is required of us by the unity of our fathers, and by love to our children, that we should hand over intact to our children the legacy of the fathers. For that purpose it is that we here come together and give each other the right hand, men and brethren, solemnly promising to remain faithful to our country and our people, and with our eye fixed on God, to co-operate until death for the restoration of our beloved Republic.

"So help us, Almighty God."

The spirit which animated the Boers throughout the desperate struggle which afterwards ensued, was clearly shown in the patience with which they suffered the annexation to take place without resistance, although even then determined to resort at last to the sword, if all other means of redress proved unavailing. The journey undertaken by General Joubert and his colleagues to London; their patient endurance of their flippant reception by Sir Michael Hicks-Beach; their return to the Cape; their second journey to England when Mr. Gladstone's ministry came into power; and their despairing return to the Transvaal are all matters of historic interest to the patriot and philosopher. Then at length all hope of human redress having fled, the few scattered Boers gave their flag to the winds, and entrusted their cause to the Lord of hosts.

And when at last peace was made; when the overwhelming force which Sir Evelyn Wood was leading, and which threatened to crush with iron hand the liberties of the Transvaal, was arrested by Mr. Gladstone's telegram, and the independence of the Republic again assured by a solemn treaty, the same Joubert who had been a humble suppliant in Downing Street, uttered these memorable words : " It was not we who conquered. It was the Lord of battles who fought on our side and struck down the English soldiers. Then he softened the British nation's heart, and caused it to be merciful unto us."*

During the whole of the disastrous occurrences from 1876 to 1882, no living man looked on with greater interest or more intense sympathy than Sir George Grey. He read with indignation and aston-ishment that terrible commission which had been secretly given to the African missionary's son, by which Sir Theophilus Shepstone carried in his hand the powers of life and death, and the destinies of multitudes of his fellow creatures. Sir George Grey's heart bled for the needless sufferings inflicted upon the countries and the peoples over which he had exercised a peaceful and beneficent influence. And he recognised in the disasters which everywhere befell our arms, that retribution which the Supreme Disposer of all things visits upon those who defy His justice and despise his laws. There was in his heart the added poignancy of the belief that all this might have been spared by the exercise of wise counsels. His longings and desires to be in South Africa were useless. He could only stand far off and mourn over the sufferings and disgrace so freely caused by the perverse actions of those in power.

* *Times*, December 29, 1881.

In South Africa itself there were thousands who wished for his presence. That feeling of which Macaulay speaks as rising in the hearts of men who had opposed Cromwell in the days of his power, when in the very streets of London they heard the distant echoes of the Dutch cannon on the Thames, and wished that the great Protector were once more alive, was strong in the hearts of men from Capetown to Delagoa Bay, from Port Elizabeth to Pretoria. More than one of the political and military leaders quoted that couplet from the song of Roland, when the King, at Roncesvalles, was encompassed by hosts of enemies :—

> "Oh, where was Roland then ?
> One blast upon his bugle horn,
> Were worth ten thousand men."

Sir George Grey remonstrated with Ministers in London, but his remonstrances were received with scant respect. When Premier in New Zealand in the early part of 1879, he sent the following telegram to the Secretary for the Colonies :—

Governor left. Excuse suggestions regarding Natal. Employ troops where practicable roadmaking. Expend little possible on purely military operations ; much for permanent settlement. For means raise Colonial loan low interest. Two cases repayment such loans, South Australia, Kaffraria. Plan greatly reproductive. Relieve England distressed people. Settle rich country permanently. Create valuable commerce for England. Ensure safety South Africa. Great saving England.

GREY.

With some of the leading men in the Orange Free State and the Transvaal he was in constant correspondence, and it afforded him sincere happiness to find that his memory and works were alike cherished.

Thus President J. H. Brand says in a letter from South Africa in 1881 : "I agree with you that if the authorities in the Transvaal had listened to good counsel, and sent correct reports to the Home Government, the unfortunate war would not have taken place." In 1886, commenting on an account in a New Zealand paper of the enthusiastic reception given Sir George Grey on attaining his 74th year, he says : "It must be a source of great happiness in the evening of your long and very useful life, to have received such sincere proofs of love and affection ; and to know, that not only there, but also in South Africa, every heart beats with warm gratitude and affection towards you, who have been such a good friend and benefactor, not only to the Cape Colony, but also to the Free State. I am sure that every one read with cordial sympathy what Mr. Froude wrote about you in 'Oceana.'

"You will, I have no doubt, be pleased to hear that at the re-union of the old students of the Grey College last month, your name was often mentioned with affectionate regard. The success of the Institution, founded by you, will also fill your heart with gladness."

In a despatch from Mr. Brand, as President, he informs Sir George that in his speech at the opening of the Volksraad, he pointed out the assistance which he (Sir George) had given the Free State in the important work of tree planting. He also enclosed a copy of a resolution passed by the Volksraad, of which the following is a translation :—"The Volksraad express their hearty thanks to Sir George Grey for this proof of the interest which he continues to take in the Free State, and request the State President to communicate this to Sir George."

The closing scene of the war in the Transvaal

seemed to Sir George Grey an appropriate ending to
the long catalogue of blunders which preceded it.   It
was right, as he believed, that peace should be made.
It was right that liberty should be restored to the
Transvaal Republic, of which it ought never to have
been deprived.   No disgrace could possibly attach to
a great nation like England by reason of its confession
that it had done wrong, and the announcement of its
effort to find a remedy.

After repeated reverses to the British arms : when
a strong sense of superiority had been established in
the minds of the Boers, and a corresponding depression
brooded heavily over the English with whom they
came in contact ; and, after constant declarations that
the road to Pretoria should be opened by British
arms, forces amply sufficient, under an able general,
actually commenced their march towards the capital
of the Transvaal.   Suddenly a telegram was received
by General Wood from the British Ministry, on
which the onward course of the army was stopped,
negotiations were opened, and finally peace was
restored.

This sudden cessation rendered indelible the arro-
gance of triumph on one side and the humiliation of
defeat on the other.   Many years must pass away
before these feelings are forgotten and their consequences obliterated.   Had Sir George Grey been in
command in South Africa, he would have withheld
the telegram until Sir Evelyn Wood had arrived at
Pretoria, taken possession, and relieved the English
garrison.   Then, having asserted the supreme power
of Great Britain, he would have proceeded, in the
names of justice and of mercy, to have arranged the
terms of peace.

The conduct of war in distant lands by the British
Government has always been characterised by weak-

ness and vacillation.   Britain has been generally
fortunate in the men who have held actual command
in her foreign wars, and her successes have been due,
as a rule, not to the wisdom of Ministers at home, but
to the capacity of generals abroad.   The same weakness and incompetence has characterised the Home
government of the English dependencies.

CHAPTER XLIX.

INDICTMENT OF THE COLONIAL OFFICE.

"Hast any philosophy in thee, shepherd?"
As You Like It.

"Shrine of the mighty! can it be
  That this is all remains of thee?"
Byron.

The government of the Colonies from Downing Street, especially since the separate existence of the Colonial Department, which dates from 1835, has been from the beginning to the present time characterised by blunders, mistakes, and crimes. The exigencies of party and the interests of political or financial cliques have often outweighed the claims of distant communities which possessed no voice in Parliament. In the long list of Secretaries since Charles Grant (Lord Glenelg), who held office in 1835, to Sir H. T. Holland (Lord Knutsford), who is now in power, not one had any practical acquaintance with the colonies or colonists. During the fifty-five years there have been no less than twenty-four Principal Secretaries of State for the Colonies and twenty-seven Parliamentary Under-Secretaries, of whom four afterwards filled the office of Chief. Of all these forty-seven noblemen and gentlemen, not one had any sufficient knowledge of the political, social, or economic condition of the multitudinous young nations over which he ruled—

some, and these men of high position, being absolutely ignorant even of the geographical position of these important dominions of the Crown. During the seven years from 1852 to 1859 there were no fewer than ten Principal Secretaries, namely, Sir John Pakington, the Duke of Newcastle, Sir G. Grey, Bart., Sidney Herbert (Lord Herbert of Lea), Lord John Russell, Sir W. Molesworth, Lord Stanley (Earl of Derby), Sir E. B. Lytton, and again in 1859, the Duke of Newcastle.

The tenure of office was necessarily unequal. The Earl of Carnarvon, as Under-Secretary, held office for two years, and twice as Chief Secretary for two and four years respectively. This is the only instance of one man being in the Colonial Office three times, and the term of eight years is the longest which one occupant has ever enjoyed, and is only equalled by that of Earl Grey. The Duke of Newcastle was in power for seven years, but Lord John Russell only for nine weeks in 1855, succeeding Sidney Herbert, who held office for three months, and being succeeded by Sir W. Molesworth, who kept in for four. Between February and November, 1855, there were four different Principal Secretaries for the Colonies.

Amid such a series of changes it cannot be expected that one fixed idea or fixed plan of government was possible. A tradition, indeed, exists in Downing Street that changes of Ministers do not mean changes of policy; but, however earnestly, however honestly succeeding Secretaries may strive to carry out the policy of their predecessors, change there must be, and that not seldom of a serious character.

The record of the successive Ministers holding office in this department since its first creation is sufficient of itself to prove that there could be no cohesion in principle, no sequence in council, in that

branch of the Government of Great Britain which
ruled the destinies of the colonies:

SECRETARIES AND UNDER-SECRETARIES FROM 1835 TO 1890.

		SECRETARIES.	UNDER SECRETARIES.
	1835	Rt. Hon. Chas. Grant (Lord Glenelg).	Sir G. Grey, Bart.
	1839	Marquis of Normanby.	Rt. Hon. W. Labouchere (Lord Taunton).
	1839	Lord John Russell.	Rt. Hon. H. V. Smith (Lord Lyveden).
	1841	Lord Stanley (Earl of Derby).	G. W. Hope.
	1845	Mr. W. E. Gladstone.	Lord Lyttelton.
	1846	Earl Grey, K.G.	Benj. Hawes.
	1846	Sir John Pakington (Hampton).	Benj. Hawes.
	1852	Duke of Newcastle.	Sir Fredk. Peel.
June 10,	1854	Rt. Hon. Sir G. Grey, Bart.	Sir Fredk. Peel.
Feb.,	1855	Rt. Hon. Sidney Herbert. (Lord Herbert of Lea).	John Ball.
May 15,	1855	Lord John Russell.	John Ball.
July 21,	1855	Rt. Hon. Sir W. Molesworth, Bart.	(1857) Chichester Fortescue.
Nov. 17,	1855	Rt. Hon. W. Labouchere.	(1857) Chichester Fortescue.
Feb. 26,	1858	Lord Stanley (Earl of Derby).	Earl Carnarvon.
May 31,	1858	Rt. Hon. Sir E. B. Lytton.	Earl Carnarvon.
June 18,	1859	Duke of Newcastle, K.G.	Hon. Chichester Fortescue (Carlingford).
April 4,	1864	Rt. Hon. E. Cardwell.	(1865) W. E. Forster.
July 6,	1866	Earl of Carnarvon.	Sir C. B. Adderly (Lord Norton).
March 8,	1867	Duke of Buckingham and Chandos.	Sir F. R. Sandford.
Dec. 10,	1868	Earl Granville, K.G.	W. Monsell (Lord Emly). H. T. Holland. Hon. R. Meade.

	SECRETARIES.	UNDER SECRETARIES.
July 6, 1870	Earl of Kimberley, K.G.	(1871) E. H. Knatch-bull-Hugesson (Bra-bourne).
Feb. 21, 1874	Earl of Carnarvon.	James Lowther.
Feb. 4, 1878	Rt. Hon. Sir M. Hicks-Beach.	Earl Cadogan.
April 28, 1880	Earl of Kimberley, K.G.	Sir M. E. Grant-Duff. (1881) Leonard H. Court-ney.
Dec. 16, 1882	Earl of Derby, K.G.	Hon. Evelyn Ashley.
June 24, 1885	Rt. Hon. Col. F. A. Stanley.	Earl of Dunraven.
Feb. 6, 1886	Earl Granville, K.G.	C. Osborne-Morgan.
Aug. 3, 1886	Rt. Hon. Edward Stan-hope.	Earl of Dunraven.
Jan. 14, 1887	Holland, Lord Knutsford (since made).	Earl of Onslow.
		(1888) Rt. Hon. Baron de Worms.

PERMANENT UNDER-SECRETARIES.

1835.   Sir James Stephen.
1847.   Herman Merivale.
1859.   Sir Frederick Rogers.
1871.   Sir Robert George Wyndham Herbert.

The Colonial Office in Downing Street seemed destined to be the grave of South African hopes. Under the great archway and up the massive stair-case had gone processions of men, hopeful even under adverse fates. Down the great steps and out from beneath the vaulted roof, through the quiet street and into the busy thoroughfare opposite Whitehall, those men had returned sad at heart. The delegates from the Orange River Sovereignty had trodden that path when they called on England not to disown her chil-dren. Sir George Grey had patiently waited there

during a long year, and at length weary and filled
with apprehensions for his beloved África, turned
away for ever.

Joubert and his comrades, bronzed by the southern
sun and desert winds, had marched upon that road
when Sir Michael Hicks-Beach ruled in the Colonial
Office, and had implored his mercy.   It is said that
when the unpolished Boers waited upon him with a
humble prayer, the young Secretary, filled with a
poetic and prophetic spirit, bade them look at the
sun—which to them, accustomed to his intolerable
brilliance, was not difficult in the London sky—and
said that as long as that sun shone in the heavens,
the British flag would wave in the Transvaal.   There
again they came when, after returning to the Cape,
they heard that the Ministry of Mr. Gladstone had
succeeded to power; but again in vain.   Then out
from the quiet court they went, silently breathing a
prayer to the Lord of hosts to strengthen their hearts
and sharpen their swords for the day of battle against
the mighty oppressor.

There Sir Bartle Frere went, broken-hearted, on
his sad return from the Cape.   There Froude strode
up, full of pleasant anticipations, and thence he also
departed gloomy and astonished.   Into those portals
went Mr. Shepstone, filled with vague terrors; of all
these stirring, anxious hearts, he alone went away
triumphant, honoured with a knighthood, and bearing
with him that terrible commission which will ever be
accursed in the history of South Africa.

What dreadful destiny, what conjunction of evil
stars, was it that compelled the Colonial Office thus
to flout the wishes of patriots, and to inflict wounds
so great and sore upon the unoffending people over
which it ruled?

The historic lesson taught by the revolt of the

484 SIR G. GREY ENGAGES IN ENGLISH POLITICS.

American colonies, followed by the well-nigh fatal
outbreak in India, was not sufficient to teach wisdom
to the officials in Downing Street, or to the British
people. The last great wound inflicted upon British
prestige and the solidarity of the Empire, was dealt
in South Africa between 1874 and 1881. That sore is
yet open—the scar is still unhealed.

Such gross and perverse conduct must bring punishment. It is far from impossible that the final result
of the action taken by Lord Carnarvon may be a confederation indeed of the States in South Africa, but a
confederation independent of Britain, and under an
alien standard. Australasia may also choose to leave
the shadow of the old flag.

The impotent folly which characterised the colonial
policy of 1853, which, while it rejected the absolute
dominion of the Southern Ocean, invited the nations
of the Old World to occupy with armed forces the
harbours and strategic points of many island groups,
threatening the commerce and safety of Australasia,
is not forgotten. The last ten years have borne ample
testimony to the weakness of England's foreign and
colonial policy. Australian federation will soon be
an accomplished fact. If the Empire is to continue,
there must be a different system of Government and
different principles of action to those which have
hitherto generally controlled the Colonial Department.

Nor can the Colonial Office escape the influence of
that subtle power which we call " public opinion."
The student of history will, in pondering the records
of the last fifty years of colonial development, trace
certain main currents of thought and action, obtaining
at different periods, manifested by different policies,
and producing different results. From 1835 to 1845,
the period during which the existing mighty Empire

was in great part founded or enlarged, there was an evident determination to extend that Empire on every hand. New colonies were founded, new territories annexed, new responsibilities undertaken. South Australia, Victoria, New Zealand, Natal, many parts of India, were annexed or founded during this decade, so fruitful in great conceptions. From 1845 to 1853, the predominant aim was to consolidate and strengthen the great dependencies. This was the era in which political Constitutions were granted and the leading colonies became self-governing. During the six years 1846—1852, one mind directed this part of the colonial destiny.

Earl Grey, called in 1846 to direct the affairs of the rapidly growing children of England, saw that to make stable governments there must be a wide foundation of political power, and a direct responsibility of the rulers to the people. Amid the revolutions and changes which shook Europe to its foundations in 1848, the mind of this astute statesman ever recognised the necessity for colonial self-government. To keep these great and ever-growing communities loyal to the Crown and the Empire he saw that they must be permitted to rule themselves, that Downing Street could only drive them into rebellion as it had driven America. Although the gift of responsible government had not been bestowed in full upon the great dependencies when Earl Grey gave up the seals of his office in 1852, yet the work was practically done. Some few reactionary steps were indeed taken by Sir John Pakington, who succeeded him, but the result was neither seriously delayed nor greatly altered except in the case of New Zealand.

Side by side with this growth of local self-government there marched a theory which, had it been carried into such constant practice as its teachers wished, would have shattered the Empire to pieces, and set back the history of civilisation by a hundred years.

The economists became gradually powerful during the period when the colonies experienced their self-governing and constitutional birth. By 1854 they had obtained control of both parties, and Liberals and Conservatives had tacitly consented to the abandonment of the colonies and the dismemberment of the Empire.

CHAPTER L.

" Look here upon this picture and on this,
The counterfeit presentment of two brothers."

Hamlet.

THE two representative Colonial Ministers of the rival parties in Great Britain during this period are undoubtedly Earl Grey and the Earl of Carnarvon. If we consider length of service, political and social position, the periods during which they respectively held office, the importance of the questions and exigencies which they were called upon to meet, and the respective time of life of each when holding office, it will be seen that no other Colonial Ministers are able to dispute with them the pride of place. Earl Grey, then Lord Howick, had been made Under-Secretary for the Colonies at the early age of twenty-nine, at the time when Lord Carnarvon was born. When Earl Grey took the seals of office in 1846, Henry Howard Herbert was still at Eton. 1852, which finally severed Earl Grey's official connection with Downing Street, heard "the bonny bells of Christ Church" ring sweet music to the young Earl of Carnarvon, for the honours list revealed him as a first in classics; and within six years Carnarvon entered the Colonial Office, from which Earl Grey had for ever departed.

VOL. II.   O

Lord Howick had been Under-Secretary for the Colonies at twenty-nine; Lord Carnarvon accepted the same honourable position at twenty-seven. For the seventeen months during which he continued as Under-Secretary, from February, 1858, to June, 1859, his chiefs in Downing Street were Lord Stanley (Earl of Derby) and Sir Edward Bulwer Lytton. Earl Grey was principal Secretary from 1846 to 1852, between his forty-fourth and fiftieth years; Lord Carnarvon occupied the same position twice, first from 1866 to 1867, when he was thirty-five years old, and again from 1874 to 1878, between his forty-third and forty-seventh years. The heads of great houses, wealthy, cultured, enjoying public favour both in Parliament and in social life, holding the same positions during practically the same periods of their lives, and for the same length of time, called upon to act in circumstances of great difficulty, and to exercise control of distant nations at perilous crises in their histories, when a single false step meant ruin and death to thousands, and possible disgrace and defeat to the Imperial power of Britain, they may be fairly compared.

There is a trite and humorous saying, used by many well-known writers, that "comparisons are odious"; but no reader of history, studying biography from the Lives of Plutarch to Macaulay's Essays, will deny that the truest appreciation of character is to be obtained by contrasting the acts of different men under similar circumstances and trials.

On judging the acts of public men, Earl Grey thus writes:

"A retrospect of public affairs necessarily implies that the conduct of those who have taken part in them should be made the subject of comment, which cannot always be of a favourable character, and it is for the general interest that these matters should be canvassed without unnecessary restraint. It tends to keep up a due sense of their responsibility in the minds of those who are engaged in the exciting scenes of political life, that they should know that all they may do is liable to be reviewed and discussed when time and the results of their acts shall have thrown a light on their character." *

That they are responsible to the nation is not only clear, but admitted.

"Though the Secretary of State entrusted with the department of the colonies receives much assistance from his colleagues, and though the most important measures which it is his duty to carry into effect ought to be decided upon with their advice and concurrence, still the main responsibility for all errors that are committed properly rests with him." With full knowledge of public responsibility, and offering themselves and their actions for the approval of history, it may, especially at this epoch of rapid growth in the influence of the colonies in Imperial matters, be wise to "review and discuss their deeds when time and the results of their acts shall have thrown a light upon their real character."

Even to minute details and occurrences, the similarity between the two men is remarkable. One instance may illustrate this fact. Lord Howick threw up his position and left his colleagues in 1833 because his own wish for the immediate abolition of slavery in the colonies was not followed. Lord Carnarvon gave up the seals of the Colonial Office in 1867 to the Duke of Buckingham because he differed from the Cabinet on the subject of reform.

* Colonial Policy of Lord John Russell's Administration, 1853. —Earl Grey. Richard Bentley.

The contrast exhibited between the conduct of the two statesmen will not illustrate the difference between the two political parties, for Earl Grey never held with his party upon the dismemberment craze, which was the main colonial policy elaborated between 1850 and 1870 by the Liberals. An important lesson may, however, be learned from this comparison, arising from the dangers attendant upon the present personal and irresponsible government of the colonies.

The leading events connected with the colonial government in the career of both may be shortly stated. Earl Grey resigned his position in 1833 because the slaves in the British colonies were not immediately set free. On taking office thirteen years later he was met by two difficulties. The Governor of New Zealand requested him to obtain the consent of Parliament to the suspension of their own Act, and the Canadian colonies were lapsing into a state of anarchy.

In 1849, believing that, as labour was scarce in the colonies, colonists would gladly receive convicts of comparatively good conduct, Earl Grey sent to several parts of the world numbers of these unfortunate people. During the whole term of his office, 1846 to 1852, Earl Grey had to deal with the grave question of colonial self-government. This was the era of colonial Constitutions. It was fortunate that the Colonial Office retained as its head during these six years a statesman who combined the wisdom of a philosopher with the charity of a philanthropist and the vast power of a British Minister.

When Lord Carnarvon was first in office in 1858-59, the South African States were disposed to confederate under the English flag, thus reversing the plan of dismemberment. During his two official years, 1866-67, the method of appointment of Governors to the great colonies was decided. On his final holding of the colonial seals, the problem of South Africa, including the Zulu war and the annexation of the Transvaal, presented itself for solution.

Earl Grey left his colleagues in 1833 because they would not go fast or far enough in bestowing freedom.

The Earl of Carnarvon threw up office in 1867 as a protest against the Parliamentary reform contemplated by his chief, Lord Derby.

On many occasions Earl Grey found his plans opposed and his wishes thwarted, either by the Governors of the colonies or by the colonists themselves. His earnest desire to assist the New Zealand Company in their claims to native lands; his determination to grant to New Zealand the representative government which was embodied in the Charter and Constitution Act of 1846, which it was feared would have secured to the New Zealand Company an undue and unlawful power and control over the native lands; his strong wish to settle the better part of the English convicts in the different colonies; his purpose of instituting in the colonies a State Church and granting to it immense endowments—each and all met with stern and uncompromising opposition. From some Sir George Grey dissented; from others the colonists turned fiercely indignant.

The result was always the same. Eager to advance the interests of the colonies, Earl Grey was ever ready to listen to arguments urged against his views. He showed a disposition towards extreme justice by always permitting reasons to be given against his own plans and opinions, no matter how strong those opinions might be. He was frequently astonished at the violence, amounting sometimes to antipathy, displayed against measures which he believed to be fraught with good. But he never failed, when his convictions of a righteous popular wish or of the justice of the arguments opposed to his belief became assured, to set aside his own judgment and to act in a manner consistent with the new light which he had gained.

He could not understand the passionate earnestness with which the Cape colonists refused to receive convicts. He felt compelled by the correspondence from New Zealand upon the Treaty of Waitangi and the Constitution Act to surrender absolutely every position which he had taken up. Once convinced that the public good required the sacrifice of his own opinions, that sacrifice, however painful, was made. There was a natural goodness, a wonderful impartiality in his judgment, so that he was able, when reviewing the circumstances of his defeated plans, to see all things in the "dry light" of which Bacon speaks, and to give ungrudging praise to those whom he believed praiseworthy, although they might have defeated his most cherished projects.

The merits of this great statesman were not solely of a negative kind. His exertions for the welfare of the many kingdoms over which he ruled were ceaseless. His energy was untiring, his one aim being to secure the greatest happiness for colonists in every part of the earth. He did not permit party feelings to deter him in his choice of instruments. In 1846 the state of Canada made it absolutely necessary that a Governor of peculiar abilities should be appointed. "As our object was not to make the selection with a view to party interests, but to intrust the management of the largest and most important of the British colonies, in a season of great difficulty, to the ablest hands we could find, Lord Elgin was recommended to the Queen for this appointment, in preference to any of our own party or personal friends."*

It must not be forgotten that Lord Elgin had five years before seconded the amendment to the address which defeated Lord Melbourne's ministry in 1841. In another part of his book Earl Grey says: "I consider it to be the obvious duty and interest of this country to extend representative institutions to every one of its dependencies where they have not yet been established, and where this can be done with safety."† Acting upon this principle, the noble Earl devoted thought and influence to this momentous work. Canada, Australia, New Zealand, and in part South Africa, have all benefited by his arduous toils in this direction.

Earl Grey entertained the most extreme views upon the question of the waste lands of the Crown and the abandonment of the colonies. The economists had not, at the date of publication of his book, attained the full strength and influence which they afterwards usurped.

In these days of conflicting argument as to the right of local control over the waste territories of the Empire, it may be wise to regard the past utterance of the most successful Minister to whose care the colonies were ever confided.

"The waste lands of the vast colonial possessions of the British Empire are held by the Crown as trustee for the inhabitants of that Empire at large, and not for the inhabitants of the particular provinces divided by arbitrary geographical limits in which any such waste lands happen to be situated; otherwise this consequence would follow, that the first

* "Earl Grey's letters to Lord John Russell on Colonial Administration," p. 208.
† *Ibid*, p. 26.

inhabitants of any of these vast provinces (if possessing those representative institutions which arise as of
right in ordinary British colonies) are indefeasibly
entitled to administer all the lands and land revenue
of the great unexplored tract called a province of
which they may occupy an extremity, wholly without
regard to the nation which has founded the settlement, perhaps at great expense, in order to serve as
a home for her own emigrants and a market for her
own industry. For the right thus defined and claimed
by the Legislative Council (New South Wales), if
their expressions were to be strictly taken, would
belong as fully to the 4,000 inhabitants of Western
Australia as to the 200,000 of New South Wales:
nay, would equally have belonged to the first ten
families which settled in a corner of New Zealand,
and would entitle each small community from the
first days of its planting to the ownership of tracts
sufficient to maintain Empires."*

His opinions, also, upon the growing policy of
dismemberment are instructive :—

"I have thought it necessary to state thus strongly
my dissent from the views of those who wish to dismember the Empire by abandoning the colonies,
because it is impossible not to observe that this
policy—unworthy of a great nation, and unwise as I
consider it to be—is not only openly advocated by
one active party in the country, but is hardly less
effectually supported by persons occupying an important position in Parliament, and who, while they
hesitate to avow their adherence to it, hold language
which obviously leads in the same direction, and
advocate measures the adoption of which would
inevitably bring about this result."

* Earl Grey, vol. ii., Appendix, p. 324. Answer to despatch
from New South Wales.

Again in another passage occurring on pages 304 and 305 in the second volume of the work from which the foregoing quotations are made, Lord Grey states his conviction that such views will ultimately lead "by a few short and easy steps to the severance of the tie which binds the fairest portion of our Colonial Empire to the British Crown. I know that some of those who advocate the changes to which I allude are prepared for this result—if they do not regard its probability as an additional recommendation of the measures they propose; but I earnestly trust that such is not the view of this great question which is destined to gain acceptance with Parliament and with the public. For my own part, though with the consequences of the American revolution before my eyes, I certainly am not prepared to say that the loss of our Colonial Empire must necessarily be fatal to our national greatness and prosperity, still, I should regard such an event as a grievous calamity, and as lowering by many steps the rank of this country among the nations of the world. You (Lord J. Russell), I am persuaded, will concur with me in this opinion, and will feel no less strongly than myself the desire that the great British Empire may to a long futurity be held together, and preserve its station among the principal powers of the earth."

Lord Carnarvon's official career in connection with the colonies is dissimilar and opposed in every respect to that of his illustrious predecessor. He was Under-Secretary to Lord Stanley from February to May 1858, and to Sir E. B. Lytton from May, 1858, to June 18th, 1859, when the Tories were out of power. This seventeen months is a period of deeper disgrace to the Colonial Office than any other save one since the American colonies were driven out. The blackest page in the history of colonial government was written during the last period of Lord Carnarvon's authority, from 1874 to 1878.

Soon after he first took office in 1858 a long and angry correspondence began between the Colonial Office and the War Office in England and Sir George Grey in South Africa regarding the German Legion, afterwards including the scheme of German immigration. During this period, also, Sir George was compelled by the culpable negligence of Downing Street to advance £6,000 of his private income to carry on the government of British Kaffraria. It is difficult to find words capable of conveying sufficiently severe censure upon the conduct of the Colonial Office during this period. The course pursued by the Imperial Government in reference to the vote for British Kaffraria was utterly foolish as well as dishonest, and but for the prompt aid given by the Governor would have produced deplorable results. The whole matter of the settlement of the German Legion, with its discreditable repudiation of liabilities and refusal to perform promises, would also, without the wise and prudent interference of Sir George, have led to crime and bloodshed.

The recall of the Governor in 1859, and the absolute refusal of the Colonial Office to permit the question of confederation for South Africa to be entertained, was one of the greatest political blunders possible. This has since been acknowledged by all parties.

When Lord Carnarvon again took office in 1866, Sir George Grey was just bringing to a successful conclusion the fierce and bitter native war in New Zealand. Many controversies had arisen between the Governor and Downing Street. Besides these, Lord Carnarvon remembered Sir George Grey of old. The noble Earl had evidently determined to get rid of a subordinate who possessed so strong a will and acted so independently.   In addition to these reasons another existed, which in itself was sufficient to push Sir George Grey from the public service.   The Conservative party, as we have seen, presumably acting under the advice of the Earl of Carnarvon, though it is believed Mr. Disraeli was the original proposer, laid down the rule that the Governors of the great colonies must henceforth, if possible, be peers, or the sons of peers, "born in the purple," or at least married to a peer's daughter.   For this policy, which has of late years guided the appointment of Governors to all the great dependencies, Great Britain is without doubt indebted to Lord Carnarvon.

Upon his last acceptance of office in 1874, the excitement and interest of colonial government centred in South Africa.   The long years of peace which had been given to that part of the Empire by the policy of Sir George Grey had come to an end.   Sir Benjamin Pine was again Governor of Natal, and Mr. Shepstone was again his adviser.   Langabilalele's war, brought on by a gross act of tyranny, and signalised by a ferocious cruelty, which shocked even the Government in Downing Street, caused the removal of Sir Benjamin Pine and the momentous visit of Shepstone to London, which ended in the unparalleled commission entrusted to him by Lord Carnarvon.   The annexation of the diamond fields, the Zulu danger, the state of the Transvaal, and the agitation existing upon the question of confederation —all tended to swell the storm which threatened to break over our colonies at the Cape.

Lord Carnarvon was fully alive to the dangers which menaced South Africa.   In his hands the Queen and country had placed the entire control of colonial affairs.   His will was absolute, his power

unbounded. In the very prime of life, at a time
when the passions and prejudice of youth had been
tempered by a large experience and extended knowledge of the world, the English people were justified
in the belief that he would fulfil his duty to them and
to South Africa. In the performance of that duty
Lord Carnarvon signally failed.

Upon the whole volume of English history there is
no page displaying so much stubborn prejudice and
such incredible folly as the colonial administration of
England from 1874 to 1878. During no equal period
of time did such disgraceful disasters follow such
tyrannous and unconstitutional administration. There
have been periods and Ministers which bring a blush
of shame and anger to the cheek, and there have
been policies which were mistaken, and caused great
calamities before being changed, but no instance of
history equals in deliberate misconduct the actions
of the Colonial Office at this time, not does history
record a deeper disgrace or a swifter retribution.

The two questions of importance were the shaping
of a policy and the appointment of a man to carry
that policy into effect. Lord Carnarvon was well
aware that Sir George Grey had achieved an unparalleled success in dealing with South African
matters, and acquired an unparalleled influence over
the strangely diverse populations thrown side by side
in that region. He had himself recalled Sir George
in 1859 for promoting confederation. He knew,
also, that Sir George had only a few years before
applied to be sent back to that sphere where, during
his former Governorship, he had done such brilliant
service. No one in England had greater reason than
the Earl of Carnarvon to believe that the one man
who could bring South Africa safely through the
storm about to burst upon it from so many points

was Sir George Grey.   If the noble Earl took advice
at all upon this matter, it must have been from his
friends Lord Derby and Lord Salisbury, or from the
two men to whom he generally looked for aid in
South African affairs, Sir Bartle Frere and Mr. J. A.
Froude.   If Lord Derby had been asked he would,
unless altogether changed from the Lord Stanley of
old times, have advised Lord Carnarvon to forget his
prejudices, and give South Africa again to the care
of the old Governor; while Lord Salisbury had protested against Grey's recall in 1859.   It is a matter
of history that both Sir Bartle Frere and Mr. Froude
believed Grey to be the only man who could rule
in peace over that wild territory and its strange
communities.

Lord Carnarvon was equally well aware that we
were bound by solemn treaties to the Boers, the
Orange Free State, and many of the native tribes;
that a friendly offer of assistance and intervention
would, especially under Sir George Grey's authority,
cause the clouds to disperse and the dangers to pass
away; while aggression and the use of force might
set South Africa in a blaze.

Possessing full information upon every point, taking
ample time for deliberation, fully conscious of the
tremendous consequences which might follow his acts,
Lord Carnarvon yet offered advice to his Sovereign,
which set in motion forces unconstitutional in themselves, pregnant with disgrace and disaster, and well
nigh certain to scatter war and ruin over vast territories and different races of men.

The Commission which Lord Carnarvon obtained
from Her Majesty for Sir Theophilus Shepstone was
such as no Minister should have advised, and such as
the Crown, with all respect be it written, had no right
whatever to give.   It was a gross breach of the law

of nations, it was a crime against humanity, it was in direct defiance of the justice of God.

Had not the Earl of Carnarvon been blinded by prejudice against the Boers and against Sir George Grey, he must have seen that in Grey's appointment to power, and his wonderful influence and sagacity lay, humanly speaking, the only path to peace. Had he not been infatuated with a belief in his own foresight and the invincible power of England, he would have paused before he pledged his country to a certain policy of war, of annexation, and of shame. The story of that sad time in which we waged war against the Kafirs and Zulus, annexed the Transvaal, violated treaties, and spread ruin and desolation far and wide, will cause wonder and surprise to our children's children. The end feared and predicted by Sir George Grey soon came, prefaced by the disasters of Isandlawhana, Laing's Nek, and Majuba Hill. The English people, roused at last to the enormity of the offence which had been committed by Lord Carnarvon, retraced their steps as far as possible, and caused right and justice to prevail once more.

After his retirement from active connection with the government of the colonies, Lord Carnarvon placed the last finishing touch to the sharpness of the contrast between himself and Earl Grey. Earl Grey considered and treated the great territorial possessions of the Crown in the colonies as a sacred trust for the British people. Lord Carnarvon, with his cousin, Sir Robert Herbert, and other gentlemen, took advantages under a charter to obtain a block of land in Western Australia (a Crown colony) of sixteen millions four hundred thousand acres, an area half as large as England, more than three-quarters that of Ireland, and nearly five times as large as Wales. The conditions upon which the title to this magnificent estate was to be given to those from whom Lord Carnarvon and his friends afterwards acquired large estates are somewhat doubtful. The influences which were used to obtain this Imperial concession are not known to the public. When an ex-Secretary of State for the Colonies and a permanent Under Secretary for that department become in part potential owners of estates greater than some kingdoms, in a colony subject directly to the control of the Colonial Office, in which their influence is paramount, two statements will naturally be made, first that the identification of great Ministers of State with such a proceeding must be regarded with reprobation, and second that men who engage in such enterprises, however lofty their position, are more anxious to secure great estates for themselves than to conserve the public lands for the benefit of multitudinous families of the toilers of the nation.

It is said that Lord Carnarvon himself had only contracted to acquire 64,000 acres of this huge estate, while Sir Robert Herbert had to be content with the same area. Be that as it may, the statement of the facts is sufficient to arouse public attention, and to illustrate the different opinions held upon the subject of the waste lands of the Crown by Earl Grey and Lord Carnarvon.

Earl Grey has long passed the allotted span of human existence. Nearly ninety years of age, although it cannot be said of him, as of Moses, "that his eye is not dim nor his natural force abated," even yet with clear reasoning and critical judgment he is able to speak with great wisdom upon all matters connected with that mighty Colonial Empire which he governed so well, and has done so much to benefit.

As from the calmness and the quiet of life's evening

he looks back upon his career as colonial arbiter, how gratifying must it be to pass in review the events not only painted upon his memory, but carved in the history of his country's greatness.   No blot stains the page, no jarring chord disturbs the harmony, no regret brings back a pang.   As he regards the birth and infancy of the innumerable family of nations confided to his care, he can behold with serene and lofty pleasure the development of great principles, the accomplishment of great thoughts.   It has fallen to the lot of no other man, living or dead, to mould the political institutions of so many future nations. No statesman of ancient or modern times has shown greater patience, a more sincere self-denial, or more earnest devotion in the discharge of great public duties than Earl Grey displayed in his connection with the colonies of Britain.

His epitaph will be written upon the earth's broad surface.   If in future days men ask what monument has been erected to the great Minister for the Colonies, Earl Grey, it will be sufficient to point to the four corners of the earth, where Englishmen live in possession of as much freedom as free institutions can bestow, and to answer, *Si quaeris monumentum, circumspice.*

What a different picture is presented in the outlines of Lord Carnarvon's public life! The first great error on the very threshold of his career—his determined assertion of autocratic power and the unjust dismissal of an illustrious Governor as a punishment for promoting the confederation of South Africa.   Then on his assumption of supreme authority, the exhibition of utter disregard for the wishes of colonists, leading to the establishment of a system by which the Governorships of the great colonies were to be restricted to members of the aristocracy, and no longer to be the reward of worth or merit. Finally, the ghastly series of tragedies enacted in South Africa, that history written in blood, for which he must be held in great measure responsible.

The silent, desolate rock in the African desert at whose base lie scattered to this day the bones of English soldiers, recalling that hour of carnage when the dreadful horns of the Zulu impi closed in the rear of our devoted legion at Isandlawhana; the stern, pale face of Pomeroy Colley meeting his death on Majuba Hill; the spectres of the brave men who fell at Laing's Nek and a score of other spots in the African wilderness; these must for ever darken the page which records Lord Carnarvon's connection with the Colonial Office. The form of the Prince Imperial pierced by the Zulu spears, and the weeping Empress, the lamp of her life gone out, sorrowing over the dead, protest in silent pathos against the tremendous power for good or evil exercised by one man.

Some spots of sunshine there are to relieve the darkness of the gloomy picture, but its prevailing characteristics are those of stubborn prejudice, of unconstitutional actions, of disastrous results.

The contrast of these two statesmen presents a feature of still greater importance to the Empire than the mere comparison of their personal merits. It brings prominently into view the viciousness of the system by which the colonies are governed. When the sole power of determining great questions in connection with the colonies rests in the uncontrolled will of a Secretary of State, the ties which bind the colonies to Britain are always liable to be snapped. The Sisters, with their fatal shears, are ever lurking in the corridors of Downing Street. The same bene-volence, the same wisdom, and the same patience, which made Earl Grey's control a perennial spring of blessing to the colonies, may be displayed by others under the benignant sway of the Crown to its many dependencies; but on the other hand the same obstinacy and prejudice which threw the American colonies into revolt, and in later times brought disgrace and suffering upon England and South Africa under the guidance of Lord Carnarvon, may again be seen.

If English statesmen wish in sincerity to retain the supremacy of Britain among the family of nations, they must discover some wiser and safer plan of governing the colonies than that of committing their destinies to the arbitrary will of a Secretary of State.

It is with extreme pain that a contrast so unfavourable to the character of Lord Carnarvon has in truth to be sketched. In so many ways and under so many aspects has the Master of Highclere endeared himself to the people of Britain that it is distasteful to disparage a character and life otherwise worthily held in estimation. In the household, in the Church, and in the world, blameless and unspotted, the errors of his conduct in relation to the colonies are partly traceable to his want of training in that great competitive Chamber where nearly all English statesmen have gained wisdom and experience.

Of the participators in the mismanagement of South African affairs, there remains but one who can be dealt with by public opinion in England. Sir Theophilus Shepstone, if still alive, is in South Africa. He also was but, in himself, an insignificant personage, little more than an instrument in the hand of Ministers and officials. Lord Carnarvon has since the former pages were written gone to " that bourne from whence no traveller returns." To him the praise or blame of men is immaterial. South

African disasters, Australian land ventures, federation of the colonies, will vex his soul no more.

One actor in that terrible historic drama yet remains. Sir Robert Herbert still lives, and controls the destinies of the Colonial Office. Perhaps the principal responsibility rests upon his shoulders. The errors of judgment which were committed, the deplorable want of foresight betrayed by all concerned, must cloud the memory of those public men to whose account history will place this tragedy. Probably notwithstanding the elevation of Sir Robert to the peerage, future generations will hold him guilty of conduct which amounted to a gigantic blunder, if not to a political crime.

SIR GEORGE GREY'S LIFE IN NEW ZEALAND, 1870—1892.

CHAPTER LI.

KAWAU.

" How blest is he who crowns in shades like these
A youth of labour with an age of ease." ·

Goldsmith.

FOR three years Sir George Grey remained in quiet retirement at Kawau. This island, some five miles by two, is situated eight or nine leagues from Auckland, to the northward of the Hauraki Gulf. It lies about four miles from the mainland, and contains several harbours, in one of which a whole navy could anchor, safe from every wind. Half a century back copper was worked upon the beach; and the shafts filled with clear sea water still remain, silent witnesses to the busy throng once gathered there.

Kawau is one mass of low hills, in a few spots lifting themselves to a greater height. It abounds in beautiful scenery. Upon the rocky coast the Pacific, clear and blue as the sapphire skies above, rolls its waves gently. A dwelling-house, replete with every comfort and many luxuries, is sheltered in a small bay. Round the house, in gardens, orchards, and plantations, is the most varied and most complete collection of trees in the world. From every part of the earth Sir George had obtained choice specimens of trees and plants. It was unrivalled. Travellers coming from distant regions saw with surprise and delight the familiar foliage, flowers, and fruits of home growing with more than native vigour upon this far off strand.

Within the mansion the same rule obtained. The walls were hung with pictures painted by great masters during many centuries. In the entrance hall and upon the stairways were clustered the weapons and the ornaments of a hundred islands in the Southern Ocean. Books, rare and precious, of all ages and in all tongues, adorned the shelves. The windows looked down upon a sea so calm that its waves never raised their tones above a whispered song.

All that gilds life with refinement, all that can inspire the human soul with love for the beautiful and true in nature and in art was found in that lonely paradise. It is a spot once seen never to be forgotten. In that calm and secluded corner of the earth, where the fierce din of conflict was unheard and the roar of worldly tumult was softened to a drowsy murmur, life's tide swept calmly by.

But the beautiful solitude of the island was daily broken. This is an age of travel. Duty, pleasure, illness, art, science, literature, politics, religion, athletics, discovery, and a score of other causes urge people nowadays to and fro upon the earth's broad surface. Australia and New Zealand figure largely as resorts for those voyagers, vulgarly termed "globe trotters." How large a section of those who visited New Zealand went to Kawau to see Sir George Grey it is impossible to say. Their name was legion, for they were many. Soldiers who had fought in many lands, sailors whose ships had breasted the surges of every sea, went there. Poets wrote beneath the shady trees, artists sketched sitting on the rocks or on the grass lawns by the sea. Novelists drew inspiration from the glorious sunlight and fresh breath of the great Pacific. Historians canvassed there the records of ancient states, and drew parallels between England and old Rome. There statesmen took counsel with their host upon the rapid changes of modern politics. and forecasted the probabilities of the days to come. Missionaries there told of sufferings endured and triumphs won among the savage races of the earth. Lovers went there and dreamed of paradise. There great scholars discussed the achievements of the modern schools, and compared them with the triumphs of the Athenians. The disappointed and the vanquished went for consolation, the triumphant and victorious for sympathy and praise.

There, too, on all holiday and gala days would the people and children of Auckland flock in armies. It would be difficult to imagine a more charming picture than Kawau presented on such an occasion.

The glorious framework of nature; the brightly-clad troops of merry children; the host benignant and hospitable, especially to the little ones, whom he loved; the servants of the establishment, staid but respectful, like retainers of some ancient baron; the merry laughter, tho joyous sunlight of a thousand happy eyes—these may be described: but the deep happiness, the untroubled bliss of the children, cannot be depicted by pen or pencil.

Alas that such a condition of things should pass away! The halcyon days of Kawau are ended. Nevertheless, for nearly twenty years Sir George Grey's island home was one of the happiest and most perfect spots upon the earth.

It was there that he welcomed Prince Alfred on his

voyage in the Galatea, and renewed the friendship commenced twelve years before in England and South Africa. Not the least claim which the Prince had to the regard and esteem of the people of Auckland was the affectionate respect with which he evidently regarded this friend and host of his youth.

It was there that the Maori King, Tawhiao, who was about to visit England, came to ask Sir George's advice as to his conduct, when Sir George, knowing the weakness of the savage prince, became a total abstainer in order to prevail upon Tawhiao to do the same. With tears the Maori King pledged his word to the ex-Governor, and that word was royally kept. Never once upon his trip to England did Tawhiao touch spirituous liquors.

It was from Kawau, in 1880, that Sir George wrote a long letter of advice to Malietoa, the Samoan King —then hard-pressed by the Germans—which, in the light of subsequent events, seems like a prophecy, by which advice Malietoa was guided, so that now from being a captive he is a king once more, while his all-powerful foe, Prince Bismarck, has fallen from power into private life.

After so many years of extreme activity, both bodily and mental, it would have seemed appropriate that at Kawau Sir George should end his days, "the world forgetting, by the world forgot." But meanwhile circumstances were transpiring in New Zealand which ultimately drew him from his delightful retirement into the busy arena of political strife.

CHAPTER LII.

SIR JULIUS VOGEL'S PUBLIC WORKS POLICY.

. "An ill-favoured thing, sir, but mine own."
As You Like It.

THE New Zealand colonists were a bold and adventurous race. The blood of the Norse Vikings, the spirit of daring ancestors, filled them, and it must be confessed that the same lust of strife and gain which distinguished the fathers was plainly developed in the children. Saxon, Dane, and Norman, all had similar tendencies. The men who made our name famous in the sixteenth and eighteenth centuries were men of the same character. Drake, Hawkins, Raleigh, and Frobisher, Clive and Hastings, were all alike hard-handed, hard-headed adventurers, always ready for conflict and for plunder. Eager for excitement, they were ready to adopt any plan which promised to increase wealth and to set the streams of Pactolus flowing.

After the stirring scenes of the Maori war were over, it was but natural that some other opportunity should arise for the indulgence of the dominant craving.

In 1870, Mr. Vogel presented to the colony of New Zealand a scheme of borrowing and expenditure called " The Public Works and Immigration Policy." No sooner had the proposals been publicly accepted than it became evident that great constitutional changes were certain to be effected. Doubtful as to the result, people in Auckland turned naturally to Sir George Grey as the only person likely to afford advice and assistance when necessary. Meetings were held, and a deputation waited upon him at Kawau requesting him to accept the position of Superintendent of the Province of Auckland.

It was, of course, a matter of doubt as to whether a man who had held such high offices would condescend to fill a post so greatly inferior in rank.

The deputation had not long to wait. They found the ex-Governor willing to occupy any position in which he could be useful to the colony and its people. Elected to the Superintendency of the Province, he was next requested to take a seat in the House of Representatives.

A special reason existed for this new step. The advocates of the borrowing system found that the existence of the Provincial institutions and Legislatures stood in the way of a complete centralised system of public borrowing, and it was determined to abolish the provinces.

This struck at the root of local self-government in the colony, and the adherents of that principle prepared to gird up their loins for the coming struggle. They called upon the framer of the Constitution to come forward in defence of his own creation. Nor did they call in vain. Grey, always ready at the call of duty, cheerfully responded. It he could not wield the baton of a field-marshal, he could carry a musket in the ranks. To him the position he occupied was not equal in importance to the merits of the quarrel in which he fought.

The year 1874 beheld the unparalleled sight of one who had been a Governor for nearly thirty years taking his place as a private member in a colonial House of Representatives.

His efforts were for the time in vain. The tide of the money-borrowing spirit had set in, and nothing could withstand its flood. The constituencies were like tigers which had tasted blood—they would have more.

Every safeguard was swept away — local self-government and local responsibility; the devotion of specific loans to specific objects; the certainty of re-productive expenditure of the borrowed millions. All were overthrown and disregarded. The prudent were called pessimists; the cautious fools. Sound judgment was at a discount, and economy became hateful. The destruction of the provincial Government in New Zealand threw all power into the hands of the central authority. The borrowing and squandering mania spread. Instead of the ten millions which originally dazzled and startled the minds of colonists, over thirty millions were borrowed and spent by the Colonial Government. Harbour Boards, County Councils, Municipal Bodies, and Road Boards were invited and empowered to borrow. Millions were wasted by the General Government in useless works, or expended in purchasing political influence. Hundreds of thousands were, in the same spirit, thrown into the sea by Harbour Boards. The country became demoralised, and it was fairly represented by the majority in Parliament.

The legislation of the period in question—from 1870 to 1890—was generally bad. On some important points it was incessantly changing, and incessantly changing for the worse.

It would be useless, as well as uninteresting to the general reader, to wade through the history of twenty years of mostly corrupt legislation by which New

Zealand was disgraced during this period. Communities and Parliaments without traditions, and without clearly defined political principles and parties,
must be always liable to abuse of power and the pros-
titution of political influence for the accomplishment
of private ends. And the liability to travel in erratic
courses and in the tortuous paths of intrigue was increased by the unexampled profusion of the borrowed
money which was scrambled for in the New Zealand
Parliament during that time. An average population
of 400,000 people, in addition to the collection and
expenditure of the largest revenue in the world
per head of the community, borrowed and spent
£40,000,000 of public money in less than twenty
years.

Great Britain, with an average population of
36,000,000, had she kept equal pace with her young
child in the Pacific, would have added to her national
debt during these two decades £3,600,000,000.

Against the influence exerted by the disbursement
of such great treasures, wisdom, foresight, and prudence were unavailing. The *auri sacra fames*—the
accursed thirst for gold—which has been the ruin of
men and nations, and which is declared in Holy Writ
to be "the root of all evil," seized upon New Zealand
and held its sway during this whole period. Were it
not that the colony is full of the wealth of Nature,
that its resources are practically boundless, such a
burden would be intolerable, and would ensure
national bankruptcy.

Although the elasticity of a young country, and the
rapid increase of a wealth-producing population will
doubtless enable New Zealand to bear this burden
lightly—at any rate when a few years have passed—
the immediate concomitant of such a financial de-
bauch was that political reform was paralysed, and

the onward progress of the community in social matters absolutely stayed.

The efforts continuously made by Sir George Grey in all things great and noble were in vain. In 1877 he became premier of the colony which he had twice governed.   Even with the power and influence which this position gave, he was unable to carry his measures or accomplish his desires.   A few alterations and reforms which he effected were swept from the Statute Book, when, after a short period of office, he was betrayed by his professed supporters and defeated.

On his defeat he still continued to act as a private member until the year 1890, when he retired, owing to illness, being then nearly eighty years of age.

CHAPTER LIII.

PRINCIPAL LEGISLATIVE REFORMS ADVOCATED BY SIR GEORGE GREY, M.H.R.

" Then to side with truth is noble, when we share her wretched
    crust
  Ere her cause bring fame and profit, and 'tis prosperous to be
    just;
  Then it is the brave man chooses, while the coward stands aside,
  Doubting in his abject spirit till his Lord is crucified."
Lowell.

THE principal points to which Sir G. Grey has attempted to direct legislation during the last ten years have all tended to widen the power of the democracy, and to destroy monopoly. Two of his attempts have become embodied in Acts passed by the Legislature.

THROWING OPEN THE ENTRANCE TO THE PROFESSION OF THE LAW.

The legal profession in New Zealand was only nominally divided into the two well-known branches, barristers and solicitors. Solicitors were entitled by law to practise at the bar, and barristers had the option of practising as solicitors also. Admission as a solicitor was only to be obtained after many years' service under articles, as in England. To entitle a student to be called to the bar, he must have spent three years in the necessary studies, in imitation of keeping terms and eating dinners at one of the Inns of Court.

The legal profession, therefore, was, as in England, a close monopoly. Sir George felt that in a young colony greater facilities should be given, as in the United States, and as in the olden days of Athens and Rome, to those who were naturally capable of assuming the position of an advocate. He perceived that many young men of industry and talent were shut out from the advantages offered by the liberal profession of the law, and that such men were thus hindered from pursuing an honourable career, and the community was debarred from the benefits arising from their ability.

After continuous effort during several years Sir George managed at length to pass a " Law Practitioners Act," which threw open the practice of both branches of the profession to every man of good reputation who could pass the necessary examinations, and so the law remains. An honourable ambition has spurred many young men to extra and arduous work, and the gates of a brilliant career in life have been opened to all who choose to enter.

THE FRANCHISE.

The franchise was conferred upon all male adults of good character within the colony. There were, however, different qualifications—residential and freehold. The bulk of the voters were so by virtue of their manhood and residential qualifications; but there were many owners of property who claimed under the freehold franchise.

The elector whose franchise was residential could be but on one electoral roll, that for the district in which he resided; while the freeholder might possess land in a dozen different districts and have his name on as many electoral rolls. During a general election this state of things enabled landed proprietors to vote on the same day in many districts, and not infrequently elections were turned by this system of plural voting.

After many arduous conflicts Sir George Grey succeeded in altering the law, so that at a general election one voter should have but one vote. Thus, although the name of an elector may still remain upon numerous electoral rolls, he must choose one district in which to vote. That one vote having been recorded, a vote given by him in another district would be a breach of the law, making him amenable to fine and imprisonment as well as disfranchisement.

ELECTIVE GOVERNORS.

In other matters of legislation equally desired by Sir George Grey he was unable to gain success. It had long been his belief that the Governors of the great colonies should be *elected by the people*. In this, however, Sir George was not able to secure a sufficient following, although year by year the number of adherents to the principle of elective governors increased.

LAND TAX.

During his Premiership in 1877-78, Sir George had established a Land Tax, which his opponents, on succeeding to office, had converted to a Property Tax. To both sides it was clearly apparent that while a Land Tax, especially upon large estates, might, and under the pressure of growing public burdens probably would, be increased from time to time, a Property Tax, which was practically paid by the masses of the people, would not be so likely to be enlarged in amount.

During the ten years between 1880 and 1890, Sir George Grey's efforts were unremitting to re-establish the Land Tax. There was another active motor in his mind urging him strongly in this direction.

He had, for many years, been convinced that that increase of value in land which John Stuart Mill, in consultation with himself, had termed the " unearned increment," belonged not to the individual owner of the particular piece of land itself, but to the community whose presence and labour had given to the land such increased value. Upon a modified scale, therefore, he was conducting a warfare against the monopoly of land values, similar to that which was commenced by Gournay and Quesney under Louis XV. in France; and carried on by Mr. Wallace in England, and to a still greater extent by Henry George in America.

The landed and financial interests were too strong for him to overcome. But he uttered many eloquent vindications of the principle for which he contended, and without doubt sowed the seed of a future beneficial harvest for the people of New Zealand.

In the debates which took place at the time of his imposition of a land tax, Sir George Grey fiercely attacked that abuse of public influence by which some of the leading provincial politicians had perverted the trust of the public lands confided to them, into machinery for appropriating to themselves great estates in fraud of the people. Upon two methods by which this was accomplished he was especially severe. These were known by the names of " gridironing" and " spotting." It was in allusion to the system of " gridironing" that in his speech in the House of Representatives, on October 3rd, 1878, on the Land Tax Bill, Sir George thus spoke: " I believe that the system of administering the land which we propose will be admitted by the country to be just and beneficial. Consider, by the way of contrast, the system of land administration which has proceeded in Canterbury. How eminently unjust was that! The Government was practically saying while that existed: 'Come here, all men. In this favoured province you shall roam where you please. Pick out any spot which is fitted for your purposes, which is pleasing to your eyes, and you may become the owners by paying £2 per acre for it. The whole country lies open to you.' Then for the convenience of their surveys they say to the intending purchaser, 'You must not take a less extent of land than twenty acres, because the cost of the survey is very great.'

"How did people who wished to acquire large tracts of land interpret that? They took a road-line, and for some distance behind that line they had long sections laid out parallel to the road, and then they divided the country-side between the road and the long sections parallel to it into sections, one of twenty acres, then one of nineteen acres and so on. Then when the poor man who had saved a little money to buy a small farm, went out to select his land and choose a section he longed for, and came back to the Land Office and said: 'I will take that section'; he was told, 'You cannot select it, for it is less than twenty acres.'

"Again, perhaps, he went, his loss of time and his toil in like manner to be lost, and himself made ridiculous. Then he was perhaps told that these nineteen-acre sections might be put up to auction. How poor his chance in competition at auction with a wealthy land owner who owned the land on three sides of the section the man of small means wished to acquire!"

Sir George Grey was displeased and astonished at the fact, that men holding great public positions should use those positions for their own aggrandise-

ment.   One of the deepest and strongest causes of
the enmity with which he was regarded by many of
his political opponents was found in the persistent
denunciations which he uttered against the wrong-
doing of themselves and their friends in this way.   If
it should be thought that Sir George Grey was mistaken, either in his facts or in the necessary deduc-
tions therefrom, it is sufficient to show that other men
of position and influence, and not disposed to view
such transactions from the same standpoint as Sir
George Grey, admitted the facts upon which he had
reasoned.   An appropriate illustration of this may
be given in the following extract from " Lectures
on a Visit to the Canterbury Colony,"* by Lord
Lyttelton :—

"Nominally anyone might come in and buy any
of these lands over the squatter's head, but besides
that in these remote places it would not be worth
buying, the early squatters had what was called 'a
pre-emptive right' to buy at a fixed price of £2
per acre such parts of the land as they had made
improvements upon.   They used to 'spot,' as it
was called, these improvements on different parts of
the run—the effect being that the intermediate parts
were valueless without them, and these they thus
secured."

To one, who through his long course of public
power, had deemed it improper to acquire an acre of
land in a colony where his presence and authority
might be supposed to afford him exceptional opportunities, and whose first principle in regard to the
lives of public men was that their hands should be
absolutely clean, such conduct was naturally abhor-
rent.   And the fierceness of his attacks against individuals and political parties, believed by him to be

* Simpkin, Marshall, and Co., London, 1868, p. 31.

guilty of such practices, drew forth storms of anger which were never laid to rest.

INCOME TAX.

The property tax, as framed and sustained by his political opponents, did not touch the yearly income of those whose revenue arose either from their own personal exertions, or from any other cause. It was assessed upon the value of property, irrespective of whether the property yielded an income or not.

Sir George Grey contended that all persons who derived an income in any way from the colony of New Zealand should bear an equitable and just proportion of its public burdens. As this would have levied taxation upon many within the colony who escaped, and would also have called upon all those who, living in other lands, derived a revenue either from the public purse of New Zealand, or from private investments, it provoked stormy and bitter discussions, in which he was constantly accused of advocating a policy which was both dishonourable and inexpedient. But eventually the arguments used by Sir George Grey must prevail, because they are founded upon truth.

And Sir George perceived that there was contained in the assertion of this principle of taxation a deeper and yet more important meaning than the mere levying of taxation for the public purposes of the colony. He saw that there could be no true federation of the Empire unless its different parts were placed upon an equal footing, nor until there was a common bond of advantage and liability uniting the different members of this great family of nations.

And if the English creditor and investor in New Zealand were to occupy the position of a resident in the colony, participating in its advantages and helping

to bear its burdens, then, and then only, would the
web be firmly woven which bound the whole of the
different parts together.

Thus to his mind justice and expediency both
pointed to the propriety of the course which he proposed. And although he failed to carry his measures
in this direction, he was confident that the public
mind was sufficiently enlightened and determined to
ensure the success of his plans within a moderate
period of time.

LAND SETTLEMENT.

Recognising the fact that the welfare of a new
country depends upon the profitable settlement of its
lands, especially by a class of small yeomanry, he
was always in favour of peasant and small farm
holdings. Year after year he attempted to bring
forward in the House of Representatives his " Land
for Settlement Bill," which provided among other
things for the purchase of large estates from private
owners for the purpose of cutting them up into smaller
holdings, and for giving assistance by the advance
of Government debentures, secured upon such lands,
to *bona-fide* settlers, thus utilising the public credit
towards the productive settlement of the country, and
the absorption of surplus population upon the land.

NATIONALISING THE COAL MINES.

Sir George Grey believed that the State might with
advantage resume the possession and keep the control
of all the coalfields and mines in the colony; that
then, producing coal at the cheapest possible rate, it
would foster manufactures and increase all facilities
for commerce. In this, as in other directions, he
believed that a co-operative system of industry,
adopted and supported by the Government, would be

of incalculable advantage, and would possibly prepare the way for a wiser and better economy than that provided by the intense individualism and competition, which, while they have pushed our modern civilisation rapidly forward, have brought in their train the menacing host of labour difficulties which threaten the existence of society.   And in this belief he was strengthened by his own personal observation of the circumstances attending the Australasian strike in 1890.

CHAPTER LIV.

" Till the war-drum throbbed no longer, and the battle flags were
    furled,
In the parliament of man, the federation of the world."

Locksley Hall.

THE idea of federation had, long before " Locksley
Hall" was given to the world, been conceived in the
mind of Sir George Grey. He saw afar off the fulfilment of the promises made in the Holy Scriptures,
that a day of peace should dawn upon the earth, when
the nations should learn war no more. But believing,
as he did, that God, in His providential government
of the earth, used human instrumentalities for the
accomplishment of His purposes, Grey ever worked
towards the first great step in a federation of the
nations by striving for a federation of the English-
speaking peoples.

In 1890 he was requested by the Parliament of
New Zealand to attend the meeting of the Federal
Convention of Australasia in Sydney. He accepted
the task thus imposed joyfully, and, though recently
prostrated by sickness, was sufficiently recovered to
attend the sitting of the Convention in March, 1891.

Accompanied by his niece, Mrs. Seymour George,
and her eldest daughter, he left Auckland on February 26th, in the Tarawera, which next day called at
the Bay of Islands. Many years had elapsed since
his last visit to this historic spot. His first welcome

on arrival was given by a native, who claimed a friendship of thirty years. The Maori's appearance was not very prepossessing, and the fastidious shrank from him, but the ex-Governor chatted with him most cordially.

Directly he landed Sir George Grey bought a number of ferns, and carrying them in his hands, walked to the little grave-yard where so many gallant officers and men were laid to sleep. His gift was destined for the grave of his old friend Tamati Waka Nene. Planting the delicate ferns on that hallowed spot of earth, he spoke to some of the Maoris who had assembled of the loyalty, bravery, and true heart of the friendly chief. Some time he paused there, with many pictures rising in his memory. And then, having left instructions that the grave should be attended to, enforced by his appeal to their memories of Tamati and of himself, he returned to the steamer and pursued his way to Australia.

His arrival in Sydney was marked by a very cordial reception. Nearly fifty years had passed since he had last trodden Australian soil. While entering the beautiful harbour of Port Jackson, his memory recalled that day (in December, 1837) when he had landed for the first time in Western Australia. In the fifty-three years which had intervened, a family of young nations had been born upon the Island Continent. Great cities had been built upon sites then lonely and untenanted. The few scattered hamlets of that early period had grown into mighty centres of population.

It was remarked by more than one Australian paper that Grey linked the present to the very foundations of Australasian existence. For, without doubt, he had met and known men who had taken part in the first settlement of New South Wales.

Many of the delegates were born in the colonies they represented at the Conference. All of them were familiar with the name and reputation of the veteran statesman who, after the lapse of nearly half a century, had thus returned to Australia. But few of them had ever before met him. Middle-aged and grey-haired men, whose energies for a generation have been devoted to the advancement of the Southern Continent, were lisping their first words or crowing lustily in their cradles when Grey, having rendered such illustrious service to South Australia, sailed from Adelaide in 1845.

But there was one of the representatives of that colony at the Federal Convention who could boast a personal acquaintance with the former Governor. Addressing Grey he said: "You do not remember me, Sir George, but you form one of the most distinct of my childish memories. Fifty years ago I was present at a children's party you gave at Government House in Adelaide. There was a magic lantern entertainment, but I saw very little of it till you lifted me high in your arms and held me that I might get a good view."

In the discussions of the Convention, Sir George Grey was not always satisfied with the conclusions of the majority. Although the Convention was, on the whole, characterised by broad lines of policy, imperial considerations, and high principle, yet the greater experience of Grey made him fearful that the foundations of liberty would not be laid sufficiently wide or deep.

Amid all that was changed, he was still the same. The same purposes, the same hopes, the same earnest desire for the welfare of his fellow-men and the generations yet to be, were his as had strengthened him in the disasters and privations of his terrible exploration. And the same bright anticipations of the future filled his mind as when, upon his march from Shark Bay to Perth, he beheld in fancy the desert being changed into fruitful fields and the wilderness becoming instinct with busy life.

His ideas concerning Federation were not exactly similar to those expressed by many of the leading statesmen of Australasia. He did not believe in a hard and fast union, regulated by law, between States dissimilar in character, separated by great distances, and existing under different climates and conditions. He rather favoured a looser federation, which should leave each portion of the confederated States free to work out its own destiny and should yet enable all to join together for any great purpose; and so, in any crisis or sudden exigence, give to the whole that strength and solidity which springs from union.

He made no secret of his belief that confederation in Canada, in Australasia, in South Africa, were but steps in the progress of the great movement which should ultimately bring together the different branches of that family of nations which he had ever believed was destined, in the providence of God, to guide the races of the earth into the ways of righteousness and peace.

The likelihood of peace resulting from such a union of the English-speaking peoples was thus spoken of by Sir George Grey himself:—" The state of the nations of Europe renders it necessary they should maintain large armies, thus diminishing their power to maintain large navies. If Great Britain was free from all European perplexities, she would have far greater means of maintaining a large navy if such a thing was necessary. The United States hardly require an army and navy, and her want for these will diminish every year. The united English-speak-

ing people would require really no army if they were
masters of the ocean, and they could without the least
oppression or embarrassment maintain a navy which
would render them supreme on the oceans of the
world, and prevent the smallest possibility of sudden
invasion or attack."

Sir George Grey had spoken with many Australians who were in favour of such a federation as he
proposed, and held that, with a common language, a
common literature, a common legislation, which it
really is, and a common faith existing between all
English-speaking communities, it was their duty to
unite to give to the world at large the vast benefits
which must spring from such a union.

Recognising thus the supreme importance of this
crisis in the history of the Australian colonies, it was
but natural that Sir George should desire the constitution of the confederated states to be as just and as
liberal as possible. His intense longing to see the
federation of his dreams established led him to refuse
unconditionally a meaner substitute. Should this
great and glorious opportunity to form a union of
nations which might

> " Serve as a model for the mighty world,
>   And be the fair beginning of a time,"

be lost in the consideration of trivial details—nay,
worse, actually debased into an occasion for stifling
the popular liberties, and for laying the yoke of ser-
vitude upon the necks of these young communities ?
It should not be—not while he had the power to lift
his voice in impassioned appeal against such an abuse
of a heaven-sent privilege.

The veteran statesman would not passively consent
to the adoption of measures whose inevitable result
would be the direct antithesis of the objects which his
life had been spent in promoting. His practised eye

foresaw the future, either filled with ever-widening
liberty and happiness, honour and prosperity for succeeding generations of the children of Australasia ;
or presenting a picture of oppression and self-seeking,
which was hateful to his soul. If the inadequate proposals of the majority at the Convention were carried
into effect, he could see that the coming years would
bring ever-growing political inequality, with its inseparable evils, insecurity and decadence of the states.
Gazing down this vista, his prophetic glance ran
unchecked to the time when he should be forced to
echo that sad epitome of noble hopes frustrated :

> " Till the loathsome opposite
> Of all my heart had destined did obtain."

Some of his ideas were naturally regarded by the
majority as visionary and fanciful.

As the English Government had held him in the
matters of the Dominion of the Southern Ocean and
the confederation of South Africa to be a dreamer ;
as the Liberal party in England, headed by Mr. Gladstone and Mr. Bright, had impatiently chafed at his
suggestions for emigration, the consolidation of the
Empire, and Home Rule for Ireland ; as his opponents in New Zealand had taunted him with seeking
to legislate for " the unborn millions "—so many of
his fellow-workers in the Federal Conference feared
that Sir George Grey was attempting to create an
Utopia, and neglecting somewhat the practical solution of the task which lay before them.

The Convention had been sitting for a month when
the clause relating to the qualification of electors came
under discussion. The preceding clause of the Com-
monwealth of Australia Bill provided that " each
State shall have one representative for every thirty
thousand of its people," qualified by the proviso that
no State should have less than four representatives

until its population reached the required numbers. On investigation it appeared that the voting powers were not uniform throughout the different colonies. The members of the House of Representatives in the Federal Convention were to be elected by each State in conformity with the usual method of election to the local parliament, the qualification of electors of members of the former chamber being in each colony that which was prescribed by the law of the colony as the qualification for electors of the latter.

But here a grave injustice was apparent, for New Zealand and South Australia enjoyed the advantages of manhood suffrage, while in most of the other colonies a system of plural voting gave the propertied classes a great and unfair preponderance of power. Their representatives were elected, not by a majority of the population, but by the votes of a wealthy minority. In some colonies where regulations existed to prevent an elector appearing at more than one polling booth to record his vote on the day of election, it was quite legal for him to vote by letter in any district in which he owned property. Thus one man might record fifteen or twenty votes. Sir George Grey knew from experience how little attention the just demands of a minority, fairly representing the people of smaller States, would receive at the hands of an overwhelming majority returned as the representatives of capital. Therefore he vehemently opposed a federation on such terms, and eloquently advocated the amendment of the suffrage in *all* the States, by removing the property qualification, and allowing each elector only one vote.

The conservative tendency of the Federal Bill was intensified (1) By the constitution of the Senate, which was to be elected by the members of Parliament, most of whom were returned under the system of plural voting, or nominated by successive colonial governments; and (2) by the appointment of a Governor-General with a salary of not less than £10,000, chosen by the Imperial authorities.

Sir George moved as an amendment to the last provision, that this great officer, whose salary would not be less, and perhaps far more than that of the President of the United States, should be elected by the voices of the four millions of people over whom he was to rule. In the course of his earnest speech, he said : " I ask is it just, while so many poor people have to be taxed to pay their share of that salary, to deprive them of the honour, and, I may say, of the just pride of themselves electing some worthy man, known throughout so great an extent of country as Australia, to occupy that honourable post, with the certainty that such an example will operate upon every individual of the community, stirring noble faculties in many men, giving hope, perhaps to some thousand or more of the people that they may possibly attain to such an honour ? Is it right to make the people pay such sums of money, and to deprive them of honours to which they ought justly and rightly to look ? And when, as I shall prove by-and-bye, as we go on with the Bill, each office is closed by some restriction or other to all chance of fair competition in the country, let us, at the very first, indicate in this clause, that this great office shall be open at all times to that man in Australia who is deemed the greatest, and worthiest and fittest to hold so noble a post, and to satisfy his fellow-citizens that they have wisely chosen one who will be an honour to the whole community. Can any of us believe that if at the time of the disturbances in the United States in regard to slavery, a man had to be chosen by the British Ministry of the day in London, there was the slightest hope that such a man as Lincoln would have come to the front to achieve the great and noble objects which he accomplished? I am sure the universal admission must be that there would have been no hope of such a thing. Yet from the forests of the United States, there came one who had been a mere splitter of timber, worthy, justly and rightly, to exercise the highest power for a time in the United States, and to accomplish the great ends at which he aimed. Are we in Australia to be told that we can find no man worthy to succeed to a post of that kind?"

The view taken by the majority that a Governor-General appointed in Great Britain would introduce an aristocratic element into colonial society, and that his chief obligations would be the performance of social duties, roused the spirit of the real aristocrat at such openly-avowed snobbishness. The meaning of the term "social duties" as used in this connection he confessed himself unable to understand. With deep emotion, he sketched a career—such as he knew more than one instance of—of a young girl, friendless and poor, by dint of ability and incessant toil distinguishing herself in the schools, and ultimately taking the highest honours which the universities had it in their power to bestow. Left a widow, with a young family, her days were spent in training her children to be an ornament and a treasure to the State. Was he to be told that this was not a performance of social duties? He continued:

"Considering the openings that would be given to every inhabitant of Australasia under such a system as I propose, with so many families as will necessarily do it, directing their every exertion and effort to raise up children worthy of the great opportunities laid open to them, I ask whether this is not to us a greater social question than a few balls and dinners given at

Government House, at which none but those in the
immediate vicinity can be present? I ask what comparison is there between these two things—one great
and far-reaching, extending to millions, the other a
mere sham, as it were, representing what passes in
another place, as if one were looking through the
wrong end of a telescope at some procession that was
going on? All matters connected with Government
House are diminished here as compared with Great
Britain and the influence exercised there. There it
is the influence of a hereditary monarch descended
from a long line of ancestors. There it is the influence
belonging to certain professions—the army and navy
—who look to receiving honour from the hands of
such a sovereign. Here there are no ties whatever of
that kind; and yet for a mere imaginary show, or
what is called the performance of social duties—
entertaining strangers, and also citizens immediately
surrounding the vice-regal court, which are the only
benefits that are absolutely gained—all those benefits that I speak of are lost."

The debate waxed warm. Sir George Grey was
accused of disloyalty, of impracticability, of unmean-
ing declamation, of bringing his views forward too
early, of having lost the proper opportunity of advocating them, of springing a surprise, of becoming
tiresome by repeated allusions to the subject, and of
many other misdemeanours equally inconsistent and
irreconcilable. A division was called for. It was
not the custom for the delegates to leave the chamber,
but to repair to opposite sides. Quietly the most
aged member of the convention turned, walked to one
side of the hall, and sat down alone. All the other
members of the convention, in a body, proceeded to
range themselves opposite him. But at the sight of
that calm, noble figure, that sorrowful bowed head,

one representative of South Australia faltered, and after a moment's hesitation firmly retraced his steps and seated himself beside Sir George Grey. His example was instantly followed by another delegate from the same colony. And thus between two representatives of young Australia—Dr. Cockburn and Mr. Kingston—supported on one side by a doctor of medicine and on the other by a Queen's Counsel, Grey found himself in a minority of three, while his amendment was rejected by thirty-five voices.

Macaulay sang the story of "the dauntless three" who kept the bridge against the Tuscan host for the liberty of Rome in the brave days of old. The same spirit was displayed by Grey and his two companions as animated Horatius, when Spurius Lartius and Herminius took their stand by his side and calmly defied the whole array of their foemen.

CHAPTER LV.

A SERIES OF OVATIONS.

" Turn him to any cause of policy,
   The Gordian knot of it he will unloose,
   Familiar as his garter: that, when he speaks,
   The air, a charter'd libertine, is still,
   And the mute wonder lurketh in men's ears,
   To steal his sweet and honey'd sentences."
                                    King Henry V.

AFTER the dissolution of the Conference on the 9th
of April, Sir George Grey spent two months travel-
ling in Australia. His tour was a triumphal progress. Each city through which he passed welcomed
him with manifestations of enthusiasm and veneration.
He yielded to many of the requests made through
influential deputations, and delivered addresses in
various centres.

Thousands listened spell-bound to the pathetic
vibration of his voice, inculcating the love of justice,
the beauty of goodness, the grandeur of a noble life,
and eloquently depicting the glorious possibilities
which depended on the purposes and actions of the
men to whom he spoke. Many of them will never
forget his teachings. Some will doubtless follow in
his steps, act in the way he has pointed out, and
repeat in their lives the influence he exerted upon
them.

Convinced that the Federal Bill as passed by the
Convention was not calculated to provide for the
highest liberty and well-being of the people, Sir

George used all the weight of argument to prevent
its acceptance. He urged that in proportion as they
valued the great privilege of framing their own Constitution held out to them by the Mother Country, so
firmly should they resist any half measures. He
pointed out that while other nations had only gained
such an opportunity after ages and centuries of struggling, and after long and bloody wars, Australia enjoyed it as a free gift. Yet he would advise them to
reject Federation, though it was the dearest wish of
their hearts, unless it could be obtained under perfectly just and liberal provisions. They had a chance
such as came but once in two or three centuries, and
never more than once to any nation. Their longing
for a Federal Constitution would only make their
action more heroic in refusing to accept any form of
government but the noblest.

The various deficiencies in the Bill, its conservative and aristocratic tendency, its unjust and unequal
provisions for the expression of their views by the
great mass of the people, the nominee character of its
second legislative chamber, the hard and fast law
which declared that the Bill must be accepted or rejected as a whole, were chiefly dwelt on by the "old
man eloquent." Leaving the minor questions of commercial interests and expediency, he opposed the draft
Constitution on great principles. If it were adopted
by the different states and became binding, he believed the Australian race would hamper itself with a
yoke which it might require a century to cast off,
during which time the national development would
be arrested and dwarfed.

Sir George Grey's Australian tour roused the democratic feeling everywhere. His speeches were like
sparks to tinder. The popular sentiments wanted a
voice and found it in him. On one question, espe-

cially, his arguments carried conviction to the hearts of the majority, and consternation to those of more than one colonial ministry. That question was universal and equal suffrage—one man, one vote.

The constant allusion made by him to the necessity of reform in the voting powers of Australian colonists was severely criticised by many of the leading journals. It was said that he was always dragging in the "One man, one vote" theory, in season and out of season. Very little notice was taken of his arguments at the Convention, and it was asserted that no object would be gained by his advocacy of the movement. And yet, within a few months, the Government of Victoria had the consideration of this question forced upon it, and that of New South Wales was upset upon it.

The marvellous effect which his addresses produced upon the people of Australia was well and graphically summarised by one of the Colonial journals: "In the course of a few short weeks this physically feeble old man, but morally powerful giant, has revolutionised public opinion from one end of Australia to the other. He has imbued a whole people with a vital principle, embodying the noble ideal of the equality of man. So deeply has he instilled, and so firmly has he implanted, the principle of 'one man, one vote,' in the sentiment and mind of the masses, that it must for the future be the only basis upon which Australian democracy will consent to any change in the institutions or constitutions of the country. Sir George Grey has advised, nay, he has implored the people to subordinate every other question to the attainment of this one vital principle of the political equality of all men; and happily for Australia, signs are not wanting that his advice is being accepted and acted upon."

Sir George Grey's seventy-ninth birthday was memorable. After an absence of little short of fifty years, he was borne smoothly in a railway carriage into the heart of that beautiful city in South Australia which had been the seat of his government when he laid the foundations of prosperity in that colony. The leading citizens of Adelaide were on the platform to welcome him, some few among the oldest there being able to recall his previous coming among them. Thousands, with tumultuous cheers, thronged the roads by which he drove to the Town Hall.

As he looked upon the handsome buildings, the beautiful gardens, the whole aspect of the town—familiar, yet so changed; as he breathed the invigorating air, and rejoiced in the peculiar glory of the blue skies, what wonder that his heart was overflowing with emotion, that his brain was dizzy, both with the contrast and the likeness of the present to the past. He said he felt like a man who was dreaming, as though the glowing scenes were glorified visions suggested by memories of the past, which would presently fade away. On another occasion he described his feelings as similar to those of a man who had been dead for fifty years, and then had come to life and revisited the scenes of his youth.

At the Town Hall a more formal welcome was tendered. The front seats in the hall were reserved for those colonists who had been in South Australia during his government. Some of these old men were visibly affected by the return of their former Governor and the memories it recalled. As Sir George eagerly scanned their faces, and tried to discover the features of the young men he had known half a century before in the venerable countenances before him, his eyes also filled with tears, and his voice was scarcely audible. He spoke very few words, but those broken, unstudied utterances went straight to the hearts of his hearers.   He was so overcome with emotion as to be unable to proceed.

In the evening a banquet was given by the Mayor of the city in his honour, at which about two hundred of the leading colonists were present.   Sir George had in a great measure subdued the emotion which overmastered him at the function in the afternoon and responded at greater length to the kind and flattering speeches made by the local magnates.

His address was mainly directed to the advocacy of a humane and philanthropic policy in the government of nations, as the highest wisdom and the surest guarantee of prosperity.   He pointed to the results of the policy he had inaugurated among the natives of South Africa, as opposed to the bloodshed, the loss, and the failure which followed harsher and less just measures.   And he asserted that the methods he had adopted in his several governments had been greatly owing to the teachings and influence of the men who had first settled in South Australia, whose descendants he saw that night around him.

His closing words (delivered with such impassioned eloquence that the youthful fire of the spirit gave the lie to the testimony of the eyes which saw the bowed shoulders, the silvery hair, the withered hands) will ring long in the ears of those who heard them.   " It is my duty to tell you these truths.   It is my duty to tell you what I feel myself—that a time when men sink from old age is to me a period of the greatest joy and comfort that my life has known, in receiving welcomes wherever I go, and in knowing that rewards so far surpassing anything that mortal man could do have fallen upon me.   That should satisfy men that these principles which your forefathers brought to this country, which they strove to carry out, are the

true principles which should animate all men, and
which you, as their offspring, should adopt and do
your utmost in carrying out, thus aiding and conducting the whole world, the Old and the New, through
the troublesome times that are evidently before us.
If you follow that course you will do your duty, the
duty the greatest that for two or three centuries has
fallen upon man to perform ; you will bring out nobility
and greatness amongst your fellow-men, such as in
recent times there has been no opportunity of displaying. This great field is before you. Enter into
it.   Listen to one who knew your forefathers, and
attend to his earnest request, and follow in the steps
they would wish you to pursue, and which they pursued themselves while they remained here."

The following evening a great public meeting was
held in the Town Hall. Nearly two thousand people
were present. The effect when the veteran statesman
appeared upon the platform was most impressive.
The whole assemblage rose simultaneously, mani-
festing great enthusiasm. In the afternoon Sir George
Grey had attended an even more interesting gathering.
This was a meeting to wish success and bid farewell
to an exploring party, headed by Mr. David Lindsay,
the cost being borne by Sir Thomas Elder. This
party was setting out to explore the only district of
Central Australia yet untraversed. They were turning the last leaf in the volume whose earliest pages
had been cut by Sir George and his contemporaries.
Three members of Sturt's expedition were present,
and received with hearty applause the remarks which
the speaker made about their former leader. Grey
said he had been in Adelaide when two earlier exploring parties had set out—one under Eyre and the
other under Sturt. Now he was present at the departure of the last of these daring bands. After their

return the world would contain but little unexplored territory. It was well that the nineteenth century should fulfil its peculiar mission, and even with its last years complete the task. He wished that the final effort might be crowned with greater glory and success than any of the previous ones.

The visit to Adelaide roused other memories, more personal and more pathetic. In the cemetery there Sir George Grey's only child was buried. Had he lived he would have been nearly fifty years of age. During those long decades how often must the mind of the father have pictured that son by his side. The merry winsome child, the honest, healthy schoolboy, the enthusiastic student

" Nourishing a youth sublime
With the fairy tales of science, and the long result of time,"

the man of generous impulses and sober judgment, all must in turn have been present to his imagination. A son to love, to train, to confide in, to study—always a sympathetic companion, a kindred spirit—a character like his own in many ways, but with endearing traits of individuality. All these hopes were buried in the little grave at Adelaide, which the father visited from day to day, and beside which he stood in silent grief.

From Adelaide Sir George proceeded to Broken Hill where he met with a great reception. His next addresses were delivered in Melbourne before the Trades' Hall Council and at an immense public meeting. On his way thence to Sydney, every town through which he passed received him with demonstrations of welcome. In response to a cordial invitation from the Mayor, he broke his journey at Goulburn. Arriving on Saturday, May 23rd, he remained there over Sunday, leaving on Monday morning. In spite of the fatigues of the first day, which, commencing with an early disembarkation from the train, included a public welcome, a drive round the town, the reception of three deputations and many private friends, Sir George was present at a complimentary banquet, and made a speech at a thronged public meeting in the evening, as clear, as eloquent, and as impressive as any he had given in Australia. This was the fifth address he had delivered that day.

The coping-stone to the triumphal arch of his Australian reception was added at the tremendous meeting held on the following Tuesday in the vast Centennial Hall, which is the largest in any British colony south of the line. The ovation he received was a fitting close to his tour. The great hall—estimated to hold eight thousand persons—was crowded in every part long before eight o'clock, the people beginning to muster as early as half-past six. This was regarded as practically the opening of that grand room for the democratic purposes for which it was built by the people out of the national funds. Hundreds were standing in the galleries, hundreds of tickets for the ladies' gallery were refused prior to the meeting, hundreds—even thousands—assembled outside the doors and in adjoining corridors. The effect was electrical when, on the entrance of the eagerly-expected statesman, the whole audience rose to their feet, waving hats and handkerchiefs, while the cheering was deafening. Those who were present at the receptions given to Mr. Gladstone during his campaign in Midlothian were witnesses of enthusiasm similar to that exhibited on this occasion. It was like the public rejoicing at the return of a victorious general, though unmarred by the tears of the bereaved. An English member of Parliament who was present declared that in all the great meetings he had attended in the Old World, he had never witnessed any equal in numbers, unanimity, or enthusiasm within the four walls of a building. He considered it "the most magnificent manifestation of the good-will of a people" he had ever seen. "Magnificent is a tame word with which to describe the reception Sir George Grey met with," said the *Australian Star*.

Another newspaper wrote: "The veteran Sir George Grey may be said to have had at the Centennial Hall the other evening as near an approach to what may be called a living apotheosis as ever fell to the lot of mortal."

An account of the scene, written by an eye-witness, presents it very vividly: "A noble spectacle! The grandest that has ever been seen in glorious young Australia! The spectacle of between seven and eight thousand free men and their intelligent wives held spellbound, carried out of themselves, by the magnificent eloquence of one great and good man. . . . Every seat was occupied inside of fifteen minutes from the opening of the doors, and then the wide aisles were packed with men well satisfied to stand for nearly three hours without room to move, so long as their ears could drink in the words of wisdom, sweet inspiring words, that they were certain would be spoken to them. . . .

"Once filled, the scene presented to the eyes of the gazer from above was a curious and wonderful one. The long rows of chairs with their occupants were broken at each side by the standing throngs, the effect being flats and ridges, almost like the waves and levels of the sea, and like the sea was the incessant moaning, murmuring sound of many thousands of voices echoing through the vaulted dome; and like the surge breaking on a long, level strand, were the intermittent, peculiar roars when the voices were raised in acclaim, and the ' Kentish fire' from many

feet hurled its thunderous echoes through the vast
space and out into the wide galleries and corridors
beyond. The sight and sound even at this time
were unique, but what pen can describe the scene
when the grey head and bowed form of the venerable
orator appeared ascending the stairs in the centre of
the platform? The people rose at him! and cheered
again and again: The sound was tremendous, the
sight one calculated to stir to its very depths the
coldest heart. The mighty throng arose as one, and
hats and handkerchiefs were waved in the air, while
their owners gave voice to their admiration and affection in ringing cheers that shook the very atmosphere,
and made the reeds of the noble and beautiful organ
sound a responsive echo.

"After once bowing, and twice repeating it, Sir
George sat down, but was compelled to rise twice to
again and again acknowledge the ovation he received.
And it was quite five minutes before the immense
audience settled back into a calm. After the chairman's introductory remarks he introduced the speaker
of the evening, who on rising to begin his address
had to stand with bowed head, evidently deeply
moved, while another storm of cheering arose and
subsided. Looking out over that vast sea of faces, all
raised expectant, the thoughts that stirred that great
mind must have been many and complex. Sir George
says himself that the one paramount was the reflec-
tion, a sad one, of 'Alas! how many of this vast
multitude will have gone back to the earth from
which they sprang without having had the blessing
of reaping the benefits, of garnering the harvest,
which will spring from the seed we are now sowing.'
Then he began his speech in a voice which faltered
and trembled, and his first few sentences were not
audible far back in the hall. Warming to his subject,

and overcoming his first emotion, however, his tones gained fulness and strength, and very little indeed of the subsequent magnificent oratorical effort was unheard, even in the furthest corners of the huge building. Throughout the whole address there was not one unfriendly sound from the front. The most rapt, respectful attention was exhibited throughout, while the applause which greeted each noble utter-ance was unanimous and tremendous. The audience was with the speaker throughout, and it may truly be said that the best of seed fell on the richest of soils. The mighty throng felt and knew that the orator spoke words of wisdom and truth. . . . While swaying the crowd at will, he did not exert that will to excite to incendiary thoughts and deeds, but left the minds of all who heard him purified and exalted, calmed and resolved, all in one. The ordinary dema-gogue excites and irritates ; this grand democrat urges, yet soothes, and at the same time leads the straying feet of Demos into the easiest paths to follow to attain his ends.

" Such a hearing is rarely won for a speaker, such a speaker rarely is heard to so deserve it. The fact was clear that the venerable knight not only in-structed the minds of his hearers, but he reached and won their hearts, and when he closed the grandest speech Australians have ever heard, he was applauded as no man has ever been before in this or any other Australian city. It is safe to say that not a single individual of the vast multitude which assembled within the walls of the Centennial Hall on Tuesday night will ever forget the privilege he or she enjoyed thereby."

During the course of his address, the appearance of one or two unpopular public men on the platform occasioned a great uproar in the hall. Sir George

seized the opportunity to administer a gentle but just
rebuke to those who refused to hear an opponent :

"One good plan," he said, "in our new Common-
wealth would be to silence the opinions that you
think wrong, or that I think wrong, by fair and open
argument, and not by noise."

On the following Friday, Sir George spoke to a
great meeting of over three thousand in Wallsend,
and the night after to an equally large assembly in
the Newcastle Skating Rink, being received on each
occasion with the utmost enthusiasm.   His last
address in Australia was delivered on Monday, June
1st, to the largest audience that the Gaiety Theatre
in Sydney had ever held.

Two days later the "Great Pro-Consul" embarked
on the return voyage to New Zealand, after a series of
triumphs such as Australia had never yielded to one
man before.

There are in the southern regions of Australia,
away from the seaboard, vast plains, which stretch
from the Murray across the Edwards River, the Mur-
rumbidgee, the Lachlan, and the Darling, hundreds
of miles to the west and north and east. After the
scorching sun of summer has withered the herbage,
they present the appearance of an arid and waste
desert, which, were it not for the scattered timber and
salt bush, would seem after a period of drought
almost as destitute of life as the great alkali plains
between the Sierra Nevada and Salt Lake. But there
are beneath the surface, waiting only for the reviving
influences of moisture, the ever-living roots of various
herbage. When the winter rains sweep over those
plains, so level that there is no appreciable drainage
—as level, in truth, as the sea—the whole scene
changes as if by magic. From the hot earth the
vapour arises as the soil drinks in greedily the life-

giving stream, and almost in a few hours the dusty, yellow waste is tinged with ever-increasing greenness and verdure. In a few days the plains are brilliant with flowers and rich with herbage. The whole land is changed from a wilderness into a vast field of pasture.

Such was the effect of Sir George Grey's visit to the principal cities of Australia.

There were indeed in the minds of the majority of the Australian people hopes and longings for a better state of things than that which in days gone by produced the Eureka Stockade, and in this day the Shearers' War in Queensland. Some stimulus was necessary to prompt these wishes into practical life. That stimulus was given by the presence and speeches of the ex-Governor of New Zealand. The masses of the people everywhere recognised the uselessness as well as the impropriety of force. Sir George taught them a wiser and a better way. He showed them how, by organisation and by the united use of their privileges as free subjects of the Crown, they might become a force in the Legislatures of their respective colonies potent enough to guide the main lines of legislation. As in New Zealand, in 1846, he had dared the anger of the Imperial Government and the clamours and animosity of New Zealand colonists by refusing to accept for New Zealand an imperfect and unjust Constitution, so in the Convention at Sydney he declined to accept the framework of the Federal Constitution unless it were built upon the broadest basis of popular representation in all parts of the Colonial Federation. Regarded angrily and with ill-disguised contempt by the members of the Convention, he went forth from it to the colonies which it represented.

When, on his departure, the leaders of the labour

movement came down to the wharf to bid Sir George
good-bye, there were not a few whose eyes were moist
with tears of genuine sympathy and affection. Within
a few weeks of his departure the results appeared,
and those results were marvellous. Australian politics
had undergone a new birth.

The history of the New South Wales elections is
typical of the altered state of affairs. Prior to Sir
George Grey's arrival in Sydney, and during the sitting of the Convention, Sir Henry Parkes had reached
the zenith of his power and popularity. Praise was
lavished upon him from all quarters. He was one of
the three "empire builders" of whom Mr. Stead made
much. The *Times*, ever ready to ignore true genius
and to applaud success, contrasted him with Sir
George Grey in articles which spoke contemptuously
of Grey, but alluded to Sir Henry Parkes in terms
which would have been eulogistic if applied to Washington.

What is the position now? A few speeches from
Sir George Grey revealing the true and oppressive
nature of the proposed Government which they were
asked to support, the tortuous and shameful course
which they, being free men, were asked to tread, and
dwelling upon the glorious future which awaited them
if true to themselves and to their country, and Sir
Henry Parkes was compelled to adapt his policy to
that of his rival and opponent.

Australia is politically regenerated, and an example
has been set to the labouring classes of the world
which will never be forgotten. Without doubt the
example will be followed in Great Britain, and a new
force in Imperial politics will arise. The Parliament
of New South Wales was dissolved. A new force—
the Labour Party—came into existence, and its members were returned in sufficient numbers to hold the

balance of power between political parties. Acting upon the instructions of the labour unions, Mr. E. J. Houghton, the Secretary of the Trades and Labour Councils of New South Wales, on June 30th, 1891, sent a letter to Sir George Grey containing the following paragraph: "I can hardly express the gratitude felt towards your noble self by the workers of this colony for the great amount of good which resulted from your timely visit, and the beautiful words of advice you spoke when about to step on board the steamer which carried you to New Zealand. These words have been quoted by myself and others of the Labour candidates at many of our meetings, and I need scarcely add that their effect has been very marked. . . . Indeed, some of our men give you all the credit, and I am not by any means disposed to quarrel with those who hold that opinion."

CHAPTER LVI.

RETROSPECT OF SIR GEORGE GREY'S PUBLIC LIFE.

" Oh, good old man, how well in thee appears
The constant service of the antique world,
When service sweat for duty, not for meed!
Thou art not for the fashion of these times
When none will sweat but for promotion."
                                As You Like It.

IN the tumultuous sea of colonial politics, Sir George
Grey's integrity was as firm, and his fixedness of
purpose as unyielding, as it had ever been in the
Imperial service. Gradually he lost the support of
most of his contemporaries, not through any abate-
ment in their belief in his rectitude or wisdom, but by
reason of his unbending principle, which would not
permit of any of the political tricks, intrigues, or com-
promises which seem necessary in party warfare. So
marked and notorious had this desertion become, that
at length it was said in one of the leading newspapers
of the colony that Sir George Grey had but one
political follower left, and he was not in Parliament.
At the same time, public and private confidence in
his uprightness, patriotism, and abstract wisdom was
unbounded. His remarkable character was the theme
of respectful comment. His generous liberality was
awarded no stinted praise. Since the days when the
Athenian citizen cast his vote for the banishment of
Aristides, no stronger illustration of the inconse-
quential nature of public opinion has been afforded

than the estimation in which Sir George Grey was held by the people of New Zealand at the end of his public career, and his deserted position among politicians.

But in truth there is no great difficulty in tracing out the causes of such an incongruous and apparently strange result. George Grey was a man born to rule. As Dictator or Imperator he would have left a name which would have been handed down to the last generations of men as a symbol of wisdom, courage, and benevolence.

During the different stages of his public life his character never altered, his thoughts and purposes never changed. What he was when at five-and-twenty, filled with restless but honourable ambition, he started upon his explorations in Western Australia, he remained when with the snows of nearly eighty winters upon his head he stood before the vast audiences of Australia, waking a whole nation to its new birth.

Age had, indeed, tamed something of his fire. The frame once strong and vigorous had weakened beneath the hand of time. But the George Grey of 1891 in heart, in hope, in faith, was the same George Grey who, when Victoria ascended the throne of Britain, had gone forth, young, handsome, vigorous, to the commencement of life's busy work.

Naturally fitted for command, he found a suitable sphere for the development of a remarkable character in the perils and responsibilities of Western Australia, in the financial crisis and critical position of South Australia, in the wild turmoil and incessant struggles of New Zealand, and in the vast complications and unparalleled difficulties presented by South Africa and India between the years 1854 and 1860.

The renown of Sir George Grey attained its greatest height during this particular portion of his life. Not that he was in any sense different from the Grey of other times and other countries, but because the circumstances and developments of that period gauged his capacity and tested his genius. No page of history, either of ancient or modern times, contains a record more sound or brilliant than that of Sir George Grey in South Africa. Confronted by every form of opposition; menaced by dangers of every description; oftentimes not only unsupported but actually thwarted by his superiors; with means utterly inadequate to the ends to be attained; met by occurrences so peculiar as to be absolutely without precedent; called upon to decide at a moment's notice questions, on the answers to which depended the fate of nations; with science, religion, and literature looking to him for guidance, and the usual cares of government resting upon his shoulders; not only acting for the present, but forecasting the future with almost prophetic wisdom, he never neglected one single iota of his duty, he never failed to achieve success.

It is said by Macaulay, when speaking of Cromwell and his Ironsides, that no foeman ever saw their backs, that they never met an enemy without inflicting defeat, and that whenever they conquered, their opponents were crushed. No matter who the enemies were whom Cromwell and his Ironsides met, or how great their numbers, he always remained the master of the field. So long as Grey was in absolute command, a similar verdict may safely be passed upon his career. Especially may it be so stated of his work in South Africa. No conjunction of circumstances ever found him unready; no evil tidings stayed the hand which he stretched out to protect his people. In the storms and tempests which beat upon him at that time his courage never failed, his judgment was never wrong. No fear of consequences caused him to hesitate in the marvellous combinations which he thought out, and the wonderful steps which he took. He acted unconstitutionally, it is true, but he acted unconstitutionally to save the constitution. He levied troops without the sanction of Parliament indeed, and in defiance of law, but he gave to those regiments standards which were to wave in distant fields, where their gleam and rustle would strike terror to the heart of mutiny, and bring hope and joy to the servants of the Queen. Wise to plan, swift to decide, strong to act, his capacity both moral and physical is brought into singular prominence by the strange and unexampled events of those few years.

In spite of the carpings of his opponents, and the detractions of smaller men, his Royal Mistress followed the record of his government with pleasure, and endorsed his unconstitutional actions with her approval. The hand of Providence was apparent in sending Grey at that time to that particular portion of the world. The Governor was fortunate in serving so wise a Queen; the Queen was happy in the command of so true a servant.

His return to New Zealand with limited power and discretion, fettered upon all sides, hindered the free play of his genius, and reduced the possibility of his usefulness by exactly so much as his personal authority was lessened. His attempts to perform public service in England in 1869 and 1870 indicated indeed the grasp of his mind upon all subjects of importance to Great Britain, but as he possessed no power to enforce his belief, he failed to accomplish practically those great measures which he advocated with singular skill and eloquence.

His Parliamentary career in New Zealand proved

beyond a doubt that his influence in the management of men, and his tact in obtaining the acquiescence and the voluntary assistance of his fellows were by no means equal to his wonderful capacity for command. Here again the reasons are obvious enough. To his mind authority and influence were only desirable in order that they might be used for the happiness and welfare of others. His appeals to men for support were based upon the highest of all principles—self-sacrifice. No lust for place, or public money, or estates, or the petty greatness of official position, could offer to him any temptation whatever, or be supposed by him to offer temptation to others.

It was not, therefore, possible in the crowd, partly of selfish or ignorant men, with whom he was brought in contact, that either he, or his principles, could gain a large or permanent support. Even those who followed him for long periods of time at length fell away, because the objects they desired were not his objects and their ideas not his ideas. And so it happened that at last the press, with some show of truth, averred that all his followers, save one or two, had deserted him.

It is not given to the sons of men to be able always to command success, or at any rate, what the world believes to be success. The life of the greatest of all men ended in seeming failure. And so the seeming failure of Sir George Grey's later years will probably contain the germ of great future usefulness. For even when standing alone in the Parliament of New Zealand his mind was ever active on the side of justice and of humanity, and his tongue was always eloquent in the cause of the oppressed, and in vindication of the common rights of the whole people.

CHAPTER LVII.

NATIVE FEELING FOR SIR GEORGE GREY.

"Take away the sword.
States can be saved without it."
                    Lytton.

THE native kings and chiefs of the Pacific had learned to look on Sir George Grey as their natural guardian and adviser. His correspondence in this direction is as instructive as it is interesting, and it is full of pathos. Savage princes, menaced by the French and German officers, appealed to Grey for advice without reserve. Through him many of them more than once prayed to be admitted within the sacred circle of the British Empire. And although this great privilege was denied, they yet approached him when in peril or fear, as their protector.

Thus Malietoa came. After the English Government had refused to accept those beautiful islands of Samoa, Bismarck made no secret of his intention to annex them as German colonies. In great distress, the Samoan king, from beneath the shade of the cocoa palm and telea tree at Apia, penned a humble letter to his illustrious friend, the erstwhile Governor of New Zealand. He set forth his sad predicament. In simple language he told all his fears, and asked by the memory of olden days, and by Grey's love to the native races and their chiefs, that he would spare time to guide the King and people of Samoa in their deep perplexity.

The advice which, in reply, Sir George tendered was at once full and precise. Well aware of the grasping and overbearing nature of the German, awake to the iron determination of the Chancellor in his colonising plans, he laid before Malietoa the two methods which could be adopted in the face of a certain German aggression. The King might resist by force, or he might submit to superior power and appeal under God to the great nations with whom he was in treaty, including Germany herself.

As to resistance, he merely spoke of it to remark that it would mean destruction to Malietoa and his people, while affording an excuse to Bismarck for the occupation of the islands as a conquered territory. The only safe course was that of non-resistance. Careful to avoid meeting force by force, Malietoa must patiently endure insult and injury, trusting in God and in the justice of the nations.

Sir George explained the jealousy of Germany, England, France, and the United States towards each other in the matter of annexing new territory in the great southern seas. He added that public opinion in all civilised nations was ever becoming stronger to resist wrong, and that, if Samoa refused to enter into an unequal conflict and appealed to the great powers, Germany must ultimately yield. Even should the Germans carry him personally into captivity, he must still be patient.

Malietoa received this advice with gratitude. In 1887 the Germans carried him off a captive. Then what Sir George had predicted came to pass. England—to her shame—did not venture to interfere. Prince Bismarck had threatened Lord Salisbury that if she opposed Germany in Samoan colonisation

Germany would aid France in Egypt. But America stood up boldly. The States were firm. Germany should not have Samoa. Justice must be done to the Samoan king.

Malietoa was restored, and this failure in Samoa seems to have been the prelude to Bismarck's fall. Sir George Grey was indignant at the conduct of the German Chancellor. He was surprised as well as pained by the attitude of the English Government. The Samoan episode taught him a new truth. It convinced him that the real and efficient guardianship of the English-speaking races was transferred from Britain to the United States. Henceforth it seemed to him the redress of human grievances and the defence of human freedom must be sought, not in the Councils of London but in those of Washington. He perceived that in the future, if any community or State, especially if it were of English origin, desired protection it would turn across the waves of the Atlantic to the great nation of the West for help rather than to England. For in that young and vigorous Republic, untrammelled by Continental interests, and ambitious for the leadership of the nations, there were wisdom to perceive and courage to vindicate the claims of universal justice, and the blessings of universal liberty.

The feeling of the Maoris towards the Government of the Queen was generally that of a fixed and steady loyalty. Even when the king movement had become settled and organised, there was not, until a fierce and bitter war had been waged between the races, any desire to throw off paramount allegiance to the Crown. The king was looked upon as a sort of provincial superintendent, and as the provinces made their own laws, which were submitted to the Governor for his assent, so the king natives desired to make their laws, and submit them also to Her Majesty's Representative.

It was not until fire and sword had been carried through the Island that the fierce passions of the Maori tribes caused them to throw off all sense of loyalty, and to assume an absolutely independent position.

It might be supposed that when the forces of General Cameron and General Chute had over-powered the scattered bands of the natives the rebellion was suppressed, and the authority of the Crown restored. This, however, was not the case. When the Imperial troops were withdrawn a sort of tacit peace was inaugurated. The Maori King still existed, and his authority was supreme in the centre of the North Island. A line was drawn called the Aukati. Within that line the Queen's Writ did not run, and for many years Europeans only crossed that fatal boundary at the peril of their lives.

Thieves, murderers, criminals of all sorts, once within that pale were safe from pursuit. No police, no armed colonial force dared to penetrate save secretly and at night.

But in all other parts of the two islands, save in the so-called King Country, the chiefs and people were nearly all loyal to the Crown. They returned members to the New Zealand Parliament, they prosecuted their claims in the English courts, they transmuted their communal titles to land to the ordinary freehold known to English law.

To both king natives and loyal natives there was but one Queen and one Governor. To this day, when the inhabitants of any kainga or the garrison of any pah welcome Sir George Grey, the cry is still the same—" Haeremai, Haeremai, Haeremai te Kawana, Kawana Kerei " (Governor Grey).

In the year 1876 a great law suit was decided in Wellington, in which the Honourable Henry Russell sued the Government — through the Government printer—for libels upon himself and the great Maori chiefs of Hawke's Bay, published in the columns of a paper supported by the Government, called the *Waka Maori* or *Maori Canoe*. After a long and interesting trial, a special jury gave a verdict against the Government for £5,000 and costs.

The proceedings had been of intense interest to the natives. Numbers of chiefs had assembled in Wellington to witness the result. Old war-scarred veterans were there, who had never before seen a European town. Chiefs who had led their tribes to battle in the far North, in the King Country, in Wanganui, on the East Coast, Hawke's Bay and Taranaki, scores of whom bore visible traces of the conflicts in which they had fought side by side with our best and bravest, had assembled to be witnesses of this legal battle, where the rifle, the bayonet, the tomahawk, the spear, and marae gave place to logical argument and the strife of tongues. With the result they were pleased beyond measure. Their loyalty and good faith were unanimously testified to by a pakeha judge and jury against the then Government of the colony.

They could no longer indulge in the ancient feasts of the conqueror, but such an occasion could not pass uncelebrated. A great banquet was given. Many hundreds of guests — Maoris and Europeans—sat down to a well-prepared and appointed dinner. Enjoyment and triumph shone upon every Maori face. The meats were well cooked, the beer and wine abundant. If the feast lacked something of the fierce element of vindictive triumph, which forty years before it would have exhibited, yet there was enough of the intoxicating influence of success to fill the native heart with pleasure, and tinge each cheek with a darker flush.

According to European custom, toasts were proposed. To the first health all Maoris and Europeans rose, and with respect and pleasure drank to "Her Majesty the Queen." The next toast was that of "The Governor." No sooner had the toast been given out than the Maori chiefs, with one spontaneous impulse, sprang to their feet, and with a great cry, shouted "Kapai! Te Kawana! Te Kawana Kerei!"

The Governor at this time was the Marquis of Normanby. But the Maoris, true to their nature, had forgotten that there was, or ever had been, any but one Governor. With gleaming eyes and heaving breasts, the chiefs and warriors who had followed Grey in war, and listened with child-like reverence to his voice in council, swept aside all mere formalities and went back to the earnest and living times, when in their simple faith the Queen was their immediate Sovereign, and Grey was their Governor and Father.

It would be impossible to adequately describe the enthusiasm, the fire, the abandonment of the native chiefs, as with one accord and roars of acclamation they toasted "The Governor—Governor Grey." It was useless for the Europeans to tell them, "The Governor—the Marquis of Normanby." All efforts were futile. The Maoris did not seem to understand the correction which was attempted, and louder and still louder rose the shouts, "Kapai! Te Kawana! Kawana Kerei!"

CHAPTER LVIII.

THE PUBLIC LIBRARY AT AUCKLAND.

" Dreams, books, are each a world; and books we know
Are a substantial world, both pure and good.
Round these, with tendrils strong as flesh and blood,
Our pastime and our happiness will grow."

Wordsworth.

TWENTY-FIVE years had passed since Sir G. Grey presented his magnificent library to the people of South Africa. During those years, by purchase, by bequest, by gifts, and by his own untiring researches and participation in active affairs, he had once more accumulated a priceless collection of literary treasures. His love of books was as keen as ever, his knowledge of what was of real interest and value only enlarged by experience. For the second time in his life he found himself the possessor of the most valuable private library in the Southern Hemisphere.

The thought that after his death this collection might be broken up, dispersed, and its component parts lost or destroyed, distressed him. To prevent such a misfortune, and also from love to Auckland, he determined to present his treasures to the city, and enrich the public of New Zealand as he had already enriched that of South Africa.

He communicated his intentions to the destined recipients of his bounty. The munificent bequest of £12,000 under the will of Edward Costley strengthened the determination of the municipal bodies to erect a suitable building, and when it was completed Sir George Grey sent his books to make their permanent home on the shelves.

The Free Public Library at Auckland was opened by Sir G. Grey on the 26th of March, 1887.

In his address he alluded to Sir Everard Home as being the first donor of valuable books to the Auckland Library. When Home lay dying in Sydney he made his will, leaving all his books to Sir G. Grey. Only a few hours before his death he sent for his will, and to it he added a wish that if Sir George ever parted with the books he would give them to the city of Auckland. Sir Everard was most anxious to see a public library established in that place, and had fully and constantly discussed the matter with his friend.

Sir George was deeply moved by the importance and interest of the opening scene, and affected by the irrepressible enthusiasm and excitement in the vast crowd which filled every chair and occupied every inch of standing room in the Art Gallery of the new Library buildings. Not only the body of the hall, but the platform, the doorway, and the steps were filled, and the outer passages blocked. The veteran scholar spoke in simple but eloquent language of the high aims which should animate the youth of the rising generation. He said the task which lay before them, though apparently different to that which had been accomplished in his lifetime, was in reality only a more advanced stage of the same work.

" I believe," he said, "that the world is now entering upon an entirely new epoch. In my youth—that is, early in the nineteenth century—the state of things was this :—For a long period of time man had been endeavouring to acquaint himself with the world. But really, comparatively speaking, little was then known regarding the surface or the inhabitants of

this earth, and that arose naturally from the difficulty
of communication from place to place, the slowness
with which persons could travel, the difficulty of
collecting information, and other impediments of that
kind. We knew nothing of Africa. The sources of
the Nile were unknown. The continent had been
found so unhealthy that its interior had never been
traversed by persons who could leave any useful
account of what they saw. Little indeed was known
of its capabilities, or of the populations which inhabited it. Little was known of China ; little was
known of a great part of America, and but very little
was known of Australia. It was imagined that a
great inland sea existed there, and regarding what
an exploration of the interior might unfold nothing
was known. Little was known of New Zealand,
nothing but the accounts of Captain Cook. Little
was known of the islands of the Pacific. In fact, a
great portion of the earth lay hidden from man. The
duty, therefore, of the nineteenth century was to
clear up all these points, to make man acquainted
with the planet which he inhabited, to let him know
what its resources were, what kind of people it contained, and what were the limits of the available
territory within which mankind were to be confined,
and within which alone their efforts for their support
could be exerted. Therefore, the duty of the nineteenth century was to see that countries were ex-
plored and examined, that their contents were ascertained, that unknown tongues were mastered, and
that all dialects should be compared by comparative
philology so that we might be able to get some idea
of the way in which human beings had distributed
themselves over the earth."

After pointing out how thoroughly and completely
these objects had been attained, Sir George con-

tinued, "And now, what is the work that remains to
be done? To comprehend that we must consider
how small a spot the earth has proved to be. Think
how many times in a single year any one individual
here could encompass the world now, and go round
and round it. How little an orb, and yet countless
millions will be compelled to find their existence
upon it. And on the youth of the generation coming
rests an immense task, and a most difficult one—the
ascertaining and deciding exactly in what manner it
is best that the waste parts of the earth should henceforth be peopled. Of this rest assured, and it is a
point never enough valued and fairly considered,
that whilst the Creator has laid down certain natural
laws, regulating the winds, the seas, the earthquakes,
regulating all things which interest man in that way,
He has left to human beings the governance in all
other respects. You are either His ministers to give
effect to His desires for the welfare of His creatures,
or are turning traitors to that duty, to prevent His
wishes for the welfare of all being carried out. You
may say, 'Oh, no design is necessary to determine
how the world is to be hereafter peopled, and by
what races different portions of the globe are to be
occupied.' But I say that if you take that view you
neglect your duty, and bring untold or untellable
miseries upon the generations who are now coming
into the world."

After instancing the case of the West Indies, in
which the injustice and cruelty of the slave trade had
borne fruit in the atrocities of the negro descendants
of the slaves, who have become the dominant race in
many islands of the group, he pointed out the dangers
and difficulties which had attended the occupation of
New Zealand, but which having been surmounted,
were thought of no more.

"In most of these islands Christianity is now established. But what shall I tell you in regard to that—that soon after Christianity is established in these islands a total forgetfulness takes place of the evils, which were removed by the early pioneers of Christianity. How many of you sitting here now ever realize to yourselves what was the state of New Zealand in former years? Which of you can imagine human sacrifices continually taking place, human victims habitually being slain for the purpose of being consumed by their fellow-men, all the scenes of bloodshed and atrocity which went on, and the numbers that were annually sacrificed to habits of that kind? All that we have forgotten. We take New Zealand as it is. And so it will be with each of those other islands. And then when the question of how they are to be peopled arises, as it is rising now, I say, if you leave all to chance, all to haphazard, if you forget your duties which will fall upon you in the next few years, you will repeat in some other form, or cause to be repeated, not exactly the same evils which took place in the West Indies, but evils equally great, and which will produce proportionate unhappy results. Not only that, but if you allow the world to be widely peopled in the few parts still remaining open to us, if no care is taken for the regulation of such things, you will fail in your duty, and you will, as I say, not have shown yourselves worthy ministers of your Creator, but you will simply become men, who, in pursuit of their own objects, forget the most sacred and the greatest of duties."

After several other speeches had been made, Sir George performed the ceremony of placing a few valuable books on the shelves, and declared the Library formally open.

Grey's munificent gift to the people of Auckland and the Colony of New Zealand is a fitting measure of the love which he has ever borne towards that "Corinth of the South," that beautiful city between two seas, upon whose strand he first trod New Zealand soil. It is fitly shrined in a handsome and commodious building. To the Library and Art Gallery Sir George Grey is not the only donor. Mr. S. T. Mackelvie, during his lifetime, and afterwards by his will, contributed large numbers of valuable pictures and works of art, as well as a very large sum of money; while other citizens and friends of Auckland gave with no niggard hand.

But without deducting from the worth and value of other benefactions, it is certain that the chief glory of the Auckland Library and Gallery lies in the "Grey collection."

Gods are there, idols of wood and stone from many lands, worshipped amid strange shrines for centuries; weapons uncouth and fearsome, wielded by savage hands in deadly fight: implements of agriculture and the chase—wonderful stone axes, and fishhooks made of bone; spears and assegais, war hatchets and poisoned arrows; shells which had formed the currency of savage tribes; pictures, models, and specimens—all are there; medals of gold, silver, and bronze, gathered from every part of the earth. Older than the occupation of New Zealand by the Maoris is the matuatonga, a stone image now in the Art Gallery. It was brought by the first party of that race who, launching their frail canoes from the shores of the contested Hawaiki, crossed the broad ocean in safety and landed on the coast of these islands, to multiply and live in undisturbed possession for many hundred years.

There are the fragments of that marble cross which

Bartholomew Diaz built at the Cape of Good Hope four centuries ago, to commemorate the doubling of the stormy headland, the extension of the dominions of the King of Portugal, and the mercy of God. Before that symbol of salvation the storm-tost mariners of Spain and Portugal once knelt in prayer. Little did they dream of a future day when the Cape of Good Hope would be subject to the Crown of England, and the fragments of that cross before which they worshipped would be borne two thousand leagues still further over the stormy seas, to be wondered at as a relic of the past in the remotest parts of the earth, in a land where the red cross of Britain also floated. The residue has been taken as a memento of her palmy days to the capital of Portugal. By their side is the silver spade which turned the first sod for the first railway in South Africa. There, too, is a bronze cast of the head of Napoleon, modelled after death by Antomarchi, his medical attendant. It is curious to note how the features had reverted to their appearance in his youth. The likeness to portraits taken in later life is not nearly so strong as to those of Napoleon in early manhood.

In the Library the treasures are still greater. The most complete collection of the Scriptures in all the world is there deposited. The drafts are there of some of Cromwell's last despatches, in the handwriting of Mr. Secretary Thurloe, scored in many places by the stern writing of England's great Protector—in one place he having altered the too gentle sentences of his courteous secretary to his own iron words, one written when the shadows of death were already creeping over his undaunted heart.

These despatches are of considerable national importance. With them is the treaty concluded in the time of Richard Cromwell with the Hanseatic towns, and signed by most of the members of the Council of State as well as the foreign ambassadors. There are allusions in the last letters written to Cromwell by the British Ambassador in Sweden, Sir Philip Meadowes, to the suggestions made to the Protector to assume the title of King of England. The Swedish king is represented as expressing great surprise at Cromwell's persistent refusal to assume the dignity of the Crown, and as stating his belief that such a step would tend to strengthen Cromwell's Government, and ensure the peace and the prosperity of England. One such passage runs thus: "The king told me he wondered His Highness, my master, so prudent and experienced a prince, took no more effectual care to extricate himself out of those necessities, and that he who had achieved so many brave actions, though accompanied with manifold dangers, should now at last scruple that which would be his best and most visible security. This he spoke in reference to assuming the title of king."

The "necessities" alluded to in this paragraph are those which arose from "the non-payment of those moneys (subsidies), from the dissolution of Parliament before provision was made for the supply of my master's treasury." It is curious to note how little the real lesson of Charles the First's deposition and death was understood at the time. The Swedish king evidently implied that if Cromwell were to assume the title of king, he would be independent of his Parliament in the matter of supplies.

On the 16th of August, 1658, Sir Philip Meadowes alludes to the death of the Protector's favourite daughter in these words: "Yesternight I received your Honor's of the 6th instant, from Hampton Court, advising me of the sad breach which it hath pleased

God to make upon the family of Hiš Highness by the death of the Lady Elizabeth."

The authorities of the British Museum have endeavoured to induce Sir George Grey to send these documents to that national institution. But Sir George, anxious to bestow such precious relics upon the Library at Auckland, declined, thinking that a new colony ought to possess such valuable historic records. He believed that the possession of such treasures would stimulate among the youth in a new community a passion for learning and research. And he thought that the manuscripts at the Cape and in Auckland would afford the means by which in after years new authors would build up great names.

Sir George did, however, offer these letters to Carlyle some time before his death, to add to a new edition of his ' Life and Letters of Cromwell." But the Sage of Chelsea declared that he was too old to undertake a fresh task, and said that it ought to be given to some younger man.

There, also, is a wonderful and priceless collection of ancient missals and illuminated manuscripts. There is the first Dutch Bible, printed at Delft in the year 1477. In a magnificent Latin manuscript of the Bible, in two volumes, folio, there was found, in altering the binding, a note containing the self-complacent boast that by the wonderful process of printing men were in the year 1477 able to produce as much in a day as they had been to accomplish by the old process of writing in a year. Little did the old fathers in the school of wooden block type and black-letter printing dream of the perfection to which their art would come, and the revolutions it would effect in human society.

The mere perusal of the catalogue of the Grey collection in the Auckland Public Library carries the

reader back into the distant past, and into the most
remote parts of the earth. There are fifty-three well
authenticated manuscripts in Greek, Latin, Coptic
and Arabic, some of them within a few years of their
millennium. Twenty-four editions bear the date of
the fifteenth century, and sixty of the succeeding
one.

It is not the size of the Grey collection which
renders it so valuable, but the rarity and interest of
most of the works. It comprises about 12,000 volumes,
and is particularly complete in the philological and
theological sections. In the latter there are 374
Bibles, or portions of Holy Scripture, in 160 languages, for the most part belonging to modern times,
but including many ancient tongues.

Not the least interesting department in the Library
is that of the autograph letters, numbering two or
three thousand, and including communications from
Her Majesty Queen Victoria, from explorers like
Livingstone, Speke, and Sturt, from missionaries
and philanthropists, from statesmen and men of
letters, from scientists and philosophers, from rulers
and poets, from emissaries of peace and men of
action. The mere enumeration of such names as
Carlyle, Florence Nightingale, Selwyn, Lyell, Moffat,
Colenso, Whately, Froude, Huxley, Sir John and
Lady Franklin, Gladstone, Herschell, Speke, Sturt,
Patteson, Humboldt, Darwin, Bunsen, Lubbock, and
Henry George calls up a bewildering variety of ideas,
and the perusal of their letters will give future generations many interesting glimpses at the inner history
of this century.

But the charm of the treasured relics of many ages
and many lands gathered in the Library at Auckland
is greatest when Sir George Grey himself acts as
guide. The gorgeous and enduring colours and thick

gold on the pages of the illuminated missals draw
forth the wonder and admiration of all visitors, but
Sir George finds a deeper interest in reading between
the lines the life history of the patient monks whose
work is so faithful and so beautiful. Here and there
an almost imperceptible blemish will catch his keen
eye, and he will paint in a few words the picture
which is presented to his mind, of the remorse of
the devoted toiler, of midnight penance in the lonely
cell. Any little touch of human feeling is dear to
him.

At the end of one of the most beautifully illuminated
of these volumes there is such a message from the
dead. It takes the form of a most humbly-implied
hope that the dark sins of the unworthy scribe may
be in some slight measure atoned for by the fulfilment
of his self-imposed task. Unexpressed but quite as
evident as the sincere penitence and humility, are the
satisfaction and delight the writer felt in his accomplished work, and his conviction that such a worthy
offering must be accepted by Heaven.

With such keys to the feelings with which they
were wrought, the pictured pages are found doubly
eloquent. The hope of eternity, and the desire of
offering a perfect tribute to the glory of God, inspired
these holy recluses. In such service no care was too
great, no detail insignificant. In the complicated
tracery round the sacred pages; in the beautiful
miniature designs which adorn the initial letters of
chapter and verse; in the lavish embellishments with
crimson, gold and purple, whose brilliancy the centuries have not been able to dim, are read—beyond
the pride of the artists in the beauty of their work—
the agony of human souls striving to achieve their
own salvation.

To walk through the Library with Sir George Grey

is to enter a magnificent picture gallery. Taking down a book at random from the shelves, with a few words he will conjure up the forms of the mighty departed, not as spectres, but as breathing, living personalities. The "heroes of a hundred fights" reveal some softer aspect of their natures, the barbaric tongues of naked savages utter words of heaven-taught wisdom and eternal truth. The vices, the follies, the trivialities of past ages may pass unnoticed, but the attention of Sir George's listeners is continually drawn to deeds and words of heroism and virtue, for these are what his mind best loves to dwell upon.

But it is in the little recess which contains trans-slations, vocabularies and works in many languages, written with infinite labour and research by the missionaries, that the most thrilling pictures of noble self-devotion are drawn by him. There exist and live that noble band of whom the world was not worthy. From the solitary heroic figure upon the bleak Patagonian coast, to the lonely exile in the coral-circled islets of the South Pacific, surrounded by the utmost beauty and luxuriance of vegetation; from Father Damien, giving his life for the lepers, to Livingstone, the emissary of peace in Central Africa, struggling wearily against the languor and weakness of deadly fever, which had thinned the ranks of his little band, undergoing privation and sickness, renouncing all that most men consider makes life worth living. All are there, and when interpreted by him who was their friend and correspondent, still live and speak.

It was in this building that Sir George Grey showed Stanley, the eminent African explorer, a volume which he had heard was in existence but had never seen, containing a map drawn nearly three hundred years ago, on which the course of the Congo was correctly

To

Sir George Grey K.C.B.

In recollection

of the beloved giver

from

his Widow

Victoria[?]

March 1869

'traced. On one of its shelves also is treasured a copy of the "Early Life of the Prince Consort," doubly precious from the autograph inscription by Her Majesty to Sir George Grey, dated March 6th, 1869.

In many features the Library at Auckland is not equal to that presented by Sir George to the Cape of Good Hope, but in some respects it is superior. It was his desire to aid in making Auckland a seat of learning. He hoped not merely to inspire the youth of his favourite city with an eager appetite for knowledge, but to draw from distant places to Auckland students and those who, in the pursuit of literature, would deem it wise to consult portions of the vast mass of authorities which his unrivalled industry had enabled him to bestow upon the people of Auckland. He was pleased to think that in the days to come, future generations would resort to this mine of wealth and spread its riches far and wide in the literary world.

The vast extent of the literary, scientific, and artistic treasures which fell into the hands of Sir George Grey, and were divided by him between Cape Town and Auckland, represented not merely the result of great industry, knowledge, and the expenditure of money in purchasing. It proceeded partly from the widely-scattered gifts and contributions which during so many years he bestowed upon different races and repositories of learning. The natural consequence of his own boundless liberality was the return to him of many curiosities of a like nature. Thus, from all quarters and from all classes, from savage chiefs and men of letters, from scientific discoverers and kings of the earth, he continually received acknowledgments reciprocal to his own generosity. It was thus that from innumerable sources these collections accumulated, which now excite, and will for ever continue to excite the astonisment and delight of visitors.

Since the opening of the Library, Sir George Grey has continually added to it choice and valuable gifts. Under skilful management, the great mass of valuable correspondence is being steadily and surely reduced into system and order.

CHAPTER LIX.

GREY'S ACHIEVEMENTS, FAILURES, AND PERSONAL CHARACTERISTICS.

"The meaning of life here on earth might be defined as consisting in this: To unfold your *Self*, to work what thing you have
the faculty for."—*Carlyle.*

As the British Empire is now entering upon an epoch
of change in social, political, and economic doctrines,
it may be useful to summarise those matters of importance in which Sir George Grey's efforts have
resulted either in success or failure, and to draw
notice to his views and opinions.

He himself ever attributed his success in great
measure to the aid he received from many noble
friends, amongst whom were chiefs of so-called
barbarous races.

Submitted thus in a bird's-eye view, the mind will
perceive those "signs of the times" which contain
lessons of wisdom beyond price.

Twelve or fourteen great achievements, in which he
was completely or partially successful, immediately
present themselves to the mind. They are:

1. Prevention of the establishment of a State Church
in Australia and New Zealand.

2. The maintenance of the integrity of the Empire.

3. The fulfilment of treaty obligations with the
natives of New Zealand and other countries.

4. The framing of a model Constitution for colonial possessions.

5. The establishment in the Australasian Colonies of the principle of equal and universal franchise.

6. Framing of a Constitution for a Free Church of England in New Zealand, which has since, in its main features, been adopted in other places.

7. Cape Breakwater and Harbour, the value of which to British commerce can hardly be estimated.

8. Pacification of New Zealand.

9. Pacification of South Africa.

10. Establishment of beneficent institutions in all his governments—Libraries, Hospitals, Schools, Universities, Public Reserves, &c., &c.

11. Providing from his own resources for the purchase of native lands for European settlement, for the carrying on of government in Kaffraria and for colonisation.

12. Largely assisting in the saving of India by taking immense personal reponsibility.

13. Opposition to land monopoly, and the granting of facilities for *boná-fide* settlement in South Australia, New Zealand, and South Africa.

14. Encouragement and assistance to the efforts of explorers, missionaries, students, reformers, and writers.

15. Important additions to scientific knowledge in Natural History, Ethnology, and Philology, and the wide diffusion of such knowledge.

In many of the great purposes which George Grey set himself to achieve he has failed. For some of them the possibility of success has for ever passed away. The enumeration of these attempts now can only recall the memory of disasters which might have been averted, the vision of blessings which might have been secured.

Round some the waves of political strife are still fiercely surging. Some are bound eventually to prevail as they contain the living germs of truth and necessity. Others are yet possible, and would bring great blessings if persevered in. Among these is the confederation of South African States, though under different conditions to those formerly existing. As the theory that members of different religious bodies were incapable of agreeing in common council on measures for the common good has been proved false: so Sir George Grey believes that a similar theory in regard to subjects of different forms of government is false. He holds that delegates from monarchies and from republics might well deliberate on questions affecting the welfare of all.

His plan, briefly stated, is : That the States should contract that they would each (whenever the majority of the contracting parties thought good that a law should be made upon any subject) send the number of deputies agreed upon to a common conference. That the conference so summoned should be empowered to make a general law, and that the deputies on returning to their respective States should introduce the general law passed by the conference as an Act of their own Legislature, each State passing the law according to its own customs. This plan would enable Free States, Sovereignties, and Republics to join in a common federation without interfering with each other's legislation. If it succeeded in South Africa it could be extended to other lands.

In all these attempts Sir George Grey has advocated wide views, noble principles, and an imperial policy. Their mere consideration is ennobling after a dispiriting experience of legislation conducted in the interests and the spirit of Little Peddlington.

It is something at least to hear the voice of the

prophet from his lonely mountain height proclaiming the beauties and the grandeur of the wide extended view, even if he stand alone. It is something to see with his eyes for a moment, even if we will not lift our own from the lower ground. The utterance of such truths will inspire some souls to soar upwards, although the majority may scoff at the prophet and his visions. And it is well for the world that he should speak, although his voice should fail, and his eye grow dim, and his heart break in the fruitless effort to make the people believe and see. It may truly be said of Sir George Grey that his failures are more glorious than meaner men's successes.

Amongst the most prominent of the things attempted, in which he failed, are the following :

1. Confederation of Southern Seas under English flag.

2. Confederation of South African States under English flag.

3. Home Rule for Ireland.

4. A national system of colonisation.

5. A complete and perfect system of self-government for the Colonies.

6. The prevention of the Zulu war.

7. The preservation of the New Zealand Constitution.

8. A pure and unselfish system of administration.

Sir George Grey has been ever a great reader of books as well as a student of human nature. His industry is even now unwearied. The lofty standard which he achieved at Sandhurst has been more than equalled by his subsequent career. His scientific attainments are matters of public notoriety. He is a philological student, and he is acquainted with many languages. The greatest of modern philosophers have borne testimony to the depth and variety of his knowledge in many branches of natural and physical science.   His reading in Constitutional and International Law is sound and extensive.

His opinions upon economic questions, which questions he believes to underlie much of the future prosperity and happiness of mankind, are simple and yet profound.   The extreme competition and selfishness which characterise modern economic science find in him no adherent.   He believes that labour has a right to share in the profits and surplus values which it creates.   And although he treads on this ground with extreme circumspection, and recognises the wonderful complexity of the web of social life in relation to the distribution of wealth, he yet holds firmly to the theory that association and mutual assistance make a safer and sounder foundation for national prosperity than bare individualism and merciless competition.   It is his opinion that the truest system of economics is built upon practical Christianity, and is based upon the two corner stones found in the utterances of the New Testament, " Whatsoever ye would that men should do to you, do ye even so to them," and "Thou shalt love thy neighbour as thyself."

Sir George Grey tells with a smile how, when once walking with the late Sir James Stephen, they saw an arbour in which Mr. Senior, a neighbour of the Colonial Under-Secretary, usually sat while writing. Mr. Senior was then believed to be preparing the new Poor Laws.

"Think of that man," said Sir James Stephen, "I would not for all the world be in his position.   He is writing upon the Poor Laws and political economy. A most amiable man, and most upright and conscientious.   Yet in the interests of what he calls political economy, which he believes to be fraught with benefits to England, he is adding unconsciously to the

sorrows and burdens of millions of his fellow countrymen."

The opinion of Sir George Grey upon the subject
of political economy were almost identical with those
of his friend, Thomas Carlyle.

As a writer, he has always evinced considerable
skill and great knowledge of the subjects under discussion. His style is clear, forcible, and sometimes
—even upon grave questions of State—dramatic in
its vividness. His correspondence has been already
several times alluded to, although not half its treasures have been brought under the notice of the
reader. Perhaps in its width and the variety and
importance of the matters comprised in it, it has
rarely, if ever, been surpassed.

His philanthropic and social plan, and their fulfilment, form part of his history of the colonies of
Australasia and South Africa.

His main political views are few and simple .—That
the franchise should be universal and equal; that
taxation should be proportionate to the power to bear
it and the benefit derived; that all public offices
should be open as the reward for merit and efficiency;
that the community has a right to a fair portion of
what John Stuart Mill calls "the unearned increment"; and that colonisation should be used for the
purpose of increasing the national safety, prosperity,
and power, are among his principal articles of political faith.

His personal character is peculiar, but ingenuous.
In a life crowded by adventures he has had no love
of adventure for itself. The strange incidents of his
career have been always merely attendant upon the
performance of some task, or have been met with in
the accomplishment of some ulterior purpose. The
pleasures by which other men are delighted have had

comparatively but little interest for him. And as his adventures, so his pleasures have mostly come during the discharge of duty. His wonderful voyages with Selwyn through the glorious islands of the Pacific, his matchless sporting expedition with Prince Alfred at the Cape, his presidency of public feasts and public festivals, his presence at great commemorations and the commencement of national undertakings, even his attendance on the racecourse, in the concert-room, and at scenes of public amusement, have all been, more or less, in the fulfilment of duties inseparable from public position.

One feature, strange enough in these days, should stand out conspicuously in a sketch of the character of Sir George Grey. This is found in the utter absence of the love of wealth which has eaten like a canker into the heart of the nation; and of any desire to acquire landed estates. Perhaps the fiercest storm that ever raged in the House of Representatives in New Zealand arose from an accusation made by a Minister of the Crown that Sir George Grey had, when Governor, participated in the private purchase of native lands. The charge, although no wrongdealing was imputed, was absolutely denied by the ex-Governor. The correspondence which was relied upon by his accuser, when produced, substantiated Sir George Grey's words and confounded his opponents. The effect of this vindication was very great, and soon afterwards the then Ministry were ousted from power, and were succeeded by a Cabinet over which Sir George Grey presided.

Not only was he thus regardless of wealth and estates. His life presents a long and unbroken record in its entire and peculiar abnegation of self, of comfort, rest, retirement, or relaxation, when likely to interfere either with public or private duties.

His firm and determined character was nowhere more clearly shown than in his resistance to wrong-doing in high places, and the rectitude of that character was exhibited in the scrupulous fulfilment of promises made to any of the numerous native tribes, however feeble, with which he was brought into contact during his official career. His sympathies with all that is good and worthy, irrespective of class, creed, colour, or race, are, and have ever been, universal and unchanging.

Any sketch of Sir George Grey's life which did not bring into strong relief the charm of his society and his deep sympathy and interest in the most trivial events affecting those amongst whom he lived, would omit one important feature of his personality. And yet these are the most difficult of all characteristics to portray. Displayed fifty times a day in conversation, in kindly words and thoughtful actions, it is yet manifestly impossible to record these speeches or incidents in full. And to write of one or two isolated examples may, perhaps, provoke wonder at their being considered of sufficient importance to chronicle.

Five minutes' conversation with Sir George Grey at any time found him eager and excited over some literary or historical discovery. Some well-known truth or established fact would have presented itself in a novel light, and led to an utterly unexpected result, explaining the motives which actuated public men, and clearing up the mystery surrounding their actions. There was always something new to be told, something of interest to be shown anyone who found Sir George at leisure for a little conversation.

His great acquirements and natural parts made him an ideal companion. His slow impressive speech never wearied his listener, his learning and attainments were never obtruded in condescension or patronage. His manner was simple in the extreme; his language couched in the purest and most unassuming English. The respect, almost homage, which was shown Sir George by all who met him, was not the result of any conscious effort on his part. On the contrary, his consideration and courtesy were extended equally to all—a peasant woman was as sure of them as a marchioness, a gumdigger as a Minister of the Crown, a naked savage as a Colonial Governor.

Mr. Murray, son of the well-known publisher, frequently spoke of Sir George as "the only person in New Zealand to whom everybody took off his hat," and he might have added with equal truth, "the only man who took off his hat to everybody." It was an amusing sight to watch the gravity and courtesy with which the "great Pro-Consul" returned the salutations of even tiny children of six and seven years old. Little shy boys pulling off their hats to him in a shame-faced way, always saw him in return bare his venerable locks with the same gesture with which he would have responded to the greeting of an archbishop.

His dignity was something deeper than the exclusiveness which refuses to recognise persons of an inferior station in life, and demands constant self-assertion. But at the same time the unconscious influence of the old aristocrat's presence checked any approach to presumption or familiarity.

Many of Sir George's friends were much scandalised at his indifference to the barriers of society. On one occasion, during his second government of New Zealand, he visited Hokitika and Greymouth, to which neighbourhood a large number of people had been attracted by the discovery of gold. The Governor held a reception, at which ladies were present as well as their husbands. "Look," whispered one of the leaders of "society" to a friend, "that is my washer-woman with whom the Governor is shaking hands so cordially." Grey remembered the faces, names, and circumstances of these humble acquaintances in a marvellous manner, a conclusive proof that the interest he showed in their concerns was sincere and not feigned.

In the early days of New Zealand's history, a Maori named Moses or Mohi, became the devoted servant of the Chief Justice and his wife. After their departure from the Colony he attached himself to Mr. Swainson, the first Attorney-General, who had been a passenger by the same vessel which brought Sir W. Martin and Bishop Selwyn to New Zealand. The homes of these three distinguished men were close to each other. About the time of Mr. Swainson's death, Sir George Grey, with his nephew and niece, Mr. and Mrs. Seymour George, and their family, left Kawau and settled in Auckland close to the lovely bay in which Mohi's two English homes had been. Immediately the old man looked upon himself as having a right to the protection and support of this, the last of his old friends.

For years Mohi was a pensioner of Sir George Grey, and when at last the shadows of death fell upon him, and he was unable to move from the little cottage which had been found for him, he sent for the ex-Governor, who was himself weak from illness, yet did not delay in acceding to the wish of the old Maori. The scene by the death-bed was most pathetic. The faithful old servant's last sensation of bodily pain was removed by Sir George, who, seeing the failing fingers struggling to loosen the band round his throat, rubbed the dying man's chest and side with firm yet gentle pressure. He often afterwards related with visible emotion how a peculiarly sweet smile crossed the native's face. On inquiring its cause, the Maori replied—"My mind has gone back many years. The last hand that touched me as you are doing was that of my mother, when she used to play with me as a child, and tickle me to make me laugh." Mohi confided to Sir George the disposition he wished made of his property, which the latter promised should be carried out. Then, having handed over to Sir George's keeping some rings which he had received from Lady Martin, the dying Maori spoke hopefully with his visitor about the future, saying he felt perfectly satisfied and at peace. Sir G. Grey was persuaded by Miss Outhwaite, another friend of Lady Martin's, to leave the bedside for a short time. When he returned, after an absence of about twenty minutes, he found that Mohi had passed calmly and quietly away, and he felt that almost the last direct link which bound him to the days of Selwyn and Martin had parted. When the bell tolled solemnly from St. Stephen's, Sir George Grey, with bowed shoulders and failing gait, headed the little procession, and stood bare-headed by the open grave. Many wondered that so much notice should be taken of the death of "a mere Maori," but the great heart of the chief mourner sorrowed for a friend.

To gratify the wishes of children was a continual delight to Sir George. His own nephews and nieces found out very early in life that they had only to wish for anything in order to receive it, so long as they expressed the wish in their uncle's hearing. A very amusing scene took place on one of these occasions at Kawau. One of his nieces, a fair-haired little maiden of some three or four summers, had sighed for a Shetland pony. There were none on the island, so Sir George sent to Auckland for one. It was car-

ried down in a small steamer, and landed on the jetty,
which ran out into the bay directly in front of the
house.   Then the child was taken to see that her wish
was fulfilled, and to watch the pony being put ashore.
Unfortunately the animal became frightened and
struggled in a most lively manner.   " Take it away,"
cried the little girl, " take it away.   I don't want it.
I won't have it."   And for a long time she could not
be persuaded even to look at her new possession.
But in the end, finding how gentle and quiet her pony
really was, she grew very fond of it.

Sir George's sympathy was not less ready towards
children outside his own household.

After endowing the Public Library in Auckland
with his magnificent collection, Sir George Grey
spent many hours almost daily in the building giving
information to the librarian, and assisting him to
catalogue and arrange the multitudinous treasures
and literary curiosities.   Leaving the Library, he
would often make his way through the adjoining
gardens of the Albert Park.   There, on several occasions, he found a schoolboy with his eyes bent on the
volume in his hand, while his companions ran races
and amused themselves in various ways.   One day
the grey-haired scholar spoke to the young student
and asked the name of the book over which he pored
so intently.   The lad coloured with embarrassment,
but replied simply that he was studying hard, with
the hope of winning a scholarship.   Sir George was
greatly interested.   After asking several questions,
and speaking a few words of encouragement, he told
the boy to let him know if he succeeded in the examination.   He did not forget the circumstance; and
when, a few months later, he received word from his
young acquaintance that the coveted scholarship was
gained, Sir G. Grey bought a large and handsome

book, in which he wrote the lad's name and sent it to him as a memento and a reward.

.   .   .   .   .   .

It is a pity that the lives of those who go forth from the older countries to encounter strange perils in the performance of duty, and to sow the seeds of future harvests for the world, are not made more familiar and easy of access.   It is impossible to believe that if the life of Sir George Grey be studied by the youth of the United Kingdom it can fail to incite a spirit of emulation in many minds.   To those who fear that the endurance and courage of our race are fading, it will bring conviction that there are yet men bred from the old stock who are fit to lead the world.   To those who are inclined to believe that scepticism and materialism are usurping the place once held by simple faith in God, the stories of such lives as this will afford consolation.   To those, and they are many, who dread the approach of almost universal confusion and anarchy, this record, typical of the lives of other men, though upon a larger scale, will give this assurance—that there are eyes which look down the vista of the future with steady gaze; that there are hearts full of courage and devotion, equal to any fate; and that among the scattered millions of our people exist intellects keen and observant, hands strong to direct the helm of State in any storm, and hearts sublime in the absence of fear, in dependence upon God, and in love to their fellow men.

CONCLUSION.

THE task of the writers is accomplished, a task pleasant in itself, and yet full of anxiety. Much that might have been included—incidents and adventures of different characters in many lands—has been of necessity omitted. Whether portions which have been written might with advantage be replaced by other records of Sir George Grey's busy life is a question which we find it difficult to decide.

As from the study where these pages have been written we look down upon the sunlit waters of the Waitemata, and away to the beautiful islands of the Hauraki Gulf, past the little church where Selwyn worshipped, and the walks, then unsheltered, now overshadowed by English trees, where Grey and Selwyn and Sir William Martin took counsel together in the early crisis of the history of New Zealand, memories of stories, of sufferings, and of achievements came crowding thickly upon us.

The figures of three great men stand out in bold relief; but behind them rise a vast number of loyal supporters in all that was good and true, who toiled for the peace and prosperity of their adopted country. Amid the scenes of conflict and of suffering that the early story of the colony presents, we can discern the forms of soldiers and sailors laying down their lives for her welfare, officers and men vying with each other in devotion and in courage; patriots and philanthropists, warm in heart, wide in sympathy, steadfast in endeavour for the good of their race; missionaries and other pioneers of civilisation, living laborious days, remote from luxury and comfort; Europeans and Maoris alike aiding the representatives of civil and religious authority and law. The majority of them are unknown to fame, their very names forgotten, yet the people of New Zealand will ever owe them a debt of gratitude which time cannot discharge. Their descendants may be proud and feel that they do well to be proud of such ancestors. Were their names and deeds to be collected and recorded, the page on which they were inscribed would be glorious, rich in all that appeals to the noblest sentiments of man—but such a page can never be compiled.

Many of the events in Sir George Grey's life must also inevitably pass unrecorded. The work of selection from such varied materials must be always difficult. Doubtless the choice has ofttimes been decided by the personal feelings of the writers. What has been omitted would but have given a deeper emphasis to the courage and wisdom of the character we have attempted to portray.

It has been our wish without exaggeration to place Sir George Grey as an example for imitation to all those who are anxious or likely to bear a part in the performance of public duty. It is true that no man can hereafter expect to be placed in the same circumstances. In this respect his record is unique. No such epoch ever before existed, nor can any practically similar ever again occur.

But in all positions of life, and under every varying phase of human existence, the same principles which animated George Grey, and the same faith which sustained him, may animate and sustain others, whether they be princes, born to an imperial throne, or peasants, whose hands must be familiar with the spade and plough.

If we have succeeded in reducing into order and historic progression the great events herein alluded to; if we have succeeded in showing how faith in God can sustain and strengthen the heart under perils and dangers most appalling; how a permanent and paramount sense of duty can nerve the heart to do and to suffer all things; and how in most trivial matters, as well as events of Imperial importance, wisdom and rectitude should control both the words and deeds of public men, we shall count ourselves well repaid. And we rest contented with the knowledge that some portion of the greatness of a great life, some of the radiance which streams from an illustrious character, will be enjoyed by those who rescue from possible oblivion the record of noble deeds, and who rear for the study and emulation of generations yet to come the figure of a man at once great and simple, powerful and unselfish.

APPENDIX.

'(NOTE A. —See pages 38 to 45.)

FREDERICK SMYTH.

IN the account of Grey's second exploration in Australia, there are two or three brief allusions to the brave lad who found a grave in the wilderness. Since that account has been in print, Sir George Grey has expressed to the writers his earnest desire that a more definite tribute should be paid to the memory of one who may be regarded as having met the death of a martyr in the cause of science and discovery, led on by personal friendship and affection for Sir George himself. Frederick Smyth came of a very good old English family. His grandfather and uncle successively represented Norwich in the House of Commons for many years.

(NOTE B.—See pages 68 to 72.)

STOKES' CHARGES AND DARWIN'S LETTERS.

THE controversy alluded to between Captain Stokes and Sir George Grey, in pages 68 to 72, led to a strange correspondence between Grey and Darwin. The great naturalist had sailed on his memorable voyage in the Beagle a few years before she was employed to convey Grey and Lushington to Australia. Mr. Stokes was at that time second lieutenant of the Beagle, and after Darwin's return to England a somewhat intimate and familiar correspondence was maintained by the author of the " Origin of Species" and the naval officer. Grey occupied the cabin formerly used by Darwin.

Captain Stokes communicated to Darwin the results of his so-called survey of the country between Perth and Shark's Bay, and asked his friend's opinion —first, as to the propriety of Grey's action; and, secondly, as to whether, in his opinion, the latter could reasonably be offended at the stand which he, Stokes, had taken.

Dr. Darwin was greatly surprised at the substance of this letter, and relying entirely upon the accuracy and good faith of his correspondent, stated in reply that he was grieved and astonished that a gentleman of Grey's character should, either by mistake or intention, have been guilty of such gross and dangerous errors.

In some strange way this letter found a place within the pages of a new book, forwarded with others by his publisher in London, to Grey, when Governor of New Zealand in 1846. Sir George, who had a great respect for Darwin, immediately enclosed this letter to its author, at the same time vindicating his own conduct and justifying the reports which he had made. The following correspondence then ensued :—

Down Farnborough, Kent, November 3rd, 1846.

My dear Stokes,—I have just received, to my great surprise, the letters of which the enclosed are verbatim copies. That with my signature was in my handwriting. I remember enclosing it to you with one of your proof sheets in answer to some query, whether Captain Grey could be offended at your manner of referring to some bay or river. I beg you to inform me immediately how it could possibly have been sent to Sir G. Grey. It places me in the position of wishing to make myself presumptuously impertinent to him—a position the very opposite to my feelings regarding him. I shall, of course, inform Sir G. Grey that I have written to you, and I should think it would be most agreeable to yourself to allow me to enclose your entire answer, or at least a paragraph from it, and I shall enclose a copy of this note. He will then see the whole part which I have been made by some means to play in this disagreeable affair.

To this Stokes replied as follows :—

November 6th, 1846.

My dear Darwin,—Your letter of the 8th, with its enclosure, has *greatly* surprised and annoyed me. I remember receiving the note of yours you have alluded to, and thought I had destroyed it at the time ; but how or by what unfair means it has been most wickedly sent to Governor Grey, I am quite at a loss to know. It gives me great concern to think that I should in any way be the means of placing you in such a disagreeable position, and rest assured it will ever be a matter of deep regret to your very faithful friend,

W. STOKES.

P.S.—I shall endeavour to find out the mischief-maker.

On November 10th, Darwin wrote to the Governor of New Zealand in these words :—

My dear Sir,—I beg to thank you for the courteous tone of your communication of the 10th of May, 1846, considering the circumstances under which it was written. I enclose a letter which I immediately wrote to Captain Stokes, and his answer. These will, I trust, exonerate us of intentional impertinence. Some most malicious person must have sent my note to you. I have been much mortified by perusing it, and though I am not presumptuous enough to suppose that you can care much for my opinion of your work on Australia, it is a satisfaction to me to be enabled to name to myself many individuals to whom I have expressed my strong opinion of the very high qualities shown in your work, of which the amusement it afforded was but a small part. Your account of the aborigines I have always thought one of the ablest ever written. As we are not likely to have any further communication, permit me to add that I have a most pleasant recollection of our former acquaintance. With much respect I beg to remain, yours faithfully,

CH. DARWIN.

Sir George, in reply, answered the questions suggested to him, and wrote in such a strain of kindliness and good feeling as to elicit a somewhat remarkable epistle from the man of · science, from which the following quotation is made :—

Down Farnborough, Kent, November 13th, 1847.

My dear Sir,—Although Your Excellency must be overburdened with business, I cannot resist the temptation to thank you cordially for the very kind, and if I may be permitted to say so, admirable spirit, with which you excuse and tell me to forget the, to me, painful origin of our correspondence. I have been the more gratified by your letter, as I had not the least expectation of hearing from you.

I am extremely glad to know how well your colony is now prospering. Ever since the voyage of the Beagle, I have felt the deepest interest with respect to all our colonies in the southern hemisphere. However much trouble and anxiety you must have had, and will still have, it must ever be the highest gratification to you to reflect on the principal part you have played in two countries, destined in future centuries to be great fields of civilisation.

You are so kind as to offer aid in any natural history researches in New Zealand. I have no *personal* interest on any point there; but there are two subjects which have long appeared to me well deserving investigation, and if hereafter your labours should be lightened, you might like to attend to them yourself, or direct the attention to them of any naturalist under you. The first is an examination of any limestone caverns. Such exist near the Bay of Islands, and I daresay elsewhere. I was prevented entering them, by their having been used as places of burial. Digging in the mud under the usual stalagmitic crust would probably reveal bones of the contemporaries of the Dinornis. . . . The second point is, whether there are "erratic boulders" in New Zealand, more especially in the Middle and Southern Islands; and their northern limit, if such occur. Most geologists are now united in considering erratic boulders to have been transported by icebergs and glaciers. I consider it a most important question, *as bearing upon the former climate of the world*, to know whether such proofs occur generally in the southern hemisphere as in the northern. I have ascertained that such is the case in South America from Cape Horn to about lat. 40°. This subject requires much care and some little knowledge, or at least thought.

As if to add assurance to assurance in confirmation of the views expressed by Captain Grey of the territory under discussion, a special correspondent despatched by the London *Daily Chronicle* traversed that district and reported upon it in the articles which appeared in that paper in August and September, 1891, under the heading, " The Outlook in Australasia."

He speaks of the very valleys indicated by Captain Grey as "the famous Greenough Flats, which the Agricultural Commission class among the richest agricultural land in all Australia." He dwells on "their deep, loamy richness, averaging wheat crops of thirty bushels per acre," and goes on to mention " the heather and innumera ble flowering shrubs, making the plains bright enough, even in winter, and encouraging a belief in all that was told us of the glorious display of flowers which the summer sun brings forth, making the country a veritable Florida, after a fashion which English imagination can hardly compass."

In a subsequent article the correspondent again returns to his description of that country, using the same terms of praise regarding large portions of it which he had already employed.

(NOTE C.—See pages 75 to 78.)

SIR GODFREY THOMAS.

THE name of Captain Grey's step-brother was inadvertently omitted. The brothers were deeply attached to one another, and Sir Godfrey made his home with Grey for many years. His early death caused deep sorrow to his brother. He was a rising public man, and bade fair to achieve a useful career.

'(NOTE D.—See page 154.)

CHURCH ENDOWMENTS IN NEW ZEALAND: SPEECH OF SIR GEORGE GREY, JUNE 18TH, 1851.

" SIR GEORGE GREY said that any information on this subject in the possession of the Government rested, he believed, solely on his own personal knowledge. All he knew regarding it was that the Agent of the Canterbury Association had read to him the draft of the letter, in which, as far as he remembered, was a recommendation that an application should be made for an extension of the block of land which was to be subject to disposal under the peculiar rules of that settlement. He had, however, heard rumours on the same subject from other sources. As far as he was informed of the intentions of the Home Government and of Parliament, he believed that they were in no way desirous that this particular mode of disposing of lands should be forced upon the inhabitants of this country. In fact, they were solely desirous of promoting the welfare of the inhabitants of New Zealand, and of consulting, as far as practicable, their wishes. It therefore was the duty of those persons who disliked the portions of the islands they lived near being subjected to such regulations to state their objections to them. The points which appeared to require attention were these :—A district containing nearly three millions of acres, including within its boundaries Bank's Peninsula, and embracing one of the most fertile districts in New Zealand, which contained also—before the present regulations were established—many persons of a different faith from that of the Church of England, was placed under the control of the Canterbury Association ; and then regulations were made, an important feature of which was that until three millions of pounds were paid for the

purposes of the Church of England, the whole of that
district could not be used, as their necessities required,
by civilised man; nor could any part of it be used for
these purposes until the proportionate part of the three
million pounds which was due under these regulations upon that part was paid over for the purposes
of the Church of England : even for the depasturing
purposes the land could not be used under the present
regulations except at a rate which, calculating that a
hundred acres would feed thirty sheep, required a
payment of nearly twopence per head per annum for
the same purposes. Now, as he understood from
rumours, it was intended to ask that a further block
of perhaps three millions or four millions of acres
should be placed under the same regulations, so that
the case would then be, that, before the whole of this
block could be used, seven millions of pounds must
be paid for the purposes of the Church of England,
and no part of it could be used until the proportionate
amount due on that portion had been so paid. This
appeared to involve questions worthy the consideration of all classes in New Zealand, as the power of
the humbler classes to acquire properties for their
families was involved in it, the amount of the produce
of the country was involved in it, and the extent and
value of the commerce greatly depended on it. The
only argument he had ever heard used in defence of
this arrangement was that Great Britain had done
much for New Zealand, and therefore had a right to
make such regulations for the disposal of its lands as
were for the benefit of the population of the whole
Empire. This argument he admitted in its fullest
extent ; but he could not consider it for the benefit of
the Mother County that one of the most fertile portions of the Empire should be closed by such restrictions, which, in as far as he understood them, placed

obstacles in the way of industrious men raising themselves from a state of want by the use of lands which, in their wild state, were useless to mankind. As a Churchman, he viewed this attempt with the utmost alarm, although on this subject he spoke with great diffidence, as he had the highest reliance upon the judgment of many members of the Association; indeed two right reverend prelates belonging to that Association were his intimate friends. Yet it did not appear to him—at the time that so large a portion of the population of Great Britain were in such distress —to be in accordance with any rule of Christianity that the poor of the earth should have closed against them by such restrictions so large a tract of fertile country which a bounteous Providence had placed at the disposal of the human race. It did not appear to him to be in accordance with the principle that those who preach the Gospel should live by the Gospel, because it wrung contributions to a Church from those who were not friendly to that Church, but whose absolute necessities compelled them to buy land necessary for their operations; and because it made the clergy, in the early stages of the scheme, dependent for their support, not upon their flocks, not upon the members of the Church, but solely upon the amount of land to be sold; so that almost involuntarily men might be led to aid in the sale of lands—a duty foreign to their calling. He thought, therefore, that this system of obtaining an endowment was objectionable, whilst he thought the endowment itself far too large, and likely ultimately to introduce habits of sloth and negligence into the Church, and thus to be injurious to its own welfare. He would rather have seen the virtuous and industrious, who could find no place at home, encouraged to occupy such a country upon terms which would have enabled them easily to acquire homes for themselves and their families, and readily to develop the resources of the country, and to have seen a busy, active clergy, by acts of kindness and Christian virtue, gaining from the members of their own Church, in that fertile district, a love and gratitude which would readily have yielded ample endowments for all their wants. He feared 'the present system would injure the Church; it led men incautiously, even in the publications issued under the authority of the Association, to hold out the clergy as a feature of attractiveness, and even to use such language in support of what is termed the religious principle as that 'the merest land speculator has an interest in the Canterbury Bishopric.' He thought that such arguments, whilst they might gain endowments for the Church, must injure the very religion they were meant to support. It therefore behoved those who objected to having the lands in their vicinity placed under such regulations to state their views upon the subject."—*New Zealand Spectator*, June 21st, 1851.

(NOTE E.—See page 246.)

CHINA ARMY AND LORD CANNING.

WE have not been able to find any evidence to show that Sir George Grey received any proper recognition of his important services on this occasion from the Queen's Ministers. Indeed it seems that Her Majesty's Advisers were so anxious to support Lord Canning, and to manifest their approval of his conduct, that they were placed in a great difficulty by Sir George Grey's continued energy in sending assistance to Bengal. Lord Canning evidently desired that only a trifling aid and horses should be forwarded. His under-estimate of the gravity of the circumstances would have been revealed if more prominent notice had been bestowed upon Grey's action. Silence, therefore, was deemed by them to be advisable. They knew Canning to be a good and able man, surrounded by difficulties of a most extraordinary character, and they desired neither to weaken his authority nor to bring discredit upon his judgment. They therefore acted wisely.

(NOTE F.—See page 264.)

GERMAN LEGION AND BOMBAY.

AT the time when Sir George Grey re-enrolled and remodelled the German Legion and sent them to Bombay, thus increasing the strength of the British army beyond that authorized by law, there were two powers with authority in India. The East India Company, which *could* increase its army, was yet the governing power, although the British Parliament and the British arms were conducting a great war in Hindostan, so great a war that Sir George Grey was confident it would result in India passing under the direct dominion of the Crown—a dominion which in truth had already commenced. Under this dual system of rule Grey fared badly. The German Legion was of invaluable service to Bombay at a most momentous crisis. Of this the East India Company was conscious, and its officers expressed their gratitude. But Her Majesty's Ministers had already condemned the illegal act of the Governor at the Cape in levying troops without authority of Parliament, and perhaps could not turn its censure into condemnation even under such pressure as the circumstances brought to bear upon them. Thus in all directions Sir George

Grey failed to receive that public recognition which his courage and foresight demanded. His sending of the China army was accredited to Lord Elgin. His continued stream of reinforcements and assistance was ignored. His recalling the German Legion, and the consequent saving of Bombay, brought upon him a censure which was never recalled.

(NOTE G.—See page 322.)

THE GREAT HUNT IN THE ORANGE FREE STATE.

IT might be thought from the description of this hunt given in the text that the destruction of such vast numbers of animals was useless and wasteful. The truth lies in the opposite direction. Many thousands of the natives joining in this unprecedented chase, obtained from its results food on which they and their families would depend through the ensuing winter. The different tribes had wagons on the field to carry off the portion of game distributed to them. This was then dried and thus turned into "bultong," and provided sustenance for communities which had little or no other means of subsistence. Nothing, therefore, was lost. In reference to this subject, see the letter of Moshesh on page 270.

(NOTE H.—See page 347.)

KAFIR SCHOOL AT ZONNEBLOEM.

THIS establishment was assisted by donations from many quarters. In particular, the Baroness Burdett-Coutts contributed very generously. Without her assistance it could not have been founded or main-

X 2

tained. Sir George Grey expressly desires that the
kindness of Lady Burdett-Coutts in this matter should
not be forgotten.

(NOTE J.—See pages 556, 557.)

AMERICA AND ENGLAND.

THE statement of Sir George Grey's opinion upon
the claims of the United States to the leadership of
the Anglo-Saxon peoples is too bald and emphatic.
It is necessary both to modify and enlarge that
opinion. The circumstances of the case of Samoa
alluded to are peculiar, and yet illustrate the weakness of the position now held by England. Prince
Bismarck had determined to enter upon a system of
German colonisation. In many places where he
desired to plant colonies he found that he was brought
into collision with British interests or with British
settlements. He had without doubt determined to
annex those islands of the Navigators Group which
pass by the name of Samoa, of which, between 1880
and 1887, Malietoa was the acknowledged King.
Finding that the Australian colonies and New Zealand resented strongly his efforts to annex the Samoan
Group, the Prince requested Sir Edward Malet, the
English Ambassador at Berlin, to convey to Lord
Salisbury his (Bismarck's) resolve, if necessary, to
treat with France in a manner which might be preju-
dicial to the interests of England if he were not
permitted to carry out his designs in regard to
colonisation. Influenced by Continental interests,
and more attentive to the chances of European complications than to the safety and the prosperity of
Australasian commerce, Lord Salisbury's representa-

tives permitted their hands to be'tied by the threats of the German Chancellor. Had it not been for the resolute action of the American Consul at Apia, who, acting under the advice of one of the writers, placed the islands under the protection of the American flag in the very presence of the German squadron, it is certain that Samoa would have been seized by Germany and incorporated in the German Empire. The cherished dream of Sir George Grey's life had been to exclude from the New World the policies, the rivalries, and the wars of the Old. And he felt that the true welfare and greatness of England, and the safety of that freedom to which she had been a bulwark for generations, were more closely connected with the intimate relations existing between Britain and her great dependencies and the United States than in the balance of power upon the Continent. He was convinced that in the terrible wars which probably will yet devastate the Old World, England could not take an effective part. He was equally convinced that England had no right, save in the interests of justice and of mercy, to interfere at all. To his mind the hopes of the world rested upon the increasing numbers of English-speaking peoples scattered in free communities upon the earth, asserting the dominion of the sea, and offering to the citizens and subjects of all nations who might choose to join them those advantages which freedom and boundless territories bestowed. The cautious—even timid attitude of England in relation to Samoa drew forth the passionate scorn of the colonies of Australasia and the Western States of the great Republic. Already in 1853 Sir G. Grey had warned the Imperial authorities on the occupation of New Caledonia by the French. It was well known that in anticipation of war between

England and other powers, plans had been prepared for the invasion of Australia and New Zealand. In the case of Samoa, it was not as if England were permitting Germany to occupy a desert and uninhabited territory; it deliberately sacrificed—under the stress of threats—a King and people with whom it was in solemn treaty to the tender mercies of Prince Bismarck. Beyond this, it was permitting a great nation to seize and fortify in the midst of the Southern Ocean a strong and fertile group of islands which directly command those great streams of commerce perpetually passing and repassing between Australasia and America, between America and China, Japan, and India; and which, without doubt, might easily dominate the commerce between Great Britain and her Australasian colonies. So vast were the interests involved, so wide the issues which depended upon this apparently trivial matter of the abandonment of Samoa to the Germans, that Sir George Grey feared England had taken a fatal step and dealt with her own hand a serious blow against her own supremacy. The inflexible resolution of all parties in the United States which prevented the annexation of Samoa by Germany filled him with delight, and convinced him that no questions of European politics, no outside entanglement with other nations, would prevent the United States from throwing its shield before the weakest community if the cause of human liberty and freedom could be thereby advanced. In his opinion, England and America should act conjointly. In all cases where it is distinctly in the interests of freedom and humanity, they should be guided by one spirit and work in unison for the same ends. So acting, the liberties of the world, as a whole, would receive a due consideration, and the Anglo-Saxon race would in all human probability be left to work-out its own destiny in undisturbed peace. Thus, in relation to the New World he thought that America and England should unite to prevent the intrusion of the quarrels and wars of the Old, and so ensure a new and happier future for large portions of the human race. But if Great Britain allowed her Ministers to be interfered with by foreign powers, or guided by considerations possibly inimical to the interests of her widely-scattered children, then the hopes and trust of the young nations of the future would be increasingly reposed in the judgment and sympathy of the United States.

NOTE K.—(See page 566.)

AUCKLAND LIBRARY.

OWING to the liberality of various donors, a sum of nearly sixty thousand pounds is invested for the maintenance of the Library and Art Gallery. This, with other great endowments for the support of education in Auckland made by Sir George Grey during his first government, not only fulfils the desire of the many contributors to these institutions, but secures for Auckland the possibility of the first place in literature and art south of the Line. So widely extended and numerous are the exhibitions and prizes open for competition among the scholars of Auckland, that clever and industrious youths from the various district schools are continually coming to the front and entering the lists of the higher teaching. If she desire it, the old capital of New Zealand may become the Bedford of the Southern Hemisphere. Thus in New Zealand the cost of education for the brightest and most industrious of her children, from the days of infancy to the highest degrees conferred by the University, is defrayed by the public purse.

———

WE cannot close these pages without gratefully acknowledging the assistance we have received from many quarters in compiling them. We feel greatly indebted, amongst others, to Sir George Buller, Colonel Rookes, Captain Shillington, and Sir George Whitmore. Of Sir George Grey's uniform kindness and consideration in giving free access to all sources of information it is superfluous to speak.

INDEX.

THE END.

PRINTED BY J. S. VIRTUE AND CO., LIMITED, CITY ROAD, LONDON.

www.ingramcontent.com/pod-product-compliance
Lightning Source LLC
Chambersburg PA
CBHW060522030726
47498CB00004B/1046